UNLUCKY DAY

A Crime Thriller

J. R. McLeay

To Tricia,

who makes me feel lucky every day

Contents

Part 1: A Dangerous Game

Chapter One

Times Square, New York City

July 4, 11:45 a.m.

W hose life will I extinguish today?
So many choices, so many worthy subjects. It's the Fourth of July in the epicenter of New York. The anthill is swarming with activity. Such easy pickings.

People are oblivious about their vulnerability as they travel about their everyday business. So lost in their little world with their self-important tasks, they can't imagine at this very moment someone could be drawing a bead on them. Mere seconds away from sudden death from the simple pull of a trigger.

There's a busy mix of tourists and native New Yorkers moving about Times Square today. It's easy to tell them apart. The natives so impatient to get from point A to B. Everybody trying to get ahead in the most competitive city on Earth. The tourists stroll about in lazy clumps, soaking up the flash and glitter of the Theater District. The locals try to wedge their way through the horde or walk onto the street to bypass the gawkers.

It's quite amusing, in an anthropological kind of way, to observe the different castes in action.

Every colony harbors insects worthy of extermination. Scanning the faces of these creatures, likely candidates

abound.   Like   the   well-to-do   tourists,   carrying   their
overstuffed Tiffany and Cartier shopping bags. What a waste
of resources. One of those fancy diamond rings could feed a
hungry child for a year.

Or the fat-cat investment banker, dressed in his bespoke
suit and five hundred dollar shoes.   How many mortgage-
backed securities has he dumped on the market today?
Building an ever-taller house of cards, poised to topple the
economy and over-indebted homeowners at any moment.

How about the muscular guy wearing a wifebeater shirt?
How many skinny kids did he torment in the playground
growing up?

So many people who deserve to die.

Power is not just bestowed by genetics or social class. It
can be wielded by anyone with sufficient motivation and will.

But I'm in no hurry to take my quarry today. I've still got
a few minutes before the appointed hour.   It's six minutes
before noon.

My rifle scope shows a crowd milling about the entrance
to the Hard Rock Cafe between 43rd and 44th Street.   A
young pregnant woman barely out of her teens is pausing to
light a cigarette. She's not wearing a wedding ring. Yet
another unplanned pregnancy by a promiscuous tramp. Will
she too abandon her baby, only to have the child bounced
from one abusive foster home to another?

So many thoughtless people in this world. My finger
presses more firmly against the trigger.

I follow the tramp as she elbows her way through the
throng northward along 7th Avenue toward Broadway. She's
giving no apparent thought to the dependent child within her.
Bouncing between one distracted pedestrian and another, she
pinballs through the crowd, toxic smoke blowing from her
lips.

Doesn't she know the prenatal months are the most
critical in a developing child's life? My anger builds as my
rifle traces her harried journey.

There are no longer any other persons of interest in my field of vision. I'm incensed. If I kill her now, at least the paramedics will arrive soon and have a chance at saving the baby. Child Services will put the baby up for adoption, and the circumstances of its delivery may find a sympathetic and caring family.

This tart isn't fit to be a mother. There is more than one way to separate an abusive parent from her offspring.

This is the child's lucky day.

The traffic light turns red at 45th Street, and the woman stops on the edge of the curb, directly facing me. I see her clearly in her red halter, a bullseye in the sea of vanilla pedestrians surrounding her.

She's waiting impatiently for the light to turn. This will be her last vision before the white light takes her somewhere else.

I glance at my phone propped on the window ledge beside my rifle. The time is just past noon. I squeeze the trigger and feel the recoil of the weapon against my shoulder.

Exactly two seconds later, pandemonium erupts at the corner of 45th and Broadway.

Chapter Two

45th & Broadway

July 4, 12:30 p.m.

J oe Bannon flashed his NYPD detective badge to the on-
duty cop as he ducked under the yellow tape surrounding
the crime scene. Accompanied by his partner Hannah
Trimble, he side-stepped a large puddle of blood trickling
over the curb onto the street. After twenty-two years as a
detective, there wasn't much he hadn't witnessed. Still, seeing
the close-up effects of violent crime always struck a personal
chord, and he swallowed hard to keep his lunch down.

"Where's the body?" he asked the attending cop.

"They took it to Lenox Hill Hospital on the East Side.
Young pregnant girl. EMS thought the baby might still be
saved."

Joe studied the chalk body outline on the sidewalk.

"Head shot?"

"Blew out half her brains. You're lucky you missed it."

"Did you see the wound before they took her away?"

"Yeah. She was shot directly between the eyes. The
back of her skull was blown almost clean off. Must have
been a hollow point bullet, judging by the extent of the
damage."

"Has forensics swept for the slug?"

"Apparently the bullet hit a man standing behind her in
the shoulder. No exit wound. You should be able to collect it
at the hospital."

Joe peered at the gawking bystanders.

"Any witnesses?"

The cop pointed behind him toward the lobby of the
Marriott Marquis hotel.

"Those folks said they were pretty close to the action. Watch where you step though. More than one person lost it when they saw the mess on the sidewalk."

Joe and Hannah walked up to a group of ashen-faced civilians sitting on the hotel lobby steps. A young woman wept while consoled by her husband. Her blond hair and white dress were splattered with blood.

"Excuse me," Joe said. "I'm Detective Joe Bannon with the NYPD. Did anyone here see the shooting?"

The bloodstained woman peered up.

"I was standing just behind and to the side of the victim. It was horrible. Who would do this? She was just a young girl. And *pregnant*!"

The woman buried her head in her partner's arms and sobbed.

"She fell backwards after being shot," her husband continued. "I think a man behind her was also struck. They took away two bodies on stretchers."

"How many shots did you hear?" Joe asked. "Were you able to tell from which direction they came?"

"I only heard one shot," the man said.

He pointed up 7th Avenue.

"It wasn't very loud. It came from uptown, quite a few blocks away. I was on the phone at the time, so I wasn't paying much attention."

Joe looked up at Hannah.

"How long did you stay on the phone after the victim was shot?" he asked

"Only a few seconds. I hung up and called 911 immediately."

"Can you check to see what time the call ended? This might help pinpoint the time of the shooting."

The man retrieved his phone from his pocket and tapped the screen a few times.

"Looks like it was right around noon," he said, turning the phone for Joe to see.

Joe pulled out his notepad and scribbled the start time and duration of the call shown on the screen.

"Did you record the call?"

He knew it was a longshot, but an audio recording could provide clues to the type of gun and firing distance.

The man looked at Joe blankly.

"Um, no. I don't think mobile calls are recorded, are they? I just use the regular features..."

"That's okay, thanks for your help. Can I get your name and contact information if we have any further questions?"

The witnesses gave Joe their particulars, and he jotted them in his notepad.

"What do you make of all this, Han?" Joe asked his partner, as he turned and walked back toward the chalk outline.

"Based on the distance of the gunshot and the degree of street congestion at the time, I'd say it was from a high-powered rifle at an elevated position. Do you think it's another terrorist attack?"

Joe took a moment to appraise the crime scene. A stream of passersby stopped to crane their necks over the crowd of onlookers at the edge of the police line before moving on.

"It's too clean for someone trying to attract attention to a cause. Terrorists try to create maximum carnage with their attacks. Why not plant a bomb or spray more shots if you're trying to make a political statement? This has the feel of a lone wolf. The shot between the eyes from a long distance— that takes special skill. Plus, I think there's a reason why he chose a young pregnant woman. We'll see if the coroner can make any more sense of this."

"Maybe the victim's next of kin can reveal a motive."

Joe peered up 7th Avenue toward Central Park.

"Not if it was a random shooting. Let's see if we can narrow down the location of the shooter."

Chapter Three

Wellington Hotel, Midtown Manhattan, 18th Floor Guest Room

July 4, 12:30 p.m.

S o this is who I'm up against. One middle-aged NYPD detective and his dutiful sidekick.

Following standard procedure, I see. Interviewing the witnesses, scoping the crime scene, probing for clues. Except in this case, there are precious few. A distant gunshot, an as-yet-unrecovered slug, no discernible motive, and no suspect. Good luck with that.

The lady cop is kind of cute, though.

What brings a woman into this line of business? This is a man's domain, the business of killing. It's a testosterone-fueled game played by angry and greedy men. No place for a lady.

She's practically bursting out of her tight slacks and blouse. I can see her nipples protruding under her blouse. My high-powered scope is useful for other things besides killing people.

Does this turn you on? Chasing bad guys, cleaning up other people's dirty business?

What to make of her partner? He's obviously in charge, asking all the questions. Clean cut, fit and trim. Probably ex-military. He doesn't waste much time, gets right down to it. Surveying the crime scene, noting the obvious, collecting relevant details from the witnesses. He looks a little shaken by the blood though, for an experienced cop. Does this hit a little close to home?

A witness is showing him his phone. The Detective is noting the time of the shooting. I can make out the number.

That could come in handy a little later. How convenient that my hotel thought to provide a pen and notepad with my free room. Perhaps we'll give the witness's friend a ring sometime. Just to remind everybody I'm always watching and keep them on their toes. A little mindfuck every now and then never hurt anyone.

They're pointing in my direction now. Can you see me? I see you. Right in the intersection of my crosshairs.

But I've had my fill today. I'll see you again, sooner than you think. Come look for me. You won't find me. I don't leave tracks.

Let the games begin.

Chapter Four

Staten Island

July 5, 11:30 a.m.

J oe knocked on the front door of a gray clapboard house in
south central Staten Island. The home had flaking paint
on its wood siding and a lopsided porch that squeaked under
his weight. A pale middle-aged woman wearing a nightgown
answered the door. Her eyes were red and swollen from
crying.

This was one aspect of his job that Joe hated.
Interviewing bereaved family members to search for clues
was never a pleasant task. He'd experienced the horror of
losing a loved one to violent crime himself and knew
firsthand how invasive a police investigation could be. He
didn't waste any time with preliminaries.

"I'm Detective Joe Bannon with the NYPD, and this is
my partner Hannah Trimble. We're investigating the shooting
of Sofia Raccheti yesterday. May we have a few minutes of
your time?"

The woman pulled the door back and motioned them
inside. A balding man in sweat pants and a sleeveless
undershirt lay in a lounge chair watching TV. The woman sat
at a vinyl-covered kitchen table in the open family room and
offered the detectives a cup of espresso.

"Thank you," Joe said. The detectives took adjacent
seats at the table. "Are you Franca and Mario Raccheti, the
young woman's parents?"

"Yes," the woman said, trying to steady a cup of espresso
between her shaking hands. "Have you found her killer?
What kind of *animale* would murder a pregnant woman and
her unborn child?"

Joe's eyes narrowed in sympathy.

"I'm sorry for your loss ma'am. This is what we're here to determine."

He noticed a photo collage on the kitchen wall showing a young girl at various stages of development. They seemed to stop around the age of thirteen or fourteen. He flashed back to when his own family mementos ended abruptly. A lone intruder had broken into his home while he was serving in the military overseas and violently attacked his wife and young son. The boy succumbed to his injuries days later.

The woman dabbed her eyes with a handkerchief and sniffed her nose, pulling Joe back to the present.

"Did your daughter mention any trouble she'd had recently?" he asked. "Anyone who might mean her harm?"

"None that I knew of. She wasn't home much. We spoke over supper two days ago. She didn't sound upset. We talked about the usual things. How she was feeling, her plans for the baby…"

The woman's back suddenly heaved and she began sobbing uncontrollably, renewing the memory of her double loss. Joe reached out and held her hand.

"Did she live here with you full time?"

"Yes—"

"When she wasn't shacking up with one *ragazzo* or another," her husband interrupted, staring impassively at the TV screen.

Joe's muscles involuntarily tensed. How a parent could be so callous about a recently deceased loved one left a bad taste in his mouth. He reached for a packet of sugar from a bowl in the middle of the table and tore off the top edge.

"Were you both here at the time of the shooting yesterday, around noontime?" he asked.

"Yes," the woman said. "We don't get out much. We've only got Mario's disability pension to get by on."

12

"I understand your daughter was unmarried. Do you happen to know who the father of the baby was and his whereabouts?"

The woman's husband snickered from the armchair.

"She didn't talk much about that," the woman said, glaring at her husband. "I don't think she knew who the father was—"

"It could have been any one of those *brutti* who always called here," the husband said. "Good luck tracking them down."

Joe emptied the packet of sugar into his cup and swirled the mixture noisily with a metal spoon. His mind wandered back almost twenty years. How much fault does a neglectful parent play in a child's premature death? Could he have saved his own child if he'd been more attentive and not far away trying to save the rest of the world?

Hannah noticed her partner's distraction and picked up the conversation.

"Did you see any bruises or signs of physical violence?" she asked.

The woman looked down at the table.

"I don't think she was having any trouble like that..."

Hannah wondered if there might be a third party interest in the child.

"Did she talk with you about her plans for the baby and who would bring it up?"

The woman sobbed again at the thought of her deceased grandchild and paused to collect herself.

"Only about her staying here so we could help care for the baby. At least until she settled down with somebody."

The woman's husband flashed a dismissive glance at his wife.

"Fat chance of that."

The woman slapped her hand on the table, spilling her half-filled cup of espresso.

"Mario, can't you be kind toward your daughter just once? She didn't deserve this. She was our *bambina*!"

Joe was torn between his desire to throttle the uncaring father and comfort the distraught mother. Stealing an angry glance in the man's direction, he drew a napkin from the centerpiece and helped the woman clean up the spilled coffee.

"I know how difficult this must be for you ma'am," he said. "We'll do everything we can to find who did this to your daughter and bring the killer to justice."

Joe's phone suddenly buzzed, and he glanced at the screen. It was a message from his precinct Lieutenant.

There's been another sniper shooting. Corner of William and Wall. Investigate asap.

Joe handed the woman his card.

"Thank you for your time, Mr. and Mrs. Raccheti. If either of you think of something that might help with this case, please call us. We'll be in touch again soon."

The detectives exited the house and walked down the rickety front steps.

"What's up, Joe?" Hannah asked. "You ended the interview pretty abruptly. Got some news on the perp?"

Joe nodded.

"Looks like he's struck again. Same M.O., different social class. Wall Street this time. He appears to be picking off his victims indiscriminately. Let's catch the next ferry and see if we can make any sense from this new hit."

"These people certainly weren't much help," Hannah sighed. "No sign of obvious foul play on the domestic front."

"Other than her deadbeat father, perhaps. Too bad we can't arrest him for willful neglect and emotional abuse."

"You almost can't blame the girl for getting knocked up under those conditions. Any excuse to escape that kind of environment."

"Maybe she just got unlucky. Twice."

Chapter Five

Office of the Chief Medical Examiner, 421 East 26th Street

July 6, 9:00 a.m.

Joe and Hannah walked into the examination room of the Chief Medical Examiner for New York City, escorted by the M.E.'s personal assistant. Two naked bodies lay draped under white sheets on adjacent stainless steel dissection tables. Only their blood-splattered faces were visible. A gray-haired doctor in a lab coat sat hunched over a microscope at a nearby desk. He peered up when the two detectives entered the room.

"Hannah, Joe, good to see you again," he said, standing to greet them. "Though as always, I wish it were under happier circumstances."

As the head forensic pathologist for one of the most violent cities in the United States, Dr. Miles Lundberg had consulted on many autopsy findings with the two detectives. Board Certified in neurosurgery and ballistics examination, he had more experience with bullet wounds and head trauma than just about anyone in America.

"Yes, Miles," Joe replied. "And this one, I'm afraid, could be a bit more troublesome than most."

Miles wrinkled his brow.

"You mean because of the similarities in the attacks?"

Joe nodded.

"Two shootings from a long-range sniper directly to the head, one day apart in heavy pedestrian traffic. It looks ominous."

"Two data points don't establish a reliable trend. Though I agree these shootings are atypical."

"How so? What have you found so far?"

"The first similarity is with the ballistics. Both slugs are of the same type and weight."

"Hollow point?"

Miles picked up two deformed bullets from a metal tray beside the microscope and held them up for Joe and Hannah to examine. The flattened tops of the bullets looked like little gray flower blossoms, their soft lead tips stripped neatly back along perforated grooves like a half-peeled banana. The stem of the bullets retained their perfect cylindrical shape, encased in a shiny brass metal coating. They almost looked to Joe like miniature sculptures until he noticed specs of blood on the lead, reminding him how they'd ended two innocent lives.

"Technically, they're jacketed soft point bullets," Miles clarified. "They don't expand and deform as much as a hollow point. Just enough to widen the bullet upon impact to increase tissue damage. But not enough to stop its travel inside the victim."

"So both bullets passed right through the victims?"

"Yes—with enough residual momentum to lodge several inches into other bystanders, based on the hospital report."

Joe took one of the bullets from Miles' hand and examined its cylindrical coatings. He could see faint parallel twisted scoring on the cylinder.

"Have you been able to compare the ballistic fingerprint?"

"Yes, they match precisely. There's absolutely no doubt they were fired from the same weapon."

Joe rolled the bullet slowly across his palm.

"Can you estimate what type of gun was used based on the weight and caliber?"

Normally this would be a job for the police ballistics department to determine, but Joe respected Miles' experience in this area and he was eager to confirm his suspicions.

"That's the other interesting thing. It's an unusual configuration. Eight point six millimeters in diameter, not nine. Weight just under 13 grams. I know this is normally

16

your domain, but I looked up the specs to see if I could find a match."

Miles reached down and clicked the computer mouse on his desk. An image of a bullet cartridge about the length of Joe's little finger popped up on the screen.

"Point three-three-eight Lapua Magnum cartridges. They match the specs exactly. Developed for military-grade long-range rifles. I'll leave it for your team to identify the specific weapon."

Joe shook his head.

"Jeesuz," he said. "Just as I feared. I was afraid we might be dealing with a highly trained sniper." He looked at the splayed tops of the bullet in his hand, imagining the kind of tissue damage it created. "Can we ascertain anything useful from the wounds?"

Miles led the two detectives to the examining tables and pointed with a gloved hand to a small red hole in the forehead of each of the two cadavers.

"There again, I found unusual distinctions and similarities. Both entrance wounds are in the center of the face. Clean concentric abrasions at the opening indicate the bullets impacted with a near-perpendicular trajectory."

Joe clenched his jaw to quell his roiling stomach. He'd seen his share of death and traumatic injury while serving in the military, but he'd never become fully desensitized to it. As a seasoned homicide detective, he didn't want to betray any sign of squeamishness.

"No powder burns?" he asked, trying to steady his voice.

"No," Miles said. "And no stippling of the skin around the wound. These shots weren't fired at close range."

Joe thought back to his crime scene interviews.

"Both eyewitness reports told of a gunshot coming from several blocks away. The streets in the vicinity of each shooting were lined with high-rise buildings on both sides. So the shooter must have been at a near ninety degree angle directly facing his targets when he took the shot."

Hannah leaned in to look more closely at the wounds.

"Both wounds are directly between the eyes," she said. "How is it possible to achieve that kind of accuracy from so far away?"

Joe had already been doing some math based on his prior military experience.

"During my tour in Iraq, special forces snipers would tell stories about taking out targets from over a mile away. Head shots each time. That was almost twenty years ago. I'm sure rifle technology has advanced even more since then."

"So we're dealing with a highly skilled sniper who can pick people off at will from a mile away?" Hannah said.

"It's beginning to look like that, unfortunately."

Joe turned to the medical examiner.

"Miles, can you tell us anything from the exit wounds about the vertical angle of the bullet? Maybe we can triangulate the sniper's height and distance with this information."

Miles stepped forward and rolled one of the cadavers onto its side to reveal a three-inch wide gaping hole in the back of its skull. Joe resisted the urge to gag. His aversion to head injuries was personal.

"The exit wound in both victims is larger than usual due to the expanded bullet diameter and severe intracranial pressure created by the high-speed bullet. You can see that the wound on the back of the head is slightly lower than the one on the front. If we take the middle of the exit hole as a reference point, I calculate the downward angle of trajectory on the first victim at a little over four degrees, and close to five degrees for the second."

Joe thought back to his high school trigonometry classes.

"From a distance of many city blocks, that equates to a pretty significant height above street level for the sniper's position. Wouldn't you agree?"

"It would seem so. But don't forget to factor into your calculations that every bullet, even one fired from a high-speed rifle, has a distinct arc to its trajectory based on the downward force of gravity. A bullet fired from the distance you've suggested would have begun to slope down considerably by the time it hit the target."

"I'll have our ballistics whizzes back at the precinct figure that one out," Joe said. "Any other details you can share that might help in identifying the shooter?"

"Only that this guy obviously was trying to make some kind of statement. A soft point bullet fired from a high-velocity weapon to the frontal lobe of the brain is all designed to create maximum damage. Most shooters use either hollow point bullets to maximize internal trauma or full metal jacket bullets to increase penetration. In this case, the killer chose the best of both worlds, so to speak. It ensured not only sudden death but also maximum mess and collateral damage."

"You mean regarding the damage to other bystanders in the line of fire?" Hannah asked.

Miles nodded.

"Yes. Maybe he just wanted to ensure a lot of blood would be spilled to increase the shock value. It wasn't enough just to kill his victims. It's almost as if he wanted everyone else to see the after-effects of the shooting. I'll leave it to your police psychologists to figure out his motivation, but this guy isn't your run-of-the-mill shooter."

Joe grimaced as he considered the implications.

"So we're dealing with a highly skilled psychopath with a high-grade military weapon roaming the streets of New York looking for random victims to satisfy his bloodlust."

Miles looked at the two detectives and nodded.

"I hate to say it, but I have a feeling I'll be seeing more of you two in the days to come. Something tells me this guy is just getting started."

Chapter Six

The Pierre Hotel, Upper East Side

July 6, 11:00 a.m.

S hortly before noon on the day after the Wall Street shooting, a young bearded man wearing a gray suit and driving cap strode into the lobby of the Pierre Hotel. Behind him he pulled a roller suitcase with a long handle. Well-dressed and purposeful, there would be no reason for the hotel staff to suspect the visitor of any ill intention.

The man walked to the main elevator bank and pressed the up button using the knuckle of his right index finger. When the elevator door slid open, he stepped into the empty compartment and snapped on a pair of surgical gloves. Then he pressed the button for the eighteenth floor and stared blankly forward as the elevator rapidly ascended.

When it reached the indicated floor, he stepped into the hallway and glanced quickly in both directions. To his right, the hallway was clear. Half way down the hall to his left, a chambermaid's cart rested in front of an open guest room. Turning left, he reached into his pocket and pulled out a one-inch square transparent acrylic cube.

As he approached the open room, he slowed and peered inside. A chambermaid had her back turned while she tucked in a set of fresh sheets on the bed. He stepped behind the cart and quickly glanced into the washroom. No toiletries were on the counter, indicating the previous guest had checked out. The man retreated from the washroom and inserted the cube into the latch hole in the door jamb then continued to the end of the hall. When he reached the exit, he opened the door and calmly waited in the stairwell.

Ten minutes later, he heard the familiar sound of a guest room door slamming shut. Pausing for a couple of minutes, he opened the stairwell door and peered down the hall. The chambermaid had moved her cart to another room and disappeared inside. He exited the stairwell and proceeded directly to room 1817. Pushing the door open without any resistance, he retrieved the cube from the latch hole and closed the door behind him.

Once inside, he checked to make sure the room was clear then he swung the security bolt to prevent unexpected entry. Moving to the window, he checked his line of sight to the south and slid the window pane open six inches. The curtains fluttered softly in the gentle breeze.

Placing his suitcase on the bed, he twisted two ends of the handle in opposite directions until it separated in the middle. He pulled a rifle barrel encased in a padded sleeve from the open handle and placed it on the mattress. Then he opened the suitcase and retrieved four objects from neatly indented foam enclosures: a hinged rifle butt, a long-range rifle scope, a noise suppressor, and a five round bullet magazine.

Picking up the rifle barrel and stock, he connected the two parts and twisted the shaft until the pieces fit snugly together. Then he took the rifle scope and inserted it into a notch on top of the stock and pressed it forward until it clicked in place.

Glancing across the street at the placid setting of Central Park, he calmly twisted the noise suppressor onto the end of the barrel. Then he picked up the bullet magazine and slapped it into the underside of the stock.

Now he just needed a stable platform to support the weapon. Next to the window, a small serving table held a tray of water bottles and chocolates. He moved the tray to the bedside nightstand and grabbed the rifle from the bed. Unhinging the stock and locking it into place, he swung the bipod support legs down and placed his weapon gently on the table. Moving a chair from the corner desk to a position behind the console, he took a seat and lifted the rifle butt to his shoulder.

Peering through the scope, he positioned the barrel facing directly south along 5th Avenue. Two blocks away, he had a clear view of the main commercial intersection at the south end of Central Park. A busy mix of tourists and office workers milled about Grand Army Plaza, centered by the Plaza Hotel. In its circular driveway, the Pulitzer Fountain sprayed a cascade of water jets in a perfect arc toward the Statue of Pomona.

What a perfect setting for an execution, the sniper thought.

Swiveling the rifle barrel a few degrees to his right, he stopped when he caught an object of interest in his sights. Reaching up with his left hand, he turned a knob on top of the scope twenty degrees clockwise. Satisfied he had made the necessary adjustments to take account of the firing distance and wind, he lifted his cheek from the side of the rifle stock and smiled.

Placing his phone on the window ledge beside his rifle, he checked the time. Ten minutes before noon. Just enough time to enjoy a bottle of water and some hors d'oeuvres before surprising another bystander who just happens to be in the wrong place at the right time.

He reached over to the bedside table and picked up the TV remote control. Clicking the On button, he scanned the channels for an appropriate distraction. Stopping at a noisy war movie, he turned up the volume then calmly unwrapped the complimentary chocolates.

Chapter Seven

NYPD 18th Precinct, 306 West 54th Street

July 6, 11:00 a.m.

Lieutenant Brady O'Neill furrowed his brow as he poured over the latest homicide file. As Detective Sections Chief for the 18th Precinct, it was his responsibility to assign homicide cases within the Midtown North jurisdiction. Normally he wouldn't take such a direct interest in an individual case, but two similar sniper shootings in as many days had him concerned.

In thirty years as a street cop and senior investigator, he'd never seen a case like this. After yesterday's repeat shooting, he called a meeting with his lead detectives to review their progress.

A tap on his glass door snapped him from his thoughts.

"You called, Chief?" Joe said, sticking his head in the doorway.

Hannah peered over his shoulder and smiled at the Lieutenant. The detective squad was a tight unit, and the three had a good working relationship. But O'Neill was in no mood for small talk this morning. He didn't waste any time getting to the subject of the meeting.

"Come in," the Lieutenant said, motioning for the detectives to have a seat. "I wanted an update on these two sniper shootings. Have you coordinated with the First Precinct?"

"Yes," Joe reported. "Unfortunately, there are no leads yet on either end. But we've found some commonalities between the two cases. It definitely looks like the same shooter."

O'Neill nodded.

"What have you got?"

"Same bullet specs, same M.O., same wound profile."

"You're referring to the head shots?"

"Yes, but these weren't ordinary head shots. Both in the middle of the face, right between the eyes."

"That's nothing new," O'Neill shrugged. "Lots of professional hits have that signature."

"Those are normally from close range using a handgun," Joe said. "These were from an elevated position using a high-powered rifle."

O'Neill leaned back in his chair.

"Have you matched the bullets with the rifle type?"

Hannah passed some photos of spent bullet slugs across the table to the Lieutenant.

"Ballistics matches the slugs to a model L115A military-grade long-range sniper rifle. It uses special bullets, 8.59 millimeter caliber. Soft point, for maximum damage."

The Lieutenant cocked his head.

"So we're dealing with a military-trained sniper?"

"Possibly," Hannah continued. "These rifles are hard to come by on the street and require a certain degree of training to use. They have extremely sensitive settings and dynamics, with a range of over a mile. Anyone who can shoot a target with that degree of accuracy has obviously had some practice."

"You say the shots came from an elevated position? How far up?"

"The M.E. estimates a four to five degree downward trajectory based on the position of the entrance and exit wounds," Hannah said. "But range and wind conditions can also affect the angle."

O'Neill nodded. His experience with murder cases over the years had given him a good working knowledge of ballistics.

"Did you interview people in the area to try to narrow down the shooter's location?"

Joe flipped open his notepad and reviewed his notes.

"We found some people in the vicinity of 55th Street and 7th Avenue who reported hearing a muted gunshot nearby. They said it came from quite a few stories above street level."

O'Neill raised his eyebrows.

"That's just a few blocks from here. Did anyone see anything suspicious? A rifle barrel sticking out of a window or someone carrying an unusual bag?"

Joe shook his head.

"Nothing. The shooter maintained a low profile and covered his tracks cleanly."

The Lieutenant stood up and walked to his office window. He separated the blinds with two fingers and looked outside in both directions.

"What's in this neighborhood that a shooter could easily infiltrate and exit under cover?" he wondered out loud.

He paused, focusing on an object upward and to his right.

"What about the Wellington Hotel? Have you talked with their staff about any suspicious traffic? Maybe some of their guests can pinpoint which room or direction the sound came from."

"That's on our to-do list today," Joe said. "We've been busy interviewing the victim's family and checking the forensic evidence with the M.E."

"Any leads from the family?"

"Nothing actionable. The pregnant woman was unmarried and had lots of boyfriends. No obvious sign of malice or financial interest. The guys downtown are saying the same about the second victim. At this point, it looks like two completely random shootings."

O'Neill crossed his arms.

"Except they appear to be from the same gun at the hand of the same shooter. That doesn't sound random to me." He picked up the case file and leafed through the pages. "Anything else of note?"

"One other thing," Joe said. "Both shootings occurred at almost exactly the same time of day—right around noon. We haven't yet put together a plausible motive for that."

"What about the victims? Any similarities that might suggest a motive there?"

"That's the strange part. You couldn't find two more dissimilar people. The first victim was a young lower-class pregnant woman from Staten Island. The other guy was a middle-aged Wall Street executive from Long Island. There just doesn't appear to be anything connecting these two events."

O'Neill turned his wrist and looked at his watch.

"It's getting close to noon. I'm worried this shooter may be preparing to strike again. I'm going to put out an APB to our guys on the street to watch for any unusual sounds and movement. If there's another shooting today I want you two on the scene to cordon the area, Code 2.

"In the meantime, I'm calling an FBI profiler in to see if they can help us connect some of the dots. Check with Ballistics. Maybe they can triangulate the shooter's elevation based on the firing distance and bullet angle. We'll scour every floor in every structure in the neighborhood if we have to. If we can't catch him in the act, we'll catch him through good detective work."

Joe and Hannah rose from their seats and glanced at one another nervously. They both had the same feeling in their gut.

Neither expected today to be very quiet.

Part 2: Raising the Ante

Chapter Eight

The Pierre Hotel, Room 1817

July 6, 11:50 a.m.

I love this scene in Inglourious Basterds, where the German sniper picks off American soldiers at will from his perch atop the clock tower. The really chilling part is seeing the unmitigated glee in the Nazi officer's faces as they sit watching the propaganda film.

Talk about schadenfreude.

The Krauts seem to have perfected the art of taking pleasure in the suffering of others. But I don't get off watching others suffer. For me, it's about control—rebalancing the scales of justice with my oppressors. I've been on the other side. I know what it's like to feel helpless and abused. No longer.

It's time to scope the kill zone. It's a sunny day in Central Park, and New Yorkers are enjoying the oasis within the city. A gaggle of children are kicking a soccer ball under the watchful gaze of their attentive mothers. A young couple lies napping on a blanket under the shade of an Elm tree, their half-finished picnic lunch carted away by opportunistic ants. Joggers in stylish running suits trot along the bridle path circling the park. It's such a peaceful scene, it almost seems a shame to shatter it with a random act of violence.

It's odd that more people aren't concerned about a killer in their midst. Haven't they heard about the previous days' shootings? It was front page in the Daily News. Perhaps not prominent enough to attract sufficient attention. There are almost four hundred murders every year in New York City, just about one every day. Perhaps New Yorkers have become desensitized to violence in their city. Maybe they think it only happens to other people—or people running afoul of the law.

I suppose they haven't yet recognized a new pattern of killings, where anybody is fair game. Under the all-seeing gaze of the mysterious rooftop sniper. They will soon learn though—because today's act raises the stakes. This one will get everyone's attention. Especially those holding the levers of power.

Authority is a perverse thing. The rules of civilized society impose order through unnatural structures and hierarchy. Lawmakers create rules governing socially acceptable behavior then the police impel citizens to comply. Children fall under the legal control of their parents or guardians, long after they've attained sexual maturity. Little mind is given to what happens behind closed doors in these supposedly protected homes.

It's a strange irony that the so-called enlightened civilization created by humankind has produced its most horrific abuses. And the worst atrocities are committed by those with the most power. Priests take advantage of defenseless choir boys. Cops target minorities and anyone who doesn't blindly submit to their authority. Politicians take kickbacks from the privileged class, maintaining the status quo and suppressing the very constituency they were elected to serve.

It's time someone started shooting holes in the veil of artificial power. It's time to expose the hypocrisy of the system and restore equality to the people. Authority figures who've abused the system must be held to account. The law can no longer be counted on to balance the scales of justice. The rules are far too entrenched, favoring the elite. Those vested with power have too much to lose from returning it to the people.

Who's in control now? Step outside. Your fate lies in the wind.

My field of vision shifts toward the south end of Central Park. A dominant figure attracts my attention in the Plaza on the southeast corner of the park. A cop on a horse mills about, chatting with tourists taking pictures of the iconic symbol. What better emblem of trusted authority than a mounted NYPD police officer?

The perfect mark.

There's just one problem. The cop is wearing a full helmet with visor. From my elevation position, I haven't got a clear shot at his eyes. The standard-issue equestrian helmet is only made of fiberglass and foam, but it's still dense enough to slow a soft point bullet from penetrating for a clear kill. This calls for a sturdier projectile.

I've got three minutes. Throwing the bolt back, I remove the soft point cartridge from the breech. Reaching into my rifle case, I see a full metal jacket bullet with a hard brass coating. Inserting it into the chamber and throwing the bolt back into position, I'm back in business.

The cop is still there. But he's a bit blurry. Turning the calibration dials on the side of my scope, he comes into focus. I can read the NYPD motto inscribed on the front of his helmet. *To Serve and Protect.* That brings a smile to my lips.

I center the crosshairs over the logo and pause. His horse is spooked by a passing carriage. It will take almost a second for my bullet to reach him. I don't want to take any chances that he won't be still during this critical interval. An inch or two off-center could deflect the bullet off the side of his helmet.

I'll only have one chance.

The time on my phone reads one minute after twelve. The cop is posing for a picture now. This should make quite the memento. I pull the trigger and the cop slumps off his horse, his feet trapped in the stirrups. The horse rears up on its hind legs, unsure what to make of its dangling master. The crowd of onlookers staggers back in horror.

Within a few short minutes, a car with flashing lights screeches into the courtyard and two familiar faces emerge to take charge of the situation. The senior detective checks the status of the officer still hanging from the horse then with the help of his female partner extracts the limp rider and lays him on the ground. He's conferring with a few onlookers, who point in my direction.

Time to make my exit. See you again, my friend. Same time tomorrow?

Chapter Nine

The Pierre Hotel, 5th Avenue lobby

July 6, 12:20 p.m.

T he sound of screaming police sirens surrounded the Pierre Hotel as scores of flashing patrol cars converged on the building. Joe and Hannah rushed into the front lobby and flashed their badges to the front desk attendant. Well-to-do hotel guests clustered together looking confused as a loud alarm permeated the marble-floored foyer.

"Detective Bannon, NYPD," Joe announced to a check-in attendant. "I need to speak with the hotel manager immediately concerning a possible shooting on the premises."

The attendant's eyes widened as he watched uniformed cops pour into the posh lobby from all sides. He craned his head and scanned the pandemonium looking for a familiar face. Catching the eye of a well-dressed man talking with some guests, he raised his hand and motioned urgently toward the detectives. The man excused himself and approached the front desk.

"I'm James Aldridge, Manager of the Pierre," he said, addressing the two detectives. "How may I help you?"

Joe pulled his jacket aside to reveal his badge.

"Detective Joe Bannon. A police officer was shot three blocks from here. We have reports of a gunshot coming from your hotel. Did you receive our message to lock down the building?"

The manager sighed, not happy with the police intrusion.

"Yes, but it will take us several minutes to finish locking all the exits. This is a large hotel—we have over thirty exterior doors to secure."

Joe signaled to a group of plainclothes detectives approaching from the 61st Street entrance.

"Our team can help with that. Do you have a floorplan of the ground floor showing these exits?"

The manager paused briefly then turned to his front desk attendant.

"William, can you supply these officers with copies of our emergency exit plan?"

The attendant rummaged under the desk and pulled out a stack of papers then handed them to Joe.

Joe passed the papers to one of the Midtown Precinct detectives.

"Tony, can you gather up some patrol officers and post a guard at each of these exits?"

Tony nodded and headed off to summon a group of uniformed cops. After distributing the maps, the officers spread out in different directions.

Joe turned back to the manager.

"Have you received any reports of unusual noises coming from any of your rooms?"

The hotel manager looked toward his front desk agent.

"Have you heard anything out of place, William?"

"A few of us on the front desk heard a loud crack about twenty minutes ago," the attendant nodded. "It sounded like it came from across the street in the park. We haven't received any guest complaints, other than the usual noisy televisions and slamming doors."

Joe peered through the 5th Avenue lobby doors at the wall of trees lining the park.

"That might have been an echo you heard from the opposite side of the street."

He turned to Hannah.

"Han, can you check with the porters and see if they can more closely locate the source of the sound?"

Hannah nodded and hurried off toward the 5th Avenue exit. Joe returned his attention to the hotel manager.

"We'll need to interview every guest and staff member and inspect the guest rooms for unusual activity."

"That will take *hours*," the manager said, crossing his arms. "We have seven hundred and fourteen rooms and over a thousand guests. Must we keep the hotel locked down during this entire period?"

Joe's face reddened in anger at the manager's indifference for the gravity of the situation.

"A police officer has just been murdered by someone in your hotel," he said, looking the manager squarely in the eye. "No one will be allowed to leave this building until they've been cleared by one of our officers. I'll also need to see your security camera footage. Are all your exits and elevators monitored?"

The manager's arms slumped to his side, realizing the balance of power had shifted out of his hands.

"Only the unlocked doors facing 61st Street and 5th Avenue. The exits to the courtyard require a guest key to enter from the outside. All of our guest elevators are monitored."

"What about staff elevators?"

"We have two at each end of the hallways. Both are unmonitored. They're used primarily by our cleaning and facilities crew."

"Do you monitor the stairwells and guest room hallways?"

"The hallways on each floor have a dome cam at every corner. The stairwells aren't monitored. When we locked the elevators, guests began making their way down from the 41st floor."

"Good," Joe said, satisfied with the manager's newfound cooperation. "We'll begin by interviewing the guests already in the lobby. You can help by reviewing your security footage of the elevators and hallways during the last sixty minutes. Watch for someone carrying a long bag or unusual case. The shooter will be looking to exit quickly, perhaps via one of side exits."

Hannah returned to the front desk and nodded at Joe.

"Two porters heard an unusual sound coming many stories above the 5th Avenue entrance about twenty minutes ago," she reported.

"Right," Joe said. "Let's get started. Mr. Aldridge, can you supply our teams with a master key for an inspection of the guest rooms? We'll start at the top floor and work our way down."

The manager hesitated.

"May I send a hotel representative to accompany them? I don't want to alarm any guests who may still be in their room. Couldn't you at least allow one of our guest relations managers to explain the situation before you barge in?"

Joe glanced at Hannah. She shrugged her shoulders. The Pierre was one of New York City's premiere luxury hotels and hosted many powerful guests. The last thing the detectives needed was a raft of new complaints to the Commissioner concerning inappropriate police conduct.

"I suppose so," Joe allowed. "But only to announce our purpose at the door. If the killer is still here, it will be too dangerous for your staff to enter the room until we've cleared it."

"I understand," the manager said.

"I'll interview the guests here in the lobby. Once everybody is cleared, they'll receive vouchers to return to their rooms. But under no circumstances is anyone to leave the building until I've given the okay to end the lockdown. If you find anything suspicious on your video feeds, please notify me immediately."

"Of course."

The manager walked away briskly with a hotel security officer. Tony returned from securing the exit doors and joined the rest of Midtown Precinct detectives at the front desk. Although Joe didn't have direct line authority over the other detectives, they informally deferred to his seniority. He was widely respected by his colleagues and had a long track record solving high profile cases.

"Han," Joe instructed. "Take Tony, Frank, and Miguel to check the rooms. Two detectives to a room. I doubt the shooter would be dumb enough to linger, but keep your safeties off and proceed with caution. If you find anyone still in the room, match their identification and hotel registration. Look for an open window with a south or west exposure, or any furniture out of position near the window. If you find anything suspicious, give me a call. I'll work with the rest of our crew down here and do likewise. Let's not let this guy slip through our fingers."

"Will do, Joe," Hannah said. "Check back soon."

****

Half a block away, a man in a gray suit pulling a carry-on bag entered Barney's department store on Madison Avenue. He walked calmly through the main floor fragrance department to the bank of elevators near the rear of the store. When the door slid open, he crowded into the compartment with other smartly dressed shoppers carrying large bags. He didn't look out of place.

At the ninth floor, he exited the elevator and approached the hostess at Fred's Restaurant.

"May I help you sir?" the hostess said.

"Table for one, facing 61st Avenue."

"Of course. Please follow me."

The man followed the hostess to a table by a window, where he paused briefly to peer in the direction of the Pierre Hotel. Seeing the swarm of flashing police cruisers still parked outside the hotel, he took his seat.

"A server will be with you shortly," the hostess said before heading back to her station.

Picking up the menu from the linen-clad table, the man scanned the lunch selections. He hadn't realized how much of an appetite he'd worked up over the last hour. When the waiter arrived at his table, the man ordered beef tenderloin and a glass of Bordeaux.

When his lunch arrived, he devoured the steak between gulps of blood-red wine. Overhearing to the idle conversations of rich Manhattan housewives and power brokers from nearby tables, he smiled as he watched the bustle of activity surrounding the Pierre Hotel.

Chapter Ten

NYPD 18th Precinct

July 7, 8:00 a.m.

J oe and Hannah approached Lieutenant O'Neill's office for their scheduled early morning appointment. They expected it to be a highly charged meeting. Three sniper murders in as many days was bad enough, but the brazen assassination of a cop in broad daylight had raised the stakes to a new level.

Normally, the anteroom outside the Lieutenant's office was a busy hive of activity with detectives chatting and making calls. Today it was ghostly silent, as all eyes followed the two detectives heading up the investigation. The worst part was that the sniper had slipped away again, leaving precious few clues. The detectives were no closer to identifying or capturing him.

The Lieutenant's office door was closed, but Joe could see an unidentified woman sitting opposite his desk through the partially open blinds. Joe tapped twice on the door as he appraised the woman through the glass. She looked to be in her mid-thirties, wearing a smart navy suit with short brown hair pulled back in a bun.

Definitely not one of ours, he thought. *Too prim and buttoned up—looks like a fed.*

"Come in," O'Neill said.

Joe and Hannah entered, and Lieutenant O'Neill stood to introduce his guest.

"This is Special Agent Kate Palmer with the FBI. She has extensive experience profiling serial killers. I've brought her in to see if she can help track our sniper."

O'Neill looked at the special agent and motioned towards Joe and Hannah.

"Ms. Palmer, these are the two lead detectives assigned to our case, Joe Bannon and Hannah Trimble."

"Pleased to meet you, Ms. Palmer," Joe said, extending his hand.

"Please, call me Kate," the special agent said, shaking each Detective's hand. "There appears to be plenty enough tension surrounding this situation already. No need to add any unnecessary formality."

"Likewise," Joe said, smiling at the special agent as he and Hannah took seats beside her.

"Right," O'Neill interjected. "Can you two update Kate with the latest information from yesterday's shooting? I understand you've gathered some new evidence from the hotel sweep?"

"Yes," Joe reported. "Most importantly, we have video footage of the suspect. It's a bit grainy and not very close-up, but we've identified it's a man in his mid- to late-twenties."

"No fingerprints?" O'Neill asked.

"The video captures the room he fired from, but our forensics team wasn't able to swab any prints beyond those traced to the previous guests."

"What about facial recognition from the video? Did you run it through the database?"

"The perp was pretty heavily camouflaged behind dark glasses, a beard and a hat, so the system wasn't able to correlate the data."

"How did he escape the cordon? Didn't you lock down the hotel within minutes of the shooting?"

"Yes, but it appears he slipped out before all the exit doors could be secured."

O'Neill slumped back in his chair and crossed his arms.

"And you have no idea as to where he went or his current whereabouts?"

"No," Joe said. "But the hotel video provides some information about his M.O. We know how he gets into the hotel, how he sets up, and how he exits. We should be able to alert other hotels to watch for similar movement in the future."

"That can work two ways," O'Neill said, cocking an eyebrow. "We might be able to prevent a recurrence, but maybe we're better off trapping him in the act than discouraging him from giving us another shot at him. Do you have the video footage with you? Why don't we give Kate a look to see if she can lend her insight?"

Joe reached into his pocket and pulled out a thumb drive.

"I've got the relevant files copied here."

He handed the thumb drive over the desk and O'Neill inserted it into the side of his laptop. He tapped his keyboard a few times then turned the laptop around ninety degrees. Kate and the two detectives pulled their chairs together to get a closer look at the screen. The video began showing a tall man in a driver's cap pulling a roller suitcase toward the elevator.

"Is that the suspect?" Kate asked.

"Yes," Joe said.

"He seems to be aware of the location of the ceiling cam," O'Neill observed. "His head is tilted down just enough to obscure his eyes. Kate, what do you make of his countenance?"

"He walks briskly and with confidence, suggesting he's done this before or at least has rehearsed his steps. He's well dressed with a neatly trimmed beard. He obviously has resources. Nobody seems to be paying him any mind at this point."

"What about his luggage? It looks a bit different than the standard carry-on. Notice the irregular handle?"

"Yes. It's a bit longer than normal and perfectly round. Possibly holds the rifle barrel? He's probably got the rest of the components neatly packed in the small case. Looks like a custom job."

All four cops watched intently as the man pressed the exterior elevator button then stepped inside.

"See that?" O'Neill said, glancing up at Kate. "He pressed the elevator button with his knuckle. No prints."

Kate nodded as she continued watching the man. "Now he's putting on gloves. No wonder you couldn't find any prints. This guy's no amateur."

The elevator cam showed the man pressing the button for the eighteenth floor, then only the top of his cap as he stood perfectly still waiting for the door to open. Kate and O'Neill shifted closer to the screen as they watched the man exit the elevator and move down the hall.

O'Neill looked up at Joe.

"We haven't got a frontal view for this shot?"

"The hotel only has hallway cams at the corners, facing the exits. You'll get a better view in a few minutes."

The man continued down the hall toward a housekeeping cart placed in front of an open guest room door. The Lieutenant's eyes widened as he watched the man quickly step behind the cart and peer into the open bathroom. He seemed to place something into the door jamb before stepping back behind the cart into the hallway. The whole sequence only took three or four seconds.

"What the hell?" O'Neill exclaimed. "Is that the normal level of security at New York's fanciest hotels? Do chambermaids routinely leave guest room doors open and unattended while they work inside? Just about anybody could slip inside that way!"

"It is, unfortunately," Hannah said. "At least on check-out days. The chambermaids are informed when guests check out, so they know when to do a thorough refresh. I guess they figure there's nothing of value in the room at this point, so they don't see the need to lock the door."

O'Neill paused the video and backed it up a few seconds.

"What was that object he took out of his pocket and inserted into the door? Can we zoom in to see what he's doing?"

"These are just basic dome cams," Joe said. "They can only sweep in circles, with no zoom capability. It looks to be some kind of jamming device, because when he returns after the chambermaid leaves, he opens the door without a key."

"Clever," O'Neill said. He watched the man walk to the end of the hall and disappear behind a stairwell door.

"No cams in the stairways?"

"No, but he reappears in about five minutes."

O'Neill pressed the fast forward button on his keyboard until the stairwell door reopened and the man walked back down the hallway.

The Lieutenant followed the man's gait as he moved toward the camera.

"That's a long shot, but at least we can see his face. What do you figure? About six feet, one-seventy?"

Joe nodded.

"Yes, he's pretty slim, but looks to be in good shape. He moves like an athlete."

The man in the video stopped and paused briefly outside the closed door to room 1817 then turned his head as if listening for any sign of interior activity. Then he pushed the door open, pulled the clear object from the door jamb, and closed the door behind him.

"At least we know how he gets into the guest rooms unnoticed," O'Neill said. "We'll have to notify all the hotel managers in the city to secure their guest rooms during future service. How long does the perp stay in the room?"

"About twenty minutes," Joe said. "He seems to be on a schedule and doesn't waste any time. He goes in to the room at 11:48 and comes out at 12:09."

O'Neill shook his head.

"Too bad this feed doesn't come with audio. Can you narrow down the exact time of the shooting?"

"Yes—once again, almost precisely at noon."

"So he's able to set up and disassemble his equipment quickly."

"It appears so. He definitely knows what he's doing."

O'Neill advanced the video to the 12:09 time mark. The door to the room reopens and the man calmly walks to the far end of the hall where he presses the staff elevator button and disappears inside.

"No cams inside that elevator?"

"No, not inside staff elevators."

"This guy's done his homework," O'Neill said. "When did you arrive at the site of the shooting and notify the hotel to lock down?"

"We got to the corner of 59th and 5th Avenue at 12:06 and identified the Pierre as the likely location of the shooter a few minutes after. We called the hotel around 12:15 and arrived there less than a minute later."

"So the perp had five or six minutes to escape before all the doors were locked down?"

"Yes. You'll see in the next clip where he gets off the staff elevator and exits to the courtyard behind the hotel."

O'Neill resumed the video and the group watched as the man emerged from the elevator and exited through a side door. The next scene showed him walking briskly away toward the East Side, his roller case trailing behind. The last time indicated on the video feed is 12:12.

"That's the last we see of him?" O'Neill asked. "And you and Hannah arrived at the hotel four minutes later?"

"Yes."

"That's one cool operator."

O'Neill turned to Kate, who'd been quiet during most of the playing of the video.

"Kate, what do you make of all this? Can you put anything together based on the clip and the M.O. from the previous shootings?"

44

Kate finished scribbling some notes on a notepad and looked up.

"From the video, we see a calm and confident young man who obviously has practiced his craft, if we can call it that. But I think there's a lot more going on under the surface that we're not seeing. Anyone with this level of broad animosity who can kill perfect strangers in cold blood obviously has a lot of issues. I've seen this time and again. Serial killers always have an agenda."

"What about his victims?" O'Neill said. "So different in each case. How can we discern a motive from that?"

"Yes, that's a bit irregular. Normally, serial killers establish a pattern of preferential targets such as young women, co-workers, or the like. In this case, we have to infer motivation. I don't think these targets were randomly selected. I think this is an angry young man who has an axe to grind and some kind of score to settle."

O'Neill spread his hands in supplication.

"Why in god's name would he start with a young pregnant woman?"

"It could be a revealing sign that he started with her. Maybe he fathered a child out of wedlock and his girlfriend had an abortion against his wishes. Or maybe he was abused by his mother and the pregnant woman was a manifestation of this. Maybe he was adopted, and this was his way of taking his anger out on a mother who rejected him."

"That's a lot of maybes."

"Yes," Kate said. "But we now have three data points upon which to connect some of the dots. The commonalities narrow the field of possibilities and begin to focus our magnifying glass."

"What do you make of his second hit? What commonalities can you establish between such widely different targets?"

"The second one was a wealthy businessman who would appear to come from power and privilege. I'm guessing this young man, whatever his current means, came from a poor upbringing. He may have been abused by his father or some other male authority figure. Maybe someone who worked in the financial district."

"And the cop? What possible connection can there be there?"

O'Neill practically spit out the words, seething at the idea of a cold-blooded killer having the nerve to target a uniformed police officer.

Kate shook her head.

"The shooter may have had trouble with the law growing up. Or this could be another manifestation of his anger for any authority figure. This might be his perverted way of reasserting his power after being in a situation where he had no control and authority figures took advantage of him."

"What about the weapon?" Joe interjected. "It's a military grade, state-of-the-art sniper rifle. Should we be looking for someone with a military background?"

"Not necessarily. He could have secured the weapon on the black market. He might just as easily have a hunting background, with practice shooting game from long distances. The military rifle might just be his way of stepping up to the latest technology."

"How about his beard and his clothes?" Hannah asked. "Can we make any conclusions based on his appearance?"

Kate nodded.

"The beard, the sunglasses, and the cap are all likely designed to mask his identity. He knew he'd be recorded going about public spaces in this expensive hotel. I think that was all calculated and not part of his normal persona."

The FBI agent turned back to Lieutenant O'Neill.

"May I have a copy of the video? Our FBI technicians might be able to clarify some of the footage. A close-up of his face could reveal more clues as to his history and identity."

The Lieutenant nodded.

46

"My suspicion," Kate continued, "is that the suit, the cap, and the cropped beard were all designed to create a persona to fit the setting. I doubt that we're dealing with a well-to-do young man with a flight of fancy or some kind of God complex. I think this is a clever but disturbed fellow who's angry at the world for multiple perceived abuses. He's likely been planning his revenge for quite some time."

"What can we make of the time of day for each shooting?" Hannah asked. "All right around noon. Is this some kind of High Noon gunslinger thing?"

Kate's eyes narrowed as she pondered the question.

"That's an interesting one. I understand you have eyewitness accounts of each shooting? The good thing about modern technology is that just about everybody nowadays carries around mobile devices that record a temporal footprint of their actions and whereabouts. Were you able to capture any of that real-time data?"

"Yes," Joe said. "In two of the three shootings, we interviewed witnesses who were on their phone at the moment of firing. In both cases the call was terminated immediately, marking the time of the shooting at one minute after noon. The guys from the first precinct weren't able to narrow down the downtown shooting beyond a few minutes either side of noon."

Kate took a moment to process the new information.

"It could be that the shooter was choosing noon as a convenient time to maximize his targets moving onto the street at lunch time. Perhaps he chose the same time of day to send a message that he's controlling the streets at this time. Maybe it's part of a scheme to shut the city down. If this were to continue, I imagine it wouldn't take long for the public to become afraid to venture outside at that time of day. If you can validate the timing in future shootings, this could help narrow down the search. In the meantime, I'll do a bit of research on the possible meaning of the 12:01 connection."

"I don't want us to just focus on *future* shootings," O'Neill interrupted. "Especially if it involves cops. That's not the way to catch this guy. If we can't protect the streets, all hope is lost for maintaining order. I want to find this guy before he does any more damage and sends the entire city into a panic. Kate, have you got any suggestions as to where we can begin looking to find this nutcase?"

"It probably makes sense to start by looking through the short list of military-trained snipers. Look for someone with a troubled record or a dishonorable discharge. Once an outcast, always an outcast. If that doesn't uncover any suspects, check the adoption records of New York City in the twenty to thirty year ago time span. I have a feeling something awful happened to this fellow in his youth that he's bottled up for a long time. See if you can cross-reference young adopted men having criminal records or a history of violence. Look for any evidence of black market trading of the sniper rifle the suspect uses, but also look for hunting rifle licenses or hunting accidents involving adoptees. I'll comb through our FBI records to see if I can find any similar connections."

O'Neill sat back in his chair, pleased with the group's progress.

"That's good work, Kate. In the meantime, I'm going to have my team contact hotel managers around the city to alert them to this sniper's M.O. At the very least we can make it harder for this guy to sneak in and out of his preferred lair. I have a meeting in one hour with the Mayor and the Commissioner to discuss next steps. The entire force is on edge. Every beat cop is looking over his shoulder, afraid to step outside. If it was the sniper's intention to create fear, he's certainly accomplished that."

O'Neill stepped up to a calendar hanging on his wall and picked up a pen.

"Kate, can you clear your schedule for the next few days? As long as this pattern continues, I'd like the four of us to meet here at the same time every day to share Intel. We'll have a better chance of finding the sniper if we work together."

"I'll check with my station manager, but there shouldn't be a problem. These serial killers always leave a trail. We'll catch him sooner or later."

O'Neill placed a large red X through the next few days on his calendar.

"It's the *later* part that worries me."

Chapter Eleven

The Mayor's Office, City Hall

July 7, 10:00 a.m.

B rady O'Neill sat in the anteroom to the Mayor's office, waiting to be invited into his scheduled ten a.m. meeting. He wasn't sure what to expect, but he knew the Police Commissioner would also be attending. There was almost certainly going to be some tough questions about the spate of sniper shootings.

The walls of the waiting room were adorned with official photos of every New York City mayor, from its first, Thomas Willett, to its currently sitting occupant, Bill Braxton. All one hundred and fourteen were men, and all but one were white. O'Neill noticed another interesting pattern among the officials. Out of sheer boredom, he began counting the number of mayors whose first name was William.

His thoughts were interrupted when he got to the fifteenth, William O'Dwyer.

"The Mayor will see you now, Lieutenant O'Neill," the mayor's secretary announced.

She opened a wooden gate separating the waiting room from the front office, then walked ahead of O'Neill and opened the door to a large room festooned with gold-embroidered U.S. flags. The whole arrangement reminded O'Neill of a courtroom. He wondered who would be on trial today.

As he entered the room, the Mayor rose from behind his large desk and walked toward O'Neill. The Police Commissioner remained seated in a leather armchair with his legs crossed.

"Brady, thanks for coming on such short notice," the Mayor said, extending his hand in greeting.

Even though the two had never met, the Mayor had no hesitation referring to him in informal terms.

I suppose you can never really take the politician out of political office, O'Neill thought.

"Please, have a seat," the Mayor continued. "Of course, you know the Commissioner, Carl Pope."

The Mayor motioned toward the police Commissioner, who slowly stood up to shake O'Neill's hand. He glanced at the Lieutenant briefly, nodded, then sat back in his chair. The two had only met tangentially at official police functions, where the Commissioner had shown little interest in O'Neill while glad-handing with higher officials.

"I've called this meeting to discuss the recent sniper shootings," the Mayor began. "In particular, the execution-style killing of a police officer yesterday. I understand your team is taking the lead on the investigation. These public shootings have begun to generate increasing interest from the press, and my office is getting bombarded with questions I'm not equipped to answer. I was hoping you and the Commissioner could get me up to speed on the status of the investigation and your plan for stopping these killings."

O'Neill looked toward Commissioner Pope to see if he would speak first. The Commissioner simply nodded back.

"My team has made some progress identifying the suspect," the Lieutenant said. "We have video footage of him breaking into a hotel to set up for the most recent attack."

The Mayor raised an eyebrow.

"Where he shot the mounted police officer?"

"Yes. We believe in all three instances, he fired from a hotel room after posing as a guest."

"Do you have any leads as to his current whereabouts?"

"No, but we've enlisted the support of the FBI. We're building a profile which has given us some clues to begin investigating."

The Mayor paused to size O'Neill up. This was their first time meeting and he wasn't sure how much he could trust his judgment.

"The sniper has attacked on three successive days at the same time of day," he said. "What's your plan for averting another attack?"

"We know how he gains entrance to the hotel rooms. We've alerted every hotel manager in the city to be on the lookout for someone matching the sniper's description and ensure all guest rooms are secured and accessible only to registered guests. We've also notified our officers on the street to watch for a slim young man carrying an unusually shaped work case."

The Mayor nodded, seemingly satisfied with O'Neill's answers so far.

"What about our officers? Are they unnerved about yesterday's shooting? Is anyone showing reluctance to resume their beat? What steps are we taking to protect them?"

O'Neill glanced at the Commissioner. This was a broader issue that was beyond the scope of his authority.

The Commissioner looked the Mayor squarely in the eyes and spoke in a confident tone.

"Our cops to a man aren't afraid to go into the line of fire. Everybody knows it's part of the job."

"I'm sure they do, Carl," the Mayor said. "But I'd like to prevent a recurrence of yesterday's circus. It looks to me, and perhaps increasingly to the public, like everybody is a sitting duck out there. Can't we equip our cops with more protection?"

"Every police officer already wears a bulletproof vest," the Commissioner said. "Plus, the mounted officer's helmet didn't provide much protection against the fatal bullet."

"What about riot gear? Don't you have more protective helmets in reserve, like the ESU team uses?"

The Mayor was reaching, O'Neill thought. *Looking for simple solutions to complex issues.*

That's what politicians do.

"Riot helmets are only designed to resist rocks and other light projectiles," the Commissioner continued, "not high-powered rifle bullets. Besides, do you really want to send all our cops out in riot gear roaming the streets of Manhattan? That will just accelerate the rising public panic."

The Mayor slumped back in his chair and looked out the window.

"So you're recommending we just operate business as usual? I hate to think what the press will say if—God forbid—another cop or pregnant woman falls prey to this sniper. One or both of our heads could be on the block next."

The room fell silent as all three considered the ramifications.

O'Neill suddenly looked up.

"We may not need to take such bold measures yet," he said. "The sniper has established a predictable M.O. He always fires to the top of the head. Every patrol cop wears a standard-issue police cap. We could jerry-rig something pretty easily to fit under their cap that could stop a bullet."

The Mayor paused for a moment then looked at his watch.

"It's already ten forty-five. We've only got a little over an hour before this guy potentially strikes again. Can you get the word out and fashion something that quickly?"

O'Neill looked at the Commissioner who shook his head skeptically.

"Every police vest has Kevlar inserts in its compartments," the Lieutenant continued. "As a temporary measure, we could ask each officer to cut out a small patch and place it under his cap. It's not perfect, but it could work at least until we come up with something more permanent."

"And just ask every cop to keep his head down?" the Mayor scoffed.

O'Neill shrugged.

"Literally, yes. So far the sniper has taken up positions some distance above the street. Assuming he sticks to his M.O., this will at least prevent a fatal head shot."

"What about the civilians?" the Mayor asked. "How are we going to protect them? We can't put bulletproof hats on everybody."

The Commissioner jumped in to defend the Lieutenant.

"I think Lieutenant O'Neill has a workable plan for protecting the principle targets. Hopefully, his other actions will block off the sniper's lairs and make it harder for him to set up. But if he does strike again, I think we should entertain some kind of public message to warn the public. At least for the narrow timeframe that he's confined his activity so far."

The Mayor threw up his hands.

"And turn the streets over to the criminals? What kind of message does that send about our ability to protect the public?"

The Commissioner shook his head.

"It's your call, Mr. Mayor. With respect, this appears to be a political issue. I think you need to decide which is the lesser of two evils: maintaining public safety with a limited curfew or risking another highly public assassination of an innocent bystander."

The Mayor paused for a long time to consider the options.

"Okay, Carl. Let's see if Lieutenant O'Neill's measures work in discouraging the shooter. If it doesn't, I want you to take the point on notifying the public about appropriate safety measures. In the meantime, I'd like to be kept informed daily of the progress you and your team are making on finding this sniper. This could quickly turn into a political landmine for all of us."

The Commissioner and Lieutenant O'Neill looked straight at the Mayor. They both knew he was setting one or both of them up to be the fall guy.

Chapter Twelve

Washington Square, Lower Manhattan

July 7, 11:30 a.m.

I t's another lovely day in Lower Manhattan. Washington Square is beautiful this time of year. Big leafy trees, the circular fountain, and the famous arch at the foot of 5th Avenue. Not quite the Arc de Triomphe in Paris, but still impressive.

And lots of young people. Smack dab in the hotbed of NYU. The students are scurrying between classes, taking an occasional break to rest their heavy backpacks and chat with colleagues by the fountain. A couple of cops are milling about, parkgoers eyeing them nervously.

It's less busy than usual in New York's public spaces today. Yesterday's shooting made the front page of the Post and the Daily News. The story finally made it above the fold in the Times. The city's finally catching on to the fact there's a new killer in its midst.

But this is no Son of Sam who operated in the dark and only targeted young couples. This killer strikes indiscriminately: young women, middle-aged men—even cops.

High Noon Sniper Strikes Again, the Daily News billed it. *Serial Killer Ups the Ante*, said the Post. *Hotel Sniper Targets Cop*, the Times reported.

Not terribly catchy. I'll have to give the press something more interesting to chew on. Let's see if they can come up with something a little more memorable.

These people don't appear to have gotten the message. It's eleven forty-five, and there's still lots of students milling about the fountain. Young people always think they're invincible. It would be so easy to pick one of them off from my perch above the park. I could have a field day, just like the German sniper in that movie.

Here we go.

Looks like the other shoe dropped. Everyone's checking the time on their phones and getting up to clear out. Slipping into cafes and under awnings. I guess the word's gotten around after all. No point taking any unnecessary chances. It's only for a few minutes. It'll be safe again shortly after noon, right?

Better to be safe than sorry. Nobody wants today to be their unlucky day.

Everyone except the cops, that is. You'd think this would be the perfect moment for them to step inside for a donut. I'm surprised they're not looking up for shiny objects and suspicious movement from above. You gotta give it to them, though. It takes a lot of guts to put yourself in the line of fire the day after one of your brothers-in-arms has fallen.

It's funny how quickly the streets can clear when the public is properly motivated. They're scurrying like ants into the safety of their anthills. Now it's only the yellow beetles marching down the thoroughfares of Lower Manhattan as we near noon. Where could you be safer than inside the steel cocoon of a taxi cab?

Everyone's ducking into automobiles now, looking for safe passage. They're probably talking about the crazy sniper who's out there watching them right now. Good thing they're safely holed up in their metal and glass cages.

There's a stream of taxis moving toward me along Washington Square North. The light turns red at the intersection where 5th Avenue ends in front of the Washington Square Arch. One cabbie is strumming the steering wheel waiting for the light to change. He knows his fare racks up faster on the move than letting the clock tick it off.

It's 12:01. The cabbie sees the traffic signal on the 5th Avenue lamppost turn yellow. As he prepares to rush out of the intersection, I size him up in my scope.

Why do people feel so safe behind fragile glass windows?

The moment the light turns green, I pull the trigger. With only one short block to travel, the bullet quickly snaps the cabbie's head back and he slumps forward onto the steering wheel. His car glides through the intersection with the horn wailing until it bumps into the lamppost on the other side. In the back seat, two passengers duck behind the backrest, cowering in fear.

This ought to give the newspapers something to write about.

Chapter Thirteen

Washington Square

July 7, 12:04 p.m.

W ithin three minutes of the shooting, flashing lights and wailing sirens pierced the peaceful setting of the park. Scores of police cruisers converged on the corner of 5th Avenue and Washington Square North. Cops poured out of their cars with guns drawn and began fanning out to block the escape of the sniper. One group raced toward the Washington Square Hotel at the northwest corner of the park.

A few short minutes later, Joe and Hannah's unmarked cruiser screeched to a stop beside the stricken taxi. Joe got out and flashed his badge to the patrol cop who was keeping gawkers at bay.

"Detectives Bannon and Trimble from the Eighteenth Precinct," he announced to the cop. "We're heading the investigation for the sniper. What time did you arrive on the scene?"

"My partner and I were patrolling the park when we heard the shot. He took off in the direction of the sound while I secured the crime scene."

"From which direction did the shot come?" Joe asked. "Can you tell how far away it was and when it was fired?"

The patrol cop nodded.

"I checked my watch just before twelve. The shot was fired a minute later. Sounded only about a block away, toward the west."

He pointed toward a building on the northwest side of the park.

"The Washington Square Hotel is on the corner. Fits the sniper's pattern. A bunch of our guys headed over there a couple of minutes before you arrived to lock it down."

Hannah looked at Joe.

"Should we follow? We know what to look for and his known escape paths."

Joe paused to look through the windshield of the taxi at the cab driver slumped over the wheel.

"One sec, Han."

He placed his finger over the bullet hole in the glass then stepped a few paces into the middle of the intersection. He lifted his arm and swung it five degrees to the left. Then he peered down his extended arm toward a high-rise building on the southwest corner and motioned for Hannah.

"There isn't a clear sightline from the hotel to this location. Too many tall trees blocking the view. Plus there's no windows on the east face of the hotel. But look at the building to its immediate left. It's taller and has a clear line of sight to this spot. The turret on top of the building would provide perfect cover for the sniper."

Hannah glanced at her watch.

"It's 12:09. We might still be able to catch him."

Joe nodded.

"I'm going to approach on foot in case we need to chase him through the back alleys. Do a circle of the block in the cruiser. If you don't see anything suspicious, meet me outside the front door in a few minutes. Then we'll head up to the roof together to block his escape."

Joe took off running up the middle of the street toward the tall building. Alternating glances between the rooftop and the perimeter of the building at street level, he searched for any sign of the sniper.

He knew there were precious few seconds remaining to block the killer's escape.

Chapter Fourteen

30 Washington Square West

July 7, 12:05 p.m.

T he sniper watched the flurry of activity at the corner of
5th Avenue and Washington Square North through his
rifle scope.   It seemed as if every police car in Lower
Manhattan had responded to the emergency dispatch.

Normally, he'd be packing up his gear and making his
way downstairs to bypass the cordon. But something held his
interest for a little longer. He wanted to see his pursuers up
close one more time. There was something intriguing about
this detective. The sniper was hoping to find some clues he
might use for future leverage. Within five minutes, two
familiar faces emerged from one of the cars stopping at the
scene.

The sniper's scope followed the senior detective as he
spoke with the attending patrol cop. He swung his rifle to a
line of cops running toward Washington Square Hotel on the
northwest corner of the park. He smiled at how easy it had
been to misdirect their attention. Shifting his focus back to
the crime scene, he watched the detective look into the front
seat of the cab and place his finger over the hole in the
windshield.

What's this? the sniper thought. *He's walking into the
middle of the intersection and pointing in my direction. Not
in the direction of the hotel—toward the rooftop of my
building. Surely he can't see me in my camouflaged position?
The sun is too high to glint off my lens. Now he's running
toward me! Shit. This is going to make exfiltration more
challenging. No time to leave in the usual way.*

The sniper quickly disassembled his rifle and packed it in his case. Then he reached into a canvas knapsack and pulled out a thick rope and two grappling hooks. He threaded one end of the rope through the eye of one hook and tied a secure clinch knot. Then he crouched down and moved to the opposite side of the rooftop elevator room.

He stopped at the south edge of the rooftop and looked across the gap to the adjacent building. The two buildings were at the same height. It was only fifteen feet across to the other rooftop. Looking down into the gap, there was a ten story drop to the top of a smaller connecting building. Just enough to kill or seriously maim the sniper if he fell. But there was no other option. He knew the cops would be rushing up to the rooftop in seconds, and there was no other way down.

He grabbed the rope three feet from the tethered hook and began to swing it up and down in widening arcs. He released the hook and flung it onto the rooftop of the adjacent building. Pulling the rope toward him, the hook caught a utility pole. He fished the other end of the rope through the handle on top of his rifle case and lifted the rope to shoulder height. The case slowly slid down the rope toward the other side until it bumped against the side of the building.

He tied the other end of the rope to the second grappling hook and secured the hook to a pipe on top of the elevator shaft. Throwing the knapsack over his shoulder, he reached up with both hands and tested the rope to be sure it would hold his weight. Then he began traversing the gap, moving hand over hand as his body dangled over the open chasm.

When he got to the other side, he detached the hook from the utility pole. Then he turned to the other building and swung the rope up in a bullwhip movement. A wave ran the length of the line until it reached the other end and made a clanging sound. The hook on the other side bumped away from the pipe atop the elevator shaft. He swung it back over to his side. Just as he heard the sound of the elevator door fly open on the other building, he scampered to the far side of the machine room on the new building. Crouching low and out of sight, he waited twenty minutes until the voices from the adjacent rooftop disappeared.

When the cops were gone, he fished two thin knife-like tools out of his pocket and inserted them into the exterior lock of the machine room. After jimmying them for a few seconds, he swung open the door and pulled his equipment inside. Finding a storage space behind some old boxes, he hid his rifle case and pulled on an old baseball cap. Then he threw the knapsack over his shoulder and began making his way downstairs.

With no sign of police on the main floor, he slipped out a side door and joined a group of students walking into the residence hall across the street. He set his knapsack down at a table on the north side of the cafeteria then watched the building across the street for the next two hours. When he was sure things had died down, he walked back across the street to the building where his rifle was stored. Taking only seconds to jimmy the lock on the side door, he made his way up to the elevator room where he retrieved his case.

Later that evening, he began planning his next move. He knew his next hit would raise the level of fear to an entirely new level and set the entire city on edge.

Chapter Fifteen

Park Slope, Brooklyn

Five Years Earlier

The young man approached a townhouse in the tony neighborhood of Park Slope with a mix of fear and excitement. He'd searched for his birth mother his entire life and hoped today to finally meet her. She wasn't expecting him and he wasn't completely sure she was his real mother. New York's adoption laws blocked the release of birth parent identities without their consent. But the young man was very resourceful and determined.

There was never any secret he'd been adopted. He'd shuttled between foster homes until a childless couple finally adopted him at the age of eight. He wondered if it was his unusual appearance that kept his natural and foster families from adopting him. He had an odd-shaped upper lip and unusually narrow-set eyes. Children at school teased him mercilessly and he'd been mistreated by his adoptive father. It was almost as if his appearance made him less human, giving others license to abuse him.

When New York changed its adoption disclosure policies, it provided him a glimmer of hope. The new law allowed adoptees over the age of eighteen to receive non-identifying information about their birth parents. This included information about the parents' race, religion, occupation, and the name of the agency that arranged the adoption. He already had his amended birth certificate, which showed his original birth date and place of birth. It wasn't too difficult to correlate the information to identify his mother's name and location.

The Adoption Information Registry revealed that his mother at the time of his birth was single, unemployed with a grade ten education, and Catholic. The adoption agency on record was St. Vincent's Adoption Services. When the agency refused to disclose his mother's identity, he returned after closing hours and used his lock picking skills to break in. After searching through the files for five minutes by his adopted last name, he found a folder under the surname Weir. It contained a copy of his original birth certificate with his name and his mother's maiden name blotted out. His father's name was listed as Unknown.

When he got home, he magnified the size of the certificate using his computer's photo editing software. Then he printed the enlarged certificate and held it over a bright lamp. He could barely make out his mother's maiden name, Sarah Feeny. His own birth name was listed as Brian Feeny. A quick internet search of the New York City white pages pulled up seven matches for a Sarah Feeny. Two were black, three were under the age of thirty-five, and one was over the age of seventy. That left only two who would have been of childbearing age when Brian was born. But only one was Catholic.

He tracked down her address and confronted her, but her reaction suggested there was no connection. As a result of his repeated childhood abuse, the young man had become super-sensitive to people's body language. He'd learned to recognize when someone meant to do him harm or when they were lying. The woman looked him directly in his eyes and spoke in a natural tone of voice. She was either a superb actor, or she wasn't related to him.

He'd hit a dead end. Where else could he search for his mother? Could she be in jail? The adoption registry information hinted at a troubled past. Research on his unique facial deformities correlated with fetal alcohol syndrome. His mother had been an alcoholic; might she also have been a junkie? Had she turned tricks to feed her drug habit? Maybe she'd moved outside the New York metropolitan area. That would make his search much longer and more problematic.

After some deliberation, it suddenly hit him. There could be a much simpler possibility. It was probable his mother had married and changed her name. After checking the public record of marriage licenses issued in New York City over the last twenty-three years, he found five women with maiden names of Sarah Feeny. Three had married in a Catholic church. Their addresses were easily traceable using the couples' married names.

Neither of the first two women demonstrated any sign of familiarity when he met them. The Brooklyn brownstone was his last chance to trace his natural mother. He hoped his appearance might trigger a memory, and that the woman's reaction would reveal the lineage. His birth mother would have noticed the unusual facial characteristics in her newborn baby and likely been informed of their cause. If he had any doubt about their connection, he was prepared to take a hair sample for DNA testing.

Walking up the steps to the front door of the expensive home, he couldn't help thinking how different his life could have been if his mother had kept him. If this was her, she'd certainly improved her standing since her high-school dropout days. Could her newfound wealth have provided a better education and more opportunities for her son? Would a loving mother have sheltered him from the abuses he received at the hands of so many vicious strangers?

He knocked on the door and straightened his hair. The sound of heels walking over a tiled floor became progressively louder as someone approached the door. It swung open and a beautiful blonde woman in her late thirties appeared. Her eyes widened as she looked at the young man. It was obvious that she recognized his face immediately.

"Mother?" the young man said.

His heart was beating a hundred miles an hour. The woman had his same hair color, and her pupils were wide as saucers, betraying her excitement.

"It's me, Brian. Your son."

The woman stood in the doorway for a long moment with her face flushed and her chest rising and falling with adrenaline.

"I—I don't know who you are," she stammered. "I don't have a son. Please...leave me alone."

She began to close the door. The young man leaped forward and placed his hand on the door.

"Please. I can tell you recognize me. I just want to talk for a few minutes. I've thought of you so often."

The woman paused. For a brief moment, it appeared as if she might acknowledge the connection and rush out to embrace her son. The sound of someone working in the kitchen behind her snapped her out of her thoughts and her expression suddenly shifted.

"I don't know what you're talking about," she said matter-of-factly. "I don't have a son. If you don't leave, I'll have to call the police."

Two little girls about the age of five or six came scrambling up the hall behind the woman and peered out the door.

"Who's that funny looking man, Mommy?" one of them said.

"Go back inside, children. It's nobody. He's got the wrong address."

The woman's eyes made contact with the young man one last time before she shut the door and bolted it from behind. In that last moment of contact, he knew from the agonized look on her face that she was his mother.

Chapter Sixteen

Battery Park, Lower Manhattan

July 7, 7 p.m.

The morning's hit on the cab driver had proven more challenging than expected for the sniper. He'd made a narrow escape under close pursuit by the two detectives. He knew he'd have to be more careful with his next attack. He also knew the detectives would be winnowing the list of suspects and that eventually he'd come under suspicion.

Tonight, he planned the perfect alibi.

At 7 p.m., wearing a mustache, sunglasses, and a baseball cap, he walked into the lobby of the Ritz-Carlton Hotel at the edge of Battery Park. He carried a heavy gym bag in his right hand. It took all his strength to hold his body straight so as not to raise suspicion as to the bag's contents. His sniper rifle dangled from a shoulder harness down the length of his back under a long coat.

When he reached the elevators, he pressed the button for the top floor with his knuckle. There would be no need for any guest room subterfuge today. No more hiding, nor rapid extraction. This time, everything would be automated.

When he got to the top floor, he walked to the end of the hall and entered the stairwell. Walking up two flights, he picked the old style door lock leading up to the mechanical room. Emerging onto the rooftop, the view was perfect. It had a raised lip around the perimeter with no tall buildings nearby for anyone to peer down on him. And he had an unobstructed view of the ferry terminal across the treed expanse of Battery Park.

He set to work immediately. He took off his coat and laid his rifle on an air conditioning unit. Then he swung the bipod legs down and pointed the barrel toward Whitehall Terminal two thousand yards to the south. Looking through the scope, he could see the bow of the Staten Island Ferry where it lay nestled in its mooring.

The 7:20 p.m. scheduled departure to Staten Island was busy loading passengers. Even at this relatively late hour, there were still many passengers boarding after a long workday in the city. The pack of bobbing heads streaming up the gangway presented an easy target. But nobody would be shot in the back of the head this evening. The sniper wondered which unlucky commuter would be in the wrong place at the wrong time on his return journey tomorrow morning.

He unzipped his gym bag and pulled out a device that looked like a waffle iron. He twisted a knob on its side, and the two sides began to separate as scissor arms connecting them elevated the upper plate. Placing his rifle butt on the top surface, he peered through the scope and swung the barrel a few degrees south. He turned the knob a couple more times and looked through the scope again. It took three or four adjustments until he had the barrel pointed where he wanted.

Then he reached into the bag and extracted three heavy sacks. He propped one behind the end of the rifle butt and the other two around each end of the bipod legs. He tried moving the rifle and it held firmly in place. Then he pulled a small black box out of the bag and placed it at the front edge of the platform. The device had an actuator arm, which he inserted into the trigger opening. Pulling out his cellphone, he tapped the screen a couple of times. A motor inside the black box whirred for a moment and the actuator arm pulled back against the trigger. The rifle clicked.

He tapped his phone again and the arm whirled forward, releasing the trigger. He pressed a button on top of the black box and a digital display blinked the current time. He quickly checked his phone to verify they matched. Then he inserted a five round clip into the stock and looked through the scope to make one final adjustment.

The last thing he pulled out of the bag was an object that looked like a small drone. At each corner of the device were six inch propeller blades encircled in a metal housing. His final step was to hook two cables attached to the bottom of the drone to eyelets on top of the rifle and the black box.

Picking up his empty gym bag, he took the elevator down to the hotel lobby and calmly walked out the front door. There was a warm, gentle breeze. As long as the weather held overnight, he'd be several miles away from the scene of the next killing.

****

Twelve hours later, the 7:00 a.m. Staten Island ferry slowly chugged toward lower Manhattan. The thirty-minute crossing of New York Harbor was one of the most breathtaking passages on earth. Steaming directly past the Statue of Liberty, passengers saw the spectacular skyline of New York City rise higher and higher as the vessel approached Whitehall Ferry Terminal.

But not many people were paying much attention this morning. Everybody was checking their email or catching a nap before starting another work day. At 7:20 a.m., the ferry sounded its foghorn announcing its arrival into port. Five minutes later, six thousand commuters shuffled through the ship's bulwark into the terminal. The bleary-eyed passengers could have no inkling that more than a mile away, an unmanned rifle was taking random aim on the crowd of faces.

On the other side of the harbor, a lone man stood on the shoreline of New Jersey watching the ship's exodus through binoculars. At 7:25 a.m., he pulled out his phone and tapped the screen twice. Three miles away, the black box atop the

Ritz-Carlton Hotel whirred and its actuator arm slowly retracted. It took almost three full seconds for him to hear the poof of the rifle after the passenger's head exploded.

Moments later, the sound of panicked screams wafted across the bay as people stampeded into the terminal. The man waited only a few short seconds before tapping new instructions onto his phone screen. A long thin object lifted off the roof of the Ritz-Carlton hotel and began flying toward Liberty State Park.

The man wondered how many people would notice the odd object flying across the harbor. No matter, he thought, because he would be long gone shortly after it landed in a heavily forested section of the park.

Two minutes later, he was on the New Jersey Turnpike headed into the haze of downtown Newark.

Chapter Seventeen

NBC Studio 1A, Rockefeller Plaza

July 8, 6:45 a.m.

P olice Commissioner Pope rested uncomfortably in the prep room for the Today Show. He was scheduled to be interviewed by the show's host shortly after it aired at 7:00 a.m. The fourth sniper killing in as many days had attracted sensational headlines from every news agency in the city. Some tabloids suggested the NYPD was inept and being outwitted by the mysterious sniper. The Mayor had asked the Commissioner to tamp down the hysteria level and assure the public that the situation would soon be under control.

The Commissioner anticipated a tough interview with many difficult questions. Worst of all, the NYPD had precious few leads as to the identity or whereabouts of the killer. The sniper had slipped through their dragnet once again, and the investigation team had no clues about where he might strike next.

A make-up technician blotted Pope's sweaty forehead as a familiar face entered the prep room and approached his chair.

"Commissioner Pope?" the man said, extending his hand. "I'm Doug Morrison, host of the Today Show. I just wanted to stop by and make sure you're comfortable before we start the interview. We'll have you join us in the main studio after the first commercial break, around 7:20. Did you have any questions?"

The Commissioner shook his head, trying to look calm.

"I've been on TV before. Something tells me this one will be a bit more challenging."

"Not to worry," Morrison assured. "We're just looking for any insights you can share on the status of the investigation and what the public can do to protect themselves."

The Commissioner eyed the host suspiciously. He knew reporters tried to sensationalize their news stories, and this one already had plenty of buzz.

"A stage manager will escort you to the studio at the appointed time," the host said. "See you in about thirty minutes."

At 7:17 a.m., the stage manager retrieved Pope and escorted him to the main set. He directed the Commissioner to sit in a high chair directly opposite the host while a stage hand attached a microphone to his suit lapel.

"We'll be going live in sixty seconds," the stage manager said.

Morrison nodded toward the Commissioner as a make-up technician performed a final touch-up. Behind the camera a production assistant called down the live feed.

"Five, four, three, two, one—*live*."

The red light atop the main camera lit up.

"We're here with New York City Police Commissioner Carl Pope," Morrison said, facing the camera. "Commissioner Pope, thank you for joining us today."

"Thanks for having me," the Commissioner replied.

"As you know, the city has experienced a raft of unusual shootings these last few days. We're hoping you can shed some light on the department's progress finding the killer and what the public can do to protect itself."

The Commissioner paused as he considered his answer.

"We've collected video footage of the suspect, and we know where he sets up. We narrowly missed apprehending him. It's just a matter of time before we find and neutralize the perpetrator."

Morrison looked at the Commissioner unconvinced.

"This sniper apparently fires from hotel rooms. What steps has the force taken to prevent unauthorized entry to these spaces and block his escape should he try to set up there again?"

"We've notified every hotel manager in the city to ensure guest rooms are locked at all times. We also have a protocol for locking down any building suspected of harboring the suspect."

Morrison's brow furrowed.

"How did the suspect evade your lockdown in four successive shootings?"

Commissioner Pope began to feel his blood pressure rise as he gripped the arms of his chair tightly.

"It takes several minutes for our first responders to arrive on the scene and identify the firing location. This killer is very clever. He seems to know exactly how long it takes for our team to respond and how to bypass our cordon."

Morrison cocked his head.

"Are you suggesting he's smarter than your cops? Haven't you got a lot more resources to work with? How many officers are working to find the killer?"

Commissioner Pope clenched his jaw. Apparently the sniper wasn't the only one ambushing his police force.

"Our entire force of thirty-five thousand officers is on alert to watch for someone matching the suspect's description. The detective squads at the Eighteenth and First Precincts are leading the investigation. We've also enlisted the help of the FBI in constructing a profile, and we're following up on some leads."

"What exactly do we know about the killer so far?"

"He's a white male in his mid-twenties, about six feet tall and 175 pounds. He uses a high-grade sniper rifle with special bullets. We're currently investigating individuals with a military background."

"You've brought a photo of the suspect," Morrison said. "May we share it with our viewers now?"

The Commissioner nodded and the camera cut to a still image of the sniper exiting the Pierre Hotel two days ago.

"That's a pretty blurry image," the host said, squinting at the photo. "Between the beard, the hat, and the sunglasses, there's not much we can make out. That could be any one of thousands of New York City citizens. Is that all you have?"

The Commissioner shifted uncomfortably in his chair.

"Our technicians are working to clarify the image quality and provide a clearer picture to share with the public. One of the distinguishing characteristics of the suspect is the unusual case he carries. It's a square black roller case with a long round handle. If any citizen sees someone matching this description, please notify the police department immediately."

Morrison nodded, satisfied with the new information.

"What can we surmise about the killer's motivation? Each of the victims was very different. Is *anybody* safe out there?"

"Our FBI profiler has established certain commonalities between the victims. We've begun to search our databases to find suspects who fit the profile."

Morrison sensed the Commissioner was holding something back.

"In each case, the sniper shot his victims in the head from a long distance. Always right around noon. What can we make of that?"

"I'm not sure we can make any conclusions just yet. I don't want to speculate until we have more information."

"Our switchboard is getting hundreds of calls a day from people who say they feel like sitting ducks when they go outside. What can the citizens of New York City do to protect themselves?"

The Commissioner nodded sympathetically.

"So far, the killer has limited his shootings to a relatively narrow time frame. Until we apprehend him, we're recommending that citizens refrain from going out in public between 11:30 a.m. and 12:30 p.m."

Morrison raised his eyebrows in surprise.

"Is this an *official* curfew?"

"At this point, it's simply an advisory."

"Does this apply to people on foot and in vehicles?"

"Yes. Hopefully this will only be necessary for a few days. We hope to apprehend the killer soon."

"So far the sniper has only struck in Manhattan. Is the advisory for the downtown borough only?"

"For now, yes. But I think all citizens of New York City should take the necessary precautions to protect themselves and their families. It may be wise for everyone to stay indoors during this time frame until we find the killer."

Morrison reached out to shake the Commissioner's hand.

"Thank you for joining us today, Commissioner. I think I share the sentiments of every citizen of New York in expressing Godspeed to the NYPD in—"

Morrison suddenly placed his finger to his ear and turned his face to the side as he listened to a message in his earpiece. Then he turned toward the camera.

"I've just been informed of a new sniper shooting at Whitehall Ferry Terminal. A passenger disembarking from the Staten Island ferry was shot during the morning rush hour."

Morrison turned back toward the Commissioner.

"Commissioner Pope, what do you make of this latest incident? It breaks from the sniper's usual pattern, with an early morning shooting. Will you extend the advisory to a wider timeframe now?"

The Commissioner pulled a mobile phone from his jacket and paused as he read something on the screen.

"We need to confirm this is the same shooter," he said. "For now, the advisory stands as recommended. We'll release a statement when we have more information. You'll have to excuse me now as I have more important business to attend to."

The Commissioner began removing his lapel microphone as the camera zoomed in on the show's host.

"There you have it, folks," the host announced. "Our city is in an unprecedented state of lockdown while the NYPD searches for a dangerous and unpredictable killer. Let's all pray for a speedy resolution of this matter so we can avoid further bloodshed and reclaim our normal lives."

With the sound of frenzied shuffling in the background, the camera cut to commercial.

Chapter Eighteen

Astoria, Queens

Twelve years earlier

The young woman sat on her living room sofa leafing through a photo album. She paused at a picture of newlyweds laughing while confetti rained on their heads. It seemed so long ago when they married, even though it had only been a few years. She caressed the image of her husband wearing his Marine uniform. He was so dashing in his dress blues, with his white peaked cap and long sword at his side.

She knew the life of a Marine officer's wife would entail stretches of time apart, but it had been many long months since she'd felt his tender caress. After the September 11 attacks, the Gulf War had pulled Joe overseas for an indefinite time. Now all she had to combat her loneliness was their five-year-old son, who sat quietly beside her playing with a toy.

As her mind wandered to memories of their wedding night, she heard a sound in the kitchen. Getting up to investigate, she told her son to stay in the living room. As she approached the kitchen with caution, she saw a shadow move along the floor. Sensing an intruder, she flipped open her phone and began dialing 9-1-1.

Just before the line started ringing, someone grabbed her from behind. She dropped the phone and her son began wailing. A man gripped her tightly around the waist and held a carving knife inches from her throat.

"Where's your cash and jewelry?" he rasped.

"I…don't keep much money in the house," she said.

Her son was cowering on the sofa, his eyes wide as saucers with fear.

"Please don't hurt us," the woman said. "I'll give you whatever you want."

The man looked at the boy on the sofa then grabbed the woman's left hand.

"Where's your wedding ring? Aren't you married?"

"Yes," she said. "My husband will be home soon."

"Don't play games with me," the man snorted. "I've been watching you. No one has come to this house in days. Give me your valuables if you don't want your son to watch his mother bleed to death before his eyes."

The woman glanced at her phone on the floor. The screen was still illuminated with the 9-1-1 number, indicating the call had been connected. She knew the operator would be tracing the call and sending a patrol car to investigate within minutes. All she had to do was remain calm and keep the intruder distracted.

"It's upstairs. Just give me a moment and I'll get it for you."

The man eased his grip and the woman instinctively reached for her son. Whatever she did, she didn't want to leave him alone with this violent stranger.

The man suddenly grabbed the boy by the back of his shirt and dragged him off the sofa.

"The child stays with me. Now hurry, if you don't want to see him harmed."

"Mommy!" the boy wailed, trying to pull away from the man. "Help me!"

The intruder placed the knife under the boy's chin.

"Let's go together," he said. "That way I can keep my eye on both of you and make sure nobody tries anything fancy."

The man saw the phone on the floor and kicked it across the room.

"Get a move on. You've got exactly one minute to hand over your jewelry."

The woman turned to head upstairs and the man followed, dragging the boy by his heels along the floor. When they got to the second floor, the woman went into the master bedroom and opened a jewelry box.

"Here," she said thrusting the open box toward the intruder. "Take everything—just leave me and my son alone."

The man used the tip of the knife to search through the box and move its contents around. It was full of silver bracelets and broaches.

"Don't waste my time. This stuff is worthless. Where's your wedding ring?"

The woman knew full well where she kept her ring. She'd gotten in the habit of not wearing it around the house while her husband was away. She didn't want to scratch it while washing dishes or playing with her son. She always kept it in a jar in the kitchen cupboard. But it held sentimental value to her and she hesitated. She just needed to keep the intruder at bay for a few more moments.

"I thought it was in the jewelry box," she lied. "Let me check the bathroom."

If she gave the intruder her ring, she was worried what else he might demand. She was wearing a flimsy nightgown, and the man was leering at her undulating breasts.

"Don't *fuck* with me!" the man yelled. "Every woman knows where she keeps her wedding ring. I'll slice your child open like a ripe tomato if you don't hand it over right now!"

He placed the edge of the knife at the side of her son's throat. The child looked at his mother and whimpered. The man grabbed the boy's hair, and the boy flinched in pain. The knife cut a thin red line across the boy's neck and blood started gushing out.

The woman screamed in horror and ran to her son. She pulled the comforter off the bed and held it up to her son's neck to stem the bleeding. But it couldn't stop the cascade pouring from his carotid artery. Blood was spurting in every direction.

"Call 9-1-1!" the woman screamed at the intruder.

For a brief moment, he looked at her as if to apologize for the accident. Then he quickly turned and ran downstairs and out the side door.

Seconds later, the sound of sirens surrounded the house.

Chapter Nineteen

T he blinds on Lieutenant O'Neill's office windows rattled as he entered the room and shut the door firmly behind him. Joe, Hannah, and Kate looked at each other expectantly on the other side of his desk. The morning's shooting had upped the stakes in the investigation and they were feeling pressure to deliver results.

"I hope you guys have something for me," O'Neill said. "I just got off the phone with the Commissioner. He's blown a gasket over this ferry shooting. He wasn't too thrilled that it happened while he was being interviewed on live TV. The Mayor and the press are looking for answers, and we've got very little to give them. What do you make of this latest incident? Is it the same shooter?"

Joe nodded.

"It breaks with his pattern of midday shootings. But it otherwise fits the profile. Another head shot fired from a long distance with a three-thirty-eight slug."

"From a hotel, like the other killings?"

"We're not sure yet," Joe said. "Eyewitnesses in the area of Battery Park said they heard a gunshot coming from the vicinity of the Ritz-Carlton. But we haven't been able to track anyone to the time and location of the shooting."

"What about the cabbie shooting yesterday? Wasn't that fired from the Washington Square Hotel?"

"We don't think so," Hannah said. "There was no clear line of sight from that location to the spot where the driver was hit. We think he fired from a co-op apartment building across the street. He had a perfect vantage point from its rooftop."

O'Neill tapped his fingers on his desk.

"How soon were you able to lock the building down?"

"We arrived on the scene in less than ten minutes and locked it down almost immediately."

"Based on the Pierre video, that should have been enough to trap him. What happened?"

Joe looked at the Lieutenant blankly.

"He slipped through our fingers. We found no trace of him."

"What about security footage from the building? Co-ops in that part of town should have pretty sophisticated CCTV systems."

"We looked at the footage," Hannah said. "There was no sign of ingress or egress from anyone matching the perp's profile at any time during the day."

The Lieutenant leaned back in his chair and crossed his arms.

"What about the roof? Did CSI scrub it?"

"They found powder residue on the northeast corner beside the elevator shaft," Joe said. "That aligns with the firing angle of the bullet through the taxi windshield."

O'Neill shook his head in exasperation.

"But no sign of the sniper? Somehow he got in and out within ten minutes without anybody seeing him?"

"It appears so," Joe said.

"What about the ferry shooting? If the sniper fired from the Ritz-Carlton, it should have cameras covering every point of entry."

Joe reached beside his chair and pulled a laptop from his bag. He flipped it open, tapped the keyboard a few times, and swung the screen around for Kate and O'Neill to see.

"Someone matching the perp's description entered and exited the hotel the night before. We found gunpowder residue on the rooftop in a location with a clear view of the ferry terminal. But the timing doesn't match. The shooting occurred twelve hours after he last left the building."

O'Neill pointed toward the screen.

"Show me the clip. Maybe we can find some clues from the video."

Joe tapped the keyboard and a video began showing a young man entering the hotel lobby.

"Looks like the same guy," O'Neill nodded. "No beard, only a mustache this time. But his frame is the same size. But he's carrying a duffel bag instead of the black roller case."

O'Neill stopped the clip.

"Kate, what do you make of that?"

"Do you mind if I rewind the tape?" she asked.

Kate tapped the keyboard a few times. Then she moved in closer to watch the screen.

"He's walking differently," she observed. "Stiff and jerky—almost like he's laboring to carry the bag. If the rifle's in there, it can't weigh that much."

Joe nodded.

"We found three sandbags surrounding the gunpowder residue on the rooftop," he said. "We're not sure what he used them for, but that could be what he had in the bag."

O'Neill squinted his eyes in puzzlement.

"Where does he go next?"

Joe tapped the keyboard. The clip showed the man getting off the elevator on the top floor, walking to the end of the hall and disappearing into the stairwell.

"There's no video showing what he's doing in there?"

Joe shook his head.

"No cams in the stairways, like the other hotels."

"Do you see him leaving the building?" Kate asked.

Joe nodded and continued the video. The four officers watched the same man walk out of the lobby thirty minutes later.

Kate pointed at the screen.

"Notice the change in the duffel bag?" she said. "And he's walking much more comfortably. He's taking a lot less out than he brought in."

O'Neill hit the keyboard and stopped the clip.

"Yes, it almost looks empty. It's virtually collapsed in the middle. He must have left the rifle on the rooftop. When did he come back?"

"There's no footage showing anyone matching his profile entering or exiting the hotel over the next twelve hours," Joe said.

"Maybe he used some kind of remote control device?" O'Neill said. "The sandbags could have been used to minimize recoil of the rifle at the time of firing."

"We considered that," Hannah said. "But we scoured the rooftop. There's no sign of the rifle."

O'Neill looked at Joe and Hannah incredulously.

"So we're dealing with some kind of magician who can make weapons disappear? And escape from the rooftops of surrounded buildings. Can he *fly* too?"

O'Neill turned to the FBI agent.

"Kate, what do you make of the shift in timing of the shooting? Were you able to make any association with the 12:01 timing?"

"The only connection I could find pertains to Bible scripture. In the Book of Romans, Chapter 12, Verse 1 there's a citation 'offering one's body as living sacrifice to receive God's mercy.'"

"Great," O'Neill said. "So now we're dealing with a religious fanatic also."

The Lieutenant turned toward Joe.

"When did the Whitehall cameras capture this morning's shooting?"

"Seven-twenty-five."

"What possible connection can there be there?"

"I'll see if I can dig up any other correlations," Kate said.

"What about the military association? Did your database uncover anything suspicious there?"

"We tracked all active and retired military snipers living in the New York City area. It was a pretty short list—there were only five. I passed that information over to your team late yesterday."

Joe looked at the Lieutenant and nodded.

"Our guys interviewed each one of them this morning. All five can account for their whereabouts during the previous shootings. They've all been ruled out as a suspect."

"And the specialized rifle? Were you able to track any black market activity?"

"If you can believe it," Hannah said, "the manufacturer in question sells it freely through registered firearms dealers. It's not semi-automatic, so it doesn't fall under the assault weapons ban. You can even order the thing online. Anyone without a criminal record can get his hands on it. Assuming they can cough up ten grand."

O'Neill shook his head.

"That's comforting to know. But ten grand is pretty steep for a single firearm. There can't be that many registered purchases."

"Checked and vetted," Joe said. "Of the two hundred and twenty registered purchasers, seventeen live in the New York metropolitan area. Every one of them has lock-tight alibis. Some of them might have been resold on the black market, but that's almost impossible to track."

O'Neill looked at Kate.

"That pretty much only leaves us with your adoption scenario. Have you begun narrowing the list?"

Kate nodded.

"Our database scanned every resident of the New York City metropolitan area. Filtering all white male adoptees between the ages of twenty and thirty, we've narrowed the list to a little over one thousand candidates."

O'Neill paused as he did some math in his head.

"Between the First and the Eighteenth Precincts, there's a total of fifty detectives on staff. That works out to roughly twenty interviews per detective. When can you supply me with that list? I'd like to share it with my counterpart downtown and get started interviewing each one immediately."

"I'll send it as soon as I get back to my desk," Kate said.

O'Neill turned back to Joe and Hannah.

"I'd like you to get the rest of our team on this right away. Identify the individuals with airtight alibis first to narrow the list. We've got five shootings. If anyone can't account for his whereabouts at the time of any of these killings, bring him in. Then we'll mobilize all our resources on building the case."

O'Neill looked at his watch. It was just before noon.

"Let's hope this guy has broken with his midday shooting pattern. With any luck, we can find him before he strikes again."

Chapter Twenty

East Flatbush, Brooklyn

July 8, 6:40 p.m.

T odd Weir sat in his apartment watching the evening news with his black Lab by his side. The morning's interview of Commissioner Pope was being rebroadcast amidst a blitz of media coverage after the ferry shooting. It was the top story on the both the local and national news. Everyone wanted to know what the police were doing to find the killer.

Weir watched with bemusement as the Commissioner squirmed to answer the host's questions. He smiled when Morrison suggested the killer had outsmarted his cops. When they showed a photo of the sniper leaving the Pierre Hotel, he leaned in closer to the screen. The man appeared unrecognizable behind a full beard and sunglasses.

He reached down and petted his dog.

"Recognize that guy, Jake?" he said, pointing to the screen.

The dog looked up and peered toward the screen then back at his master.

"Yeah, me neither. Looks like he really is smarter than the cops."

Weir's eyes widened when the Commissioner mentioned the advisory for New Yorkers to stay indoors around noontime.

"Looks like it's getting dangerous out there, buddy. Don't worry, though. Stick with me. We're untouchable."

The news feed returned to live coverage with the news anchorman.

"Shortly after Commissioner Pope's interview," the anchorman said, "there was another killing at Whitehall Ferry Terminal. The sniper shot a morning commuter as he disembarked with thousands of others from the Staten Island ferry. The timing was different, but the pattern was familiar. Another random killing from a mysterious killer who's picking people off seemingly at will. The police appear to be no closer to apprehending the sniper than five days ago when it all started."

A loud double-tap on the door suddenly snapped Weir's attention from the TV. He got up and peered through the peephole. He took a step back and looked at his dog. Then he snapped his fingers and motioned toward his bedroom.

"I need you to stay in the bedroom for a few minutes, buddy. This won't take long."

The dog obediently followed his master toward the bedroom. Weir gently pushed the dog into the room and closed the door behind him. Then he went to the front door and swung it open. Two familiar faces stood in the hallway.

"Detectives Bannon and Trimble, with the NYPD," Joe said, holding up his badge. "Are you Todd Weir?"

The dog howled from the bedroom at the sound of unfamiliar voices.

"That's my legal name," Weir replied. "But my friends call me Brian."

"May we have a few minutes of your time?"

"I suppose," Weir said, pretending to be surprised. "What's this all about?"

"We'd like to ask you a few questions about the sniper shootings."

Weir shook his head, looking perplexed.

"I can't imagine how I could help you with that."

Joe stood for a few seconds appraising the man at the door. He was clean-shaven and had the same general build of the suspect from the video. There was something about the shape of his mouth that looked vaguely familiar. Where most people had a double crease under their nose, his upper lip was completely smooth. Although that part of the suspect's face was disguised in the Pierre surveillance video, the shape was similar.

"May we come in for a moment?" Joe said. "We're simply gathering information from persons of interest."

It was Weir's turn to hesitate. Legally, he knew the detectives needed a warrant to enter or search his apartment. But he didn't want to invite suspicion by appearing overly defensive. He looked at each Detective briefly then stepped to the side and invited them in.

"Sure. I've got nothing to hide." The dog barked excitedly from the other room. "Ignore my dog—he'll quiet down in a few minutes."

Weir picked up the remote and turned off the TV. Then he motioned to the living room sofa.

"Make yourselves comfortable."

Hannah took a seat while Joe walked slowly around the living room. He stopped beside a computer sitting on a small table beside a window. The computer was turned off.

"Nice view," he said, looking across the street toward a football field.

"It's part of the high school. I like to watch the kids play sometimes after class."

Joe glanced derisively in Weir's direction.

"I bet. You have a lot of free time, do you? What do you do for a living?"

"I'm a locksmith."

Joe's forehead crinkled in surprise.

"That's convenient."

Weir tried to stifle his irritation at the Detective's tone. "How so?"

"The sniper seems to have an affinity for breaking into private places," Joe said. "Your skills would certainly come in handy in these situations."

The dog began howling from the bedroom, sensing the escalating tension in the room.

"I suppose," Weir said calmly, "but you're barking up the wrong tree. My job involves *helping* people, not hurting them."

"Uh huh," Joe said. "Who do you work for?"

"I operate my own business. Under the name Feeny Lock Services."

"Why all the aliases? Don't you like your name?"

Joe was intentionally trying to get under Weir's skin. He knew angry suspects were more likely to reveal incriminating details, if there were any to hide.

"I'm adopted, so it's not my real name. I never much liked it anyway. That's the beauty of being freelance. You can create any persona that promotes your brand."

Joe stopped at a bookcase and tilted his head to read the titles of some books standing on the shelves. *The Art of War*, by Sun Tzu, and *The Prince*, by Machiavelli.

"Interesting choice of reading material. Exactly what kind of locksmith services do you provide? Do you do any work for hotels?"

"Basic stuff, mostly. I help people get into their homes and cars when they've locked themselves out. Change locks for landlords. No hotels. They mostly use fancy card readers these days."

Joe nodded.

"Do you do most of your work in the city?"

"I take calls from anywhere in the Tri-State region. I don't discriminate about which customers I serve."

Joe picked up a photo of a blond woman walking alone down a street.

"Can you tell us where you were this morning around seven-thirty?"

"I was responding to a call in Jersey. Turned out to be a flake. Supposedly another lockout. But he wasn't there when I showed. Maybe he found a second set of keys."

"So there's no actual record of you being in New Jersey at this time?"

Weir suppressed a smile.

"I went to a convenience store in Jersey City to buy a coffee around that time. A Seven-Eleven on Burma Road, as I recall. I suppose you could check their security footage if you wanted to."

"Yes, we will," Joe replied flatly. "Can you account for your whereabouts around noon on the four previous days?"

"I was responding to calls at various locations around the city. I don't keep track of every emergency call. I'm a busy man."

"I bet you are."

Joe ran his hand over an empty shelf on the bookcase.

"You don't have many family pictures or personal mementos in your apartment. Where are all these friends you mentioned?"

Weir was growing weary of the Detective's contemptuous attitude.

"Like I said, I keep pretty busy with my business. Not a lot of time for socializing. Was there anything else I could help you with, detectives? It appears I'm not such an interesting person after all."

Joe paused as he glanced in the direction of the closed bedroom door. The dog was still barking, and he thought best not to press any further.

"I think we're done for today. Thank you for your time, Mr. Weir. We'll be in touch if we have any additional questions."

Hannah stood up from her chair, and Weir followed the two detectives to the door. He looked Hannah directly in her eyes and smiled before closing the door.

"Ma'am," he said.

Chapter Twenty-One

Medical Examiner's Office

July 9, 9:00 a.m.

"God morgon, Dr. Lundberg," Joe said as he entered the Medical Examiner's autopsy room with Hannah.

The M.E. smiled upon seeing the two detectives.

"Valkommen, min vänner," he replied in his native Swedish.

"Forgive me, Miles," Joe said. "I can never quite bring myself to say good morning when I see you here. We always seem to meet under the most unfortunate circumstances."

"It's the nature of the beast. We should get away from this Godforsaken place and have lunch sometime. I'm sure you two could use a break from the pressure trying to find this dispossessed killer."

"He's dispossessed of something, that's for sure," Joe said. "Whether it's his mind, body, or spirit, remains to be seen."

Miles nodded.

"What have your profilers put together so far?"

"All we've come up with is an angry white male with a troubled past."

"Not many surprises there."

"The FBI specialist has us chasing down every adopted male in New York City between the ages of twenty and thirty."

"I'm guessing there's quite a few of those?"

"Only about a *thousand*," Joe sniffed. "We've captured some grainy pictures of him moving about the crime scenes, so that's helping narrow the field. But without any physical evidence, we're not in a position to bring anyone in yet."

"I'm not sure how much I can help with that, but I do have some interesting details to share about the latest incidents." Miles led the detectives to his desk. "Come— have a look."

The M.E. picked up a metal tray with five bullets. He pushed two over to the side.

"These two bullets were the ones used in the initial sniper killings that you've already seen. The other three are the slugs used in the new cases."

Miles picked up one of the three new slugs and held it out for Joe and Hannah to see. It had a brass coating and a flat angled head.

"This one was used on the equestrian cop. Unlike the bullets used in the first two killings, it has a full metal jacket designed for maximum penetration. The sniper probably chose it to ensure it penetrated the officer's helmet."

Miles placed the bullet back on the tray and picked up the middle one.

"This was the bullet used to kill the cabbie—also a full metal jacket. Chosen to maximize penetration through the windshield and minimize deflection to its target."

Hannah squinted at the odd shape of the slugs.

"Why are the heads of these bullets so different?"

"The first one went straight through the officer's head and struck the hard pavement under the horse on an angle. That's why the top of the bullet is flat and slightly angled, with pock-marks from the uneven pavement. The other one appears to have gone through the driver's head, stopping in the soft upholstery of the rear seat. So it retained the pointed shape of its nose without deforming."

Joe looked at the third bullet resting among the group, recognizing the familiar mushroom shape.

"The third bullet looks like the ones used in the first two killings."

"Not quite," Miles said. He picked up the third slug and placed it in Joe's hand along with the other two from the other side of the tray.

"See how this bullet is quite a bit shorter, and the top is more flayed than the others?"

"Yes, and it doesn't have the same brass shell."

"Exactly. The one you're holding was used in the Staten Island ferry shooting. It's hollow point. The other two are semi-jacketed soft point. This one was designed to inflict maximum tissue damage and stop inside the victim. The bullets used in the first two shootings were designed to kill their victims then pass through them. I'm not sure why the sniper chose this type of bullet in the most recent shooting."

Joe rolled the bullets around in his hand.

"All eight point six millimeter?"

Miles nodded.

"Almost certainly fired from the same rifle. Your ballistics team can confirm."

"Can we conclude anything from the wounds?" Hannah asked.

"I think so," Miles said, "but I need to warn you in advance. The ferry victim is pretty messy. You might want to prepare yourself before I show you."

Miles walked to the middle of the room where three bodies lay cloaked on stainless steel tables. He pulled the sheet back on the first victim. It was the equestrian cop. Joe flinched seeing a fellow police officer in this position. He knew the risks that came with the job, but there was something about the execution-style nature of the killing that unnerved him.

Miles turned the body onto its side.

"Like the first two, this wound is clean and straight through. But there's less exit wound damage because the bullet maintained its profile as it passed through. Another head shot, this time just above the hairline."

Joe nodded.

"We know where the sniper fired from for this shot. He was closer and higher relative to the target, which explains the higher entrance wound position."

Miles pulled the sheet back from the second victim.

"This is the cab driver. Similar to the first two victims. The wound position is in the center of the forehead, just above the brow. Assuming he was looking straight ahead at the time of the shot, the bullet has an eight-degree downward angle and a three-degree medial trajectory from the cabbie's left side."

"That matches the rooftop location of the building he fired from," Joe said.

"But the third victim," Miles continued, "is a bit of an anomaly. This is pretty gruesome. Are you sure you're ready?"

Joe swallowed hard and nodded. Miles pulled back the sheet revealing a cadaver with half the side of his head blown off.

"This definitely doesn't fit the pattern of the other shootings. As you can see, the wound is way off center and higher. My guess is that the bullet grazed the top-left side of the victim's head, shearing off this part of his skull. Same thing happened in the Kennedy assassination. Except in this case, the deformation of the hollow point bullet caused a lot more internal damage. The killer definitely didn't want to take any chances that this guy wouldn't be killed. Why he shot so far off-center, I have no idea. It's almost as if he was distracted, or meant to miss. All the other shots were laser-accurate."

Joe nodded as he reflected back to the ferry shooting crime scene.

"We found sandbags beside gunpowder residue from the rifle at the location of this shooting," he said. "But the hotel video shows the sniper entering and exiting the hotel a full twelve hours before the shot was fired. Is it possible the weapon could have been fired remotely?"

100

Miles squeezed his eyebrows as he considered the question.

"That's interesting. I suppose it's possible with today's advanced electronics and robotics. But you'd have to buttress the rifle to minimize recoil if it weren't stabilized against your shoulder. That might explain the off-center shot. Maybe he fired into the crowd hoping to hit anything moving above shoulder height. But how did the rifle disappear if he didn't go anywhere near it after the time of firing?"

"That's the mystery we're trying to figure out," Joe said. "It just evaporated into thin air. We'd love to get our hands on the murder weapon. If you have any brilliant ideas, let us know."

Joe turned away from the examining table, eager to get outside for some fresh air. The image of the half-headed ferry passenger was making him queasy.

"Will do," Miles said. "I hope you find this guy soon so we can stop meeting this way. Let's schedule a celebratory lunch when you catch him."

"Thanks, Miles," Joe said. "We'll talk again soon."

"Lycka till."

The medical examiner had a grim expression on his face as he watched the two detectives walk toward the exit door. He expected they'd be seeing a lot more of one another before any celebration could be arranged.

Chapter Twenty-Two

Garret A. Morgan Elementary School, The Bronx

July 9, 10:15 a.m.

T he streets of Manhattan were eerily silent on the sixth day of the sniper attacks. Few people dared to venture into the city for fear the mysterious killer would catch them in his sights. Previously, it was only the lunchtime crowd who hid under cover. But the rush hour ferry shooting had shifted everyone's mindset. Now it was open season, and anyone was fair game.

Hotels were rapidly emptying of summertime tourists, and local airports were clogged with people trying to get out of the city. Downtown office workers had called in sick not wanting to take any chances getting caught out in the open. Even the New York Stock Exchange was operating with a bare-bones staff of employees who traveled to work exclusively underground via the MTA.

But in the outer boroughs, things were still fairly normal. In spite of the Commissioner's advisory, few people seemed concerned the sniper would strike their neighborhood. Even at noon, pedestrian and vehicular traffic hardly slowed, as local citizens went about their regular activities.

Today would change all that.

Todd Weir straddled a high-back chair with his rifle resting atop the backrest. Through the open window of the New York Housing Authority building at the corner of Park Avenue and East 169 Street, he watched the empty playground of P.S. 132. From his fifteenth-floor vantage point, he had a clear and commanding view of the entire courtyard.

The building's security had been easy to breach. Few public housing residents paid much attention to who entered their building. Unlike most residential towers in Manhattan, there was no doorman. Residents rarely noticed if anyone followed them through the main entrance.

To blend in, Weir had applied brown make-up to his face and hands, and wore a goatee along with his customary sunglasses and baseball cap. Wearing blue collar work clothes, he fit right in with the mostly Hispanic community of south-central Bronx. He had no trouble slipping through the front door during the morning rush hour. After taking the elevator to the top floor, he waited in the stairwell until he saw a young couple leave their apartment facing the school playground. It took him only seconds to pick their front door lock and slip inside unnoticed.

At 10:30, he heard the bell signaling morning recess ringing in the schoolyard. Hundreds of grade school children poured out the doors into the bright sunshine. Most of the kids ran happily around the courtyard playing tag or swinging on the playground equipment. But Weir noticed a different dynamic taking shape in a secluded corner of the courtyard behind a thick stand of trees. A big kid had cornered a much smaller boy, who was desperately trying to escape the bully's clutches. Whenever the little boy tried to run away, the bigger kid stepped in front of him.

Weir could see the fear in the young boy's eyes. It was obvious he'd been tormented by the large boy before. As the child made a desperate lunge to get past the big kid, the bully grabbed him by the collar and threw him to the ground. Then he sat on the younger boy's chest and placed his hand over the lad's mouth to stifle his screams. The youngster struggled to push the bully off him, but the larger boy grabbed his throat until he stopped moving.

Although the bully's back was turned, Weir could see him talking to the small boy. He flashed back fifteen years to his own youth, when he was teased and bullied. As he watched the bully's lips move, he recalled the taunts of his tormentors.

What's the matter, Weir-do? Can't move your tight lips? In his memories, Weir vividly heard the laughs and taunts of the other kids watching. *I bet that lip is useful for other things. Stay still while I stick you like the little toad you are...*

Weir's finger pressed against the rifle trigger. Today he would end the little boy's torment and rid him of his bully forever. He just needed the big kid to shift position a little. The back of his head was directly in line with the head of the smaller boy. If he fired now, the bullet would go right through the bully and strike the innocent boy in the face.

Keep fighting, little guy, the sniper said to himself. *I just need one clear shot.*

The youngster suddenly thrust his hips up, and the bully almost toppled over. Then he quickly repositioned himself on the boy's chest and slapped him hard in the face.

Weir saw his opening.

I've got you now, you little fucker. Two can play this game. Lights out.

Just as a Metro-North train roared past the playground along the Park Avenue rail line, Weir pulled the trigger. Nobody heard the sound of the rifle as blood suddenly spurted over the young boy's face, and the bully slumped to the ground beside him.

Chapter Twenty-Three

18th Precinct, Midtown Manhattan

July 10, 8:00 a.m.

B rady O'Neill slapped his coffee mug on his desk as he slumped into his chair. Black liquid spurted over the rim and spread onto his blotter. He grabbed a few sheets of loose paper to soak up the stains then crumpled and threw them into his waste basket.

"*Shit*," he exclaimed. "A twelve-year-old? On a school playground? How much lower can this guy get? And how much more incompetent can we possibly look?"

He rubbed his hands together to remove the coffee stains then looked at Joe, Kate, and Hannah.

"The Mayor is outraged. He's saying the sniper has free rein over the city. Please tell me you've got something— *anything*."

The three detectives looked at O'Neill blankly.

"We've been sorting through the list of adoptees," Joe finally volunteered. "Almost half of them have been interviewed."

"I assume our team's been working overtime on this?"

"Twelve hour days," Joe said. "Other than responding to new shootings, this is all we've been working on. Our guys have processed a little over three hundred of the adoptees Kate identified. I understand the detective unit from the First Precinct has processed almost as many."

O'Neill strummed his fingers impatiently on his desk.

"And?"

"Everybody's alibis check out so far."

"For every single shooting?"

"To narrow the list," Hannah said, "we've eliminated anyone with an air-tight alibi during any one of the shootings. Otherwise, it will take us six times as long to cross-reference everyone's whereabouts for every shooting."

O'Neill sat back and took a sip of his coffee.

"I suppose that makes sense. Can we also rule out the ones who don't look like the shooter from the video? There can't be that many slim white adopted males in New York City."

Joe nodded.

"The facial profile is helping."

"Even with the beard and glasses? I'd bet a months' salary that beard was fake."

"I agree," Joe said. "The Ritz-Carlton video gave us a bit more to work with since he was only wearing a mustache. The shape of the jaw, cheekbones, and mouth is helping eliminate the obvious non-starters."

"Is there video surveillance from yesterday's playground shooting? Does it reveal any new details?"

"It took a bit of extra digging to find the firing location because no one actually heard the shot. We checked all the high-rises around the perimeter of the school. Fortunately, the city recently installed CCTV cameras in the entrances, elevators, and stairwells of all public housing projects. We discovered footage of a man matching the sniper's description carrying a suspicious bag into 450 East 169th Street around the time of the shooting."

Joe reached into his pocket and pulled out a thumb drive.

"Do you want to see it?"

O'Neill waved his hand.

"Just give me the summary. Anything actionable?"

"Not really. He was wearing a goatee and a baseball cap, and he kept his head down like usual. His skin was shaded, but we're pretty sure it's the same guy."

"Did you find anything when you swept the building?"

"The elevator cam tracked him to the fifteen floor. We checked all the units facing the schoolyard and found powder residue by the window in unit 1513."

"No prints?"

"No, same M.O. He's probably wearing gloves, as before."

O'Neill exhaled deeply.

"And he disappeared into thin air as before also?"

"A convenience store cam across the street showed him walking north," Hannah said. "We lost the trail when he entered Crotona Park."

O'Neill got up and walked to a large street map of New York City hanging on his wall. He ran this finger to 169th Street and then up and to the right.

"There's an MTA station at the edge of the park at 174 Street on the 5 line," he said. "Check their cams. Maybe we can find where he exited the system and pick up his movement from there."

O'Neill turned to the FBI agent.

"Kate, what do you make of this schoolyard killing? What is the shooter's motivation for shooting a twelve-year-old?"

"Joe and Hannah said the cops on the scene indicated there'd been a fight in the yard. Apparently, a smaller kid was being bullied by a much larger kid."

O'Neill snorted.

"Like that never happens in a schoolyard. Are you suggesting that's any justification for killing a child?"

"Of course not. But it's possible this schoolyard bully personified the bullies the sniper may have encountered in his own youth."

"I grew up with three older brothers," the Lieutenant huffed. "Just about every kid gets bullied at some point growing up."

"Maybe the shooter's experience was particularly aggravated."

"What might account for that?"

"Who knows? Maybe he had an unusual tic or speech impediment. Kids can be incredibly cruel to anyone who's a little different."

O'Neill crossed his arms and leaned back in his chair.

"So we've established our shooter had a troubled youth and a possible deformity of indeterminate origin." He looked at Joe and Hannah. "I suppose that's one more thing you can watch out for as you're vetting your list."

Joe suddenly looked away, lost in thought.

"What?" O'Neill said. "Have you got something?"

"Just a hunch," Joe said. "One of the adoptees Hannah and I interviewed yesterday acted suspiciously."

"In what way?"

"To begin with, he wasn't deferential or skittish like most people are when cops knock unexpectedly on their door. He was almost *antagonistic*, like it was some kind of game."

"That definitely fits the profile of most serial killers," Kate said.

"And he's a locksmith by trade," Hannah said. "That could explain how the shooter breached the locked doors so easily at each of the known sniper sites."

O'Neill rubbed his two-day growth of beard.

"What about his face and build? Did that match from the videos?"

"His build, yes. Tall and slender. Hard to say about the face because of the facial hair the suspect had in the video footage. This guy was clean-shaven. But something Kate said just struck a chord. He had a slight facial deformation." Joe placed his finger on his lip just under his nose. "He had a smooth upper lip here instead of the normal crease that everyone else has. And there was something about his eyes that was different—more close-set than most people. I noticed it immediately."

O'Neill sat up in his chair with renewed interest.

"That might account for why the perp wears facial hair in the videos. Can he account for his whereabouts during the shootings?"

"Only during the most recent ferry shooting," Joe said. "But he has an air-tight alibi. We have video footage of him at a convenience store in Jersey City at 7:15 that morning. There's no way he could have gotten near enough to the ferry terminal from that location in time to take the shot."

O'Neill looked at the map on his wall.

"But Jersey City is right across the river from the ferry terminal. Couldn't he have taken the shot from there?"

Joe shook his head.

"The closest location from that side of the harbor is over three miles away. No rifle, not even the newest state-of-the-art military sniper rifles, can fire from that far away."

O'Neill got up and paced for a moment beside his window.

"See if we can get a warrant to search his belongings. Maybe we'll get lucky and find a murder weapon in his apartment or a hair sample that matches those found at the sniper locations."

He pulled up the blinds and cracked open the window.

"In the meantime, have our team keep working through the list of adoptees. We need to produce some real suspects to get the Mayor off my back."

****

Joe and Hannah walked through the precinct parking lot toward their patrol car.

"I knew there was something fishy about that Weir guy," Joe said. "Nobody's that cool under police questioning."

Hannah shrugged.

"Maybe he's got Aspergers or autism or something like that. It could just be a product of parent-separation issues. I imagine a lot of adopted children have anti-social personality disorders."

Joe stopped and looked at Hannah.

"You didn't feel it? He didn't seem at all suspicious to you?"

"He was definitely antagonistic," Hannah admitted. "But you were pushing his buttons. Mentioning his lack of friends, how his job was so convenient, and so on."

"Come on! A locksmith? How perfect is that? What are the odds? And what about the way he looked? Weren't you a little creeped out? If you and I reacted that quickly, can you imagine what he had to deal with growing up? Throw in the whole adoption thing, and that could easily produce one fucked up individual."

"What about his alibi?" Hannah said. "How can we get past that? He can't be in two places at the same time."

"Yes, but as Miles said, that ferry shooting was very suspicious. He seems like a clever enough guy. With his locksmith skills, he could have fashioned some kind of mechanical device to fire it remotely."

"Maybe, but without the murder weapon, we've got nothing. It's going to be questionable we'll even get a warrant to search his property."

"He couldn't account for his whereabouts for four of the five shootings. Together with the video match, I think we've got enough."

Hannah shook her head.

"I wish I shared your conviction about this guy, Joe. We'll find out soon enough."

As the two detectives got into their car to head to the courthouse, they didn't notice the young man watching them behind the window of a cafe across the street. When their car pulled out of the police lot, he looked at his phone's screen and followed the blinking red dot as it moved away from his location.

Chapter Twenty-Four

Crown Heights, Brooklyn

July 10, 12:45 p.m.

I t's a lot quieter today.
Even out here in the burbs, not many people are venturing outside. Just a few hardy souls driving cars and delivery vans. Looks like word's finally getting around. I've been upgraded in the local papers. The Post's headline today read *Sadistic Sniper Shoots Schoolboy*. Nice alliteration.

Everything stopped around noon, but only for a few minutes. Looks like I'll have to mix it up a bit to fully assimilate the animals. People are just like dogs. At first, you have to be predictable to elicit the desired reaction. Once they see the linkage between the behavior and the response, you can change the frequency and timing. It becomes hard-wired. Pavlov eventually got his dogs to salivate at the sound of the dinner bell. I guess my subjects need a bit more training.

The prospects are getting thin, though. The only ones braving the elements are those who absolutely have to be outdoors.

Here we go.

You can always count on your trusty letter carrier. What's their motto? *Neither snow nor rain nor heat nor gloom will stop them from the completion of their rounds.*

This Postie's definitely a trooper. Pulling his trusty mail cart, wearing his USPS cap. The public loves their neighborhood mailman. Especially now with everybody housebound. People can send and receive packages without even leaving home. Let someone *else* bear the risk. There's a madman roaming the streets of New York.

You'd think the postal service would equip their employees with better protection. This is too easy, like shooting fish in a barrel. I just have to wait for them to come near the surface. And there are plenty of mailmen floating about the neighborhood, walking door to door. This one will be my easiest mark so far.

Pop.

Whoa. That wasn't me. Just a passing car backfiring.

So much for the cool letter carrier. He almost jumped out of his skin. The poor guy's shaking like a leaf now, trying to collect himself. It's gotta be terrifying, not knowing if you're being watched and if you'll have any warning when your time is up.

Not to worry, buddy. I'll make this quick. You won't hear a thing. My bullet flies faster than the speed of sound. It's actually a pretty good way to go. Fast and painless with no needless suffering. It's the natural order of things, the alpha animal dispatching the weak and defenseless.

I just need you to turn in my direction. After all, I've got a reputation to uphold. People are expecting another head shot from the sharpshooter who never misses.

That's it. Coming down the front steps of another satisfied customer, walking along the sidewalk toward your next delivery. I can't see your eyes, but no matter. The USPS emblem on the front of your cap is a perfect target.

Maybe tomorrow's headline will read *Psychotic Sniper Stops Snailmail.* Yeah, that's a good one.

Time to meet your maker, my friend. See you in the afterlife. We're all sinners.

Bam.

What the fuck? I blew his cap clean off. But there's only a bruise on his forehead.

Smart, very smart. Maybe the postage service gives a damn about their employees after all. Very ingenious, lining their caps with protective material.

He's out cold. He'll wake up with a nasty concussion. That's gonna hurt. But that's not my style. It'll tarnish my reputation. We can't have that.

This might work out better than I hoped. Everyone's looking out their window at all the commotion. They're probably dialing 9-1-1 right now, summoning help for the defenseless letter carrier.

Watch carefully, everybody. This is what awaits you when you step outside.

Chapter Twenty-Five

728 E New York Avenue, East Flatbush, Brooklyn

July 10, 5:30 p.m.

T odd Weir held his barking dog at his side as he swung his apartment door open to face a phalanx of police officers. Joe and Hannah stood at the front of the group. For a few awkward seconds, Weir and Bannon stared at each other without saying a word. The rest of the officers looked ahead with clenched jaws, barely concealing their contempt for the suspected cop-killer.

"Mr. Weir," Joe said, "we have a warrant to search your premises."

He handed the court document to Weir.

"Please step aside and secure your dog."

Weir stepped back and attached a leash to his dog's collar as the police officers flooded into his apartment.

"What's this all about, Detective?" he said. "I thought you said I wasn't very interesting on your last visit. Were you able to confirm my location during the ferry shooting?"

"You've only accounted for your whereabouts during one of the murders," Joe said. "There are plenty of suspicious circumstances surrounding that incident. You still have six other ones to account for."

Weir watched a team of detectives head into his bedroom while Hannah unplugged his laptop and placed it into a plastic bag. His dog growled and pulled against its leash toward Detective Bannon.

"As I said last time, Detective, I can't account for where I am every moment of every day. My job takes me all over the five boroughs on short notice."

"So you've said. But don't worry, all that may be unnecessary if we find what we're looking for today."

Weir heard the sound of drawers opening in his bedroom. He looked down the hall and saw the detectives flip over his mattress and pass a metal detector over it.

"You won't find anything here," he said, shaking his head. "I hope I'm not under suspicion just because of my job. That seems like a flimsy proposition for a murder investigation."

"That's just one of many incriminating factors," Joe said. "You also match the physical description of the killer at the crime scene."

Weir pulled his head back in surprise.

"Really? Do you have eyewitnesses? Because I know for a fact nobody has seen me commit any murders."

Joe glared at Weir.

"You're the one who's obligated to answer questions, Mr. Weir, not me. Where were you today between noon and 1 p.m.?"

"Having lunch in the park. I usually take a break around noon from my daily routine. One needs sustenance for hard physical work, don't you agree?"

Joe ignored the comment as he watched his team deconstruct the living room.

"Which park?" he said.

"Prospect Park."

Joe's head snapped back to Weir.

"That's only a few blocks from the site of today's shooting."

"Really? What unfortunate soul was shot today?"

"A letter carrier. In broad daylight, doing his rounds. I don't suppose you'd happen to know anything about that?"

Weir pursed his lips and shook his head.

"You didn't even hear the sound of gunfire? There were two shots, seconds apart."

"It's a noisy city, Detective."

"A lot more so over the last few days."

The detective team returned from Weir's bedroom and looked at Joe, shaking their head.

"We'll need to search your vehicle," Joe said. "Where do you keep it parked?"

"In the underground parking garage. I can save you the effort though—you won't find anything there either."

"We'll be the judge of that. Please fetch your keys."

Weir's dog growled and bared his teeth at the Detective. Weir pulled the dog into the kitchen and retrieved a ring of keys from a hook on the wall. When he returned, he handed the keys to Joe.

"Do you mind if I stay here with my dog? All this commotion has gotten him pretty worked up."

Joe shook his head.

"You'll need to come with us. There will be plenty more questions for you to answer."

Joe escorted Weir to the elevator. When the door slid open, all the detectives squeezed into the small compartment. Nobody said a word during the ride to the bottom floor. When the elevator reached the underground parking level, Weir led the officers to his parked van. The words Feeny Security Services was emblazoned on the side, with the "F" fashioned in the shape of a keyhole.

Joe pressed the remote unlock button on the key fob and the detectives piled through the side doors to begin searching the van. He walked around the back and looked inside. The van was clean and well organized. Every tool, part, and piece of equipment was stored in neatly labeled plastic bins or securely bolted to the walls of the van. He reached into one of the bins and pulled out a couple of unusually shaped tools. One was a thin L-shaped wrench, and the other was a knife-like tool with deep serrated edges.

"These look like lock picking tools," Joe said.

"Every locksmith worth his salt has those," Weir nodded. "Half my jobs are lockouts. Not everybody has a key when you need one."

"I'm sure they don't," Joe said sarcastically.

He opened another bin and shifted some objects around inside. He pulled out a transparent acrylic cube about one-inch square out and held it up.

"And what do you use this for?"

Weir looked at the object and paused.

"It's just a damper," he said. "Keeps the metal keys from banging together and making too much of a racket while I'm driving."

Joe inspected the cube carefully. It had scratches along two sides and a small indentation on the third side. He pulled out a plastic bag and dropped the cube in the bag then zipped the top closed.

"You don't like loud noises when you work, Mr. Weir?"

Weir's lips curled up as he looked at Joe silently.

After twenty minutes, the detectives came out of the van and shook their head.

Joe looked at Weir.

"I'll need your mobile phone."

Weir paused for a moment then he reached into his back pocket and handed the device to the Detective.

"This won't do you much good without my passcode. You'll get locked out after too many false attempts."

"There are plenty of other ways to track your activity, Mr. Weir. We don't need your passcodes. But if you'd like to volunteer them, you might get your personal effects back much sooner."

"My Fifth Amendment rights protect me from having to provide that information," Weir said.

Joe looked at Weir evenly. He knew he hadn't found enough to arrest the suspect, and he was running out of options.

"That doesn't stop us from bringing you in for further questioning," he said.

Weir looked at the seized items in the Detective's hands.

"Other than my encrypted electronic devices and a piece of clear plastic, it looks to me like you've come up empty-handed. Do you think there's anything you can get from me at the station that you weren't able to find here? But if you feel like wasting more of everyone's time, knock yourself out."

Joe scribbled something on his notepad and handed Weir three slips of paper.

"These are receipts for the three confiscated items. We'll return them to you in due course."

Joe began to walk toward the underground parking exit with the other officers then he stopped and turned around.

"And Mr. Weir?"

"Yes?"

"Be careful out there. It's a dangerous city. You never know who might be pointing a gun at you."

Joe turned his back and walked away as the officers snickered under their breath.

Chapter Twenty-Six

J oe and Hannah sat in their favorite coffee shop taking a break from their routine. The morning's update meeting with Lieutenant O'Neill and Agent Palmer hadn't revealed any new insights into their case, and they were both feeling frustrated. The preliminary examination of the evidence seized in the Weir apartment raid had come up empty. O'Neill had asked the team to continue interviewing and ferreting out the long list of adoptees, but so far no new suspects had emerged.

Joe sat opposite Hannah at their table, cradling his warm coffee in his hands. He noticed someone reading a newspaper at the next table. The front page headline read *Sniper Takes Seventh Victim.*

"Penny for your thoughts?" Hannah interjected.

Joe paused as he watched a thin flow of pedestrians pass by his window. New Yorkers were slowly returning to the streets of Manhattan, emboldened by the unpredictable timing of sniper shootings.

I guess people figure their chances are pretty good now, he thought. *There are almost ten million people living across five boroughs. What are the odds someone will be in the wrong place at the wrong time? Especially now that the sniper has broadened his range and schedule.*

"I was just thinking how well this guy is controlling the narrative," Joe said. "He's taken the high ground, so to speak, and we have no way of touching him. The scariest thing is New Yorkers are beginning to feel immune once again."

Hannah swirled the coffee in her cup.

"You've got a golden opportunity to take back control of the narrative and influence public opinion tomorrow morning."

"You're referring to my scheduled Today Show appearance?"

Hannah nodded.

"The Lieutenant says you can use this to get the citizens of New York working alongside us rather than just being passive pawns."

Joe scrunched his brow.

"I think the brass is just trying to shift the blame down the line. The Mayor's not willing to expand the curfew—what else can we possibly say?"

"He can't close the whole city down. That would be playing directly into the sniper's hands. It made sense to issue a temporary curfew when he was shooting at the same time of day. Now he's become unpredictable. We have to treat him like every other killer and use good detective skills to flesh him out."

Joe sighed.

"That's the problem. I feel like we've already found him. This wild goose chase the Lieutenant's got us on, interviewing every adopted person in New York City, is insanity. He's right there in front of us."

"You mean Weir? You heard the Lieutenant this morning. The forensics team found nothing incriminating on his phone or his laptop."

"And the plastic cube? Don't you think that's a little incriminating?"

"Suspicious, yes. But it's not enough to hold him culpable."

"What about the scratches on the sides? Just what you'd expect from sliding it in and out of tight door latches."

"Forensics said there were too many random scratches. They don't align perfectly with the hotel rooms we identified from the CCTV footage. It would never hold up in court."

"What about his *appearance*? His build, his facial structure, his oddly shaped upper lip. Not to mention his attitude. It's almost as if he's baiting us. Everything fits. Surely you must have suspicions as well?"

Hannah took a long sip of her coffee.

"It's true," she said. "There's a lot that fits. But it's all circumstantial. He's definitely a bit...off. His foster record shows he moved around quite a bit as a child. That would screw with anybody's head and make them suspicious of authority figures."

"Jeesuz, Hannah. I think your motherly instincts are clouding your judgment. It almost sounds like you feel *sorry* for this guy."

Hannah placed her coffee mug down and looked Joe directly in his eyes.

"Look, I agree he's suspicious. We just don't have enough to bring him in. In the meantime, I think the Lieutenant is right in asking us to exhaust all the other possibilities. Without a murder weapon or an eyewitness, there's nothing more we can do."

Joe looked outside the window and tapped his foot. Hannah noticed the deep creases in his forehead and his bloodshot eyes.

"How are you holding up?" she asked.

"I'm fine. We've had tough cases before."

"You can't fool me. This one is different. I know this strikes a little closer to home. I saw how you looked at the corpses at the coroner's office. The boy in particular..."

Joe slammed his fist on the table and glared at Hannah.

"That's not fair."

He looked around the room, suddenly aware of the attention he was attracting.

"You know I don't let that get in the way of my police work," he said, lowering his voice. "That was a long time ago, and I've put it in a box. I've processed my grief and moved on."

Hannah peered at Joe sadly. She knew him well enough after ten years of working together to know that he was still wracked with guilt over the loss of his son.

"I worry about you sometimes," she said, placing her hand over his. "You and Jane never had another child. I see how personally you take some of these murder cases. Sometimes I think you internalize your loss and project your anger onto your suspects."

Joe leaned back and looked out the window.

"The last thing I need now is another shrink. We've already got one too many working on this case."

"Hey, come on," Hannah said, trying to lighten the mood. "Kate's profile of the shooter led us to your favorite suspect."

Joe allowed a slight smile.

"So you're admitting this Weir character is a valid suspect?"

"You're not the only tenacious bugger once you set your sights on someone. Maybe we'll find some actionable evidence if we dig a little deeper. Why don't we review the security footage once again? Maybe we'll find something new you can share with the public tomorrow."

Joe stood up and collected the empty cups then the detectives walked toward the exit.

"I'd rather kick this guy's door down. I know he's hiding that rifle somewhere."

Hannah opened the door and followed her partner out onto the sidewalk.

"I think the Lieutenant has made it clear he doesn't want us chasing any more ghosts."

Joe and Hannah began making their way toward their patrol car parked three stores down on the side of the street.

"For now perhaps," Joe said, fishing his keys from his pocket.

As they approached the front of their car and separated to enter their respective sides, they suddenly heard a loud metallic bang. Joe saw the front of the car buckle and an unmistakable hole in the hood.

The detectives took cover at the side of the car, crouching low behind the rear wheels with their pistols drawn. Alarmed passersby suddenly screamed and ducked into nearby stores.

"What the hell?" Hannah exclaimed.

Joe looked at his watch. It was just after twelve.

"Stay low. He hasn't got a clear shot at us from this angle."

Hannah pointed up the street.

"I heard an echo coming about a block to the west. The Millenium Hotel is at 7th and 44th. You don't think...?"

"Who else could it be? Call it in. Let's lock down the block."

As Hannah retrieved her phone and called into central dispatch, Joe began to stand up.

"Joe!" Hannah shouted. "Are you crazy? Get back down. What are you doing?"

Joe shook his head.

"This guy never misses. Let alone by several feet. If he wanted one of us dead, he could have already picked us off. I think he's sending us some kind of message."

Joe walked toward the front of the car then stepped directly into the center of the sidewalk. He spread his arms and looked down the street in the direction of the hotel.

"Joe—*please*!" Hannah begged. "You're making yourself an easy target."

"That's the point. I'll keep him distracted while you call in the location. We need to keep him stationary long enough for our guys to get to him. This might be our only chance to trap him."

"This is Detective Trimble of the 18th Precinct," Hannah spoke excitedly into her phone. "Shot fired at 58 West 44th Street. Officers pinned. Suspected shooter at Millenium Broadway Hotel. Send backup immediately!"

Joe looked up toward the top of the hotel on the side of the street nearly a block away. He couldn't see a rifle poking out from a window, but he knew the sniper was watching. He stared blankly in the direction of his adversary and sneered, daring him to shoot again.

The sidewalk between his feet spat up some loose rock as a second bullet struck the pavement directly in front of him. Joe ducked reflexively but stood his ground. If this was a game of chicken, he was determined not to be the first to blink. He thought he saw a small flare coming about half way up the side of the hotel just before the second bullet was fired.

"Han—I think I saw the rifle burst. Tell dispatch the shooter is definitely at the Millenium, roughly twenty stories up, on the south side of the building. I'll try to keep him distracted while our crew locks down the building."

"Joe, this is suicide," Hannah implored. "Don't tempt this guy. He already knows what you look like. You've antagonized him enough. Get back down here and let ESU take care of it."

Joe waved his hand behind his back.

"That's twice he's missed now by several feet. This is just his way of telling us he's watching. He knows we're getting close and he's trying to demonstrate he's still in control. If he wanted me dead, I would be."

Joe stared in the direction of the rifle flare.

"I think maybe you're right, Han. This *is* personal."

He stood still as a statue for several seconds. There were no more shots fired. The sidewalk in the surrounding area remained quiet and deserted. Joe knew the sniper was attempting his getaway.

That's right, run, you little bastard. We'll get you—if not now, very soon. We always do.

A cacophony of sirens filled the block as scores of flashing police cars surrounded the hotel. Joe motioned to Hannah, and the two detectives jumped in their car to join their colleagues. If anyone knew what they were looking for, they did. Joe didn't want Weir slipping through his grasp once more.

Chapter Twenty-Seven

NBC Studio 1A, Rockefeller Plaza

July 12, 6:45 a.m.

Detective Bannon and Commissioner Pope sat on high stools next to television host Doug Morrison preparing for their interview on the Today Show. Joe had been prepped by the Commissioner and the show's host regarding how the interview would proceed and the type of questions to be expected. This was Joe's first major media appearance, and he was definitely not comfortable with the idea of speaking in front of millions of viewers.

An early morning phone call from the Mayor hadn't helped ease his feeling of unrest. The Mayor thought it would be a good idea to introduce the lead detective on the sniper case to put a more relatable face on his media outreach. Joe knew more about the details of the case than the Commissioner, and the Mayor felt he would be able to provide more actionable Intel to enlist public support in catching the sniper.

Joe wanted to mention Todd Weir as a primary suspect, but the Mayor and the Commissioner were adamant that it was legally untenable. There wasn't enough evidence to arrest Weir or even declare him as a person of interest. They simply wanted Joe to share the relevant facts of the case and demonstrate confidence that the force would catch the killer soon.

Joe shifted uncomfortably on his stool, fidgeting with his hands and feet, unsure where to rest them.

Morrison noticed Joe's unease.

"Place your feet on the footrests at the base of the stool and clasp your hands in your lap. Relax—we're just going to ask you some questions about the latest developments in the sniper case and how the public can support your efforts. That's your area of expertise, right?"

Joe nodded and swallowed hard as the stage director began counting down the five seconds to live feed with pumping hand gestures.

"Good morning," Morrison announced, looking at the main camera as the red light flashed on.

"New York City remains under siege today by an unknown assailant, with three more assassinations of innocent civilians in as many days. The latest victims include a ferry passenger, a letter carrier, and a schoolboy. The unidentified sniper is continuing to pick off unarmed citizens seemingly at will.

"We are joined today by Police Commissioner Pope and the lead detective in the sniper case, Joe Bannon, who hopefully can shed some new light on what progress is being made to capture this vicious killer. But first, we're going to check in with our street correspondent, Elizabeth Porter, who's standing by with impressions from average New Yorkers."

The camera cut to a young woman standing on a quiet street corner holding a microphone. A middle-aged man was standing next to her, his eyes nervously darting up and to his sides.

"Liz," Morrison addressed the correspondent, "it appears the streets of New York are nearly deserted as we approach rush hour. Where are you standing right now?"

"I'm at the corner of Wall and Broad Street in the heart of the financial district," the correspondent nodded. "Normally, at this hour the streets are bustling with pedestrians on their way to work, beginning their morning routine. The streets have gotten progressively quieter since the rooftop sniper began his rampage seven days ago."

The correspondent motioned to the man standing beside her.

"Now only a few hardy souls like this gentleman standing beside me seem willing to venture outdoors in broad daylight," she said.

"What's the prevailing sentiment concerning the sniper situation?" Morrison asked.

The correspondent turned to address the man beside her and pointed the microphone towards his mouth.

"Sir, can you tell us how safe you feel traveling about the streets of New York?"

The man frowned and shook his head.

"It feels like a battlefield out here. You never know where the next shot is going to come from. I feel like I'm taking my life into my hands whenever I step outside."

The correspondent nodded.

"What brings you out this morning? Is this part of your normal routine?"

"Unfortunately, I still have a job to do. I'm a floor trader on the New York Stock Exchange and it requires me to be physically present five days a week."

"Are you taking any extra precautions traveling to and from work?"

"I'm walking a lot faster, that's for sure," the man said. "My route to work takes me mostly underground via the subway. But I still have five blocks of no man's land to pass through from the subway station to my office building every day."

"What about during the lunch hour? Do you ever go outside to grab a meal?"

"No way. Everyone I talk to is scared to be outside any more than they have to. Most non-essential personnel are working from home or calling in sick. The few who still come to work pack a lunch, so they spend the minimum amount of time outside."

The correspondent turned back to the camera, and the man quickly disappeared from her side.

"There you have it, Doug. It looks like this sniper has got a lot of New Yorkers running scared. Whatever his agenda, he's made this city feel like a war zone. New York, known for its vibrant street life, has become a near ghost town."

The camera cut back to Morrison, who turned to Commissioner Pope.

"Commissioner, when you were last here you said it was only a matter of time before you apprehended this killer. Are you any closer to capturing the sniper?"

Pope paused for a few seconds.

"Since we last spoke, our investigative team has captured new video footage of his movements and fleshed out his profile. We have a clearer picture of who we're looking for and where we might find him. We're closing the net and narrowing the list of suspects. We'll catch him soon."

Morrison looked at the Commissioner skeptically.

"What new insights about his profile have you uncovered? What kind of monster indiscriminately kills pregnant women and young children?"

Pope had anticipated the interview questions would be tougher this time. It was time to turn the spotlight over to Joe.

"I think it's best if the detective leading the investigation answers that question. He can share more details of the case and paint a clearer picture of who we're looking for."

Commissioner Pope looked at Joe and nodded. Joe stared blankly at the host.

"Detective Bannon," Morrison said, inviting Joe to speak. "Thank you for joining us today. This case certainly appears to have confounded your investigative team so far. You must have collected plenty of evidence after eight straight days of killings. Why is it proving so difficult to catch a killer who strikes so predictably every day?"

Joe could feel his pulse pounding in his head and the hair standing up on the back of his neck. Far from asking straightforward questions, the host was directly challenging his competence. Part of him wanted to blurt out everything he knew about the sniper. But in the back of his head, he could hear the Mayor and his Lieutenant's admonitions about revealing unsubstantiated information.

At least he could start by setting the record straight.

"Technically, it's been seven days. Yesterday was the first day in a week without a killing."

Morrison wasn't ready to stop stirring the pot. A fallible protagonist made for a more interesting story.

"But there was another sniper shooting yesterday, correct? Eyewitnesses saw what appeared to be sniper fire in the vicinity of 6th Avenue and 44th Street. One of our viewers submitted video footage suggesting you were the intended target."

Joe's eyes narrowed and he stared at Morrison icily. He was no longer surprised by how mobile technology had increased the transparency of the police department's business. He took a deep breath and chose his words carefully.

"It's unclear exactly who or what the shooter was targeting yesterday. No one was struck or harmed."

"Has your ballistics department confirmed the bullets were fired from the same rifle as with the previous killings?"

"Yes—"

"The footage shows you provoking the shooter..."

Morrison turned to a monitor by his side where a shaky video replayed the confrontation outside Gregory's coffee shop yesterday. Joe was seen standing his ground while the sniper took potshots around him.

"Can you explain why the sniper appears to be targeting you and why you chose to respond as you did?" Morrison asked.

Out of the corner of his eye, Joe could see the Commissioner shift uncomfortably in his seat.

"I can only surmise that the shooter knew my partner and I were covering the case and that he was sending me a warning."

"What kind of warning? Will this force you or the department to change its tactics?"

Commissioner Pope suddenly looked toward Morrison.

"The NYPD will never be cowed by acts of violence or threats directed toward its personnel," he said. "Every officer puts him or herself in the line of fire every day knowing this risk is part of the job. We will defend the safety and security of our citizens to our dying breath."

Morrison paused, recognizing the NYPD's courage in the line of duty was an unimpeachable subject after 9/11.

"This seems to be an extraordinarily calculated risk, though. Why would any officer intentionally put himself in the line of fire?"

The Commissioner looked at Joe and cocked his head as if to say 'fair question.'

Joe hesitated for a moment before responding.

"The first shot struck many feet to my side. Based on the accuracy of the sniper's previous attacks, I determined that he did not mean to harm me."

"That takes a lot of—*gumption*—if I do say, Detective."

Joe was rapidly gaining confidence in front of the cameras.

"As you said Doug, it was a calculated risk. I felt if I could hold the shooter in place long enough by distracting him, that we might have a better chance at triangulating his position. Then be in a stronger position to capture him."

Morrison pursed his lips, impressed by the Detective's courage under fire.

"Did it work?" he asked. "Did you apprehend the shooter?"

Joe hesitated, hating to admit another failure catching one of the most feared serial killers since Jack the Ripper.

"He slipped away once again. We weren't able to get to him in time."

Morrison looked briefly toward Commissioner Pope then changed his mind and turned back toward Joe. The Detective had an impressive command of the facts and the host recognized when a good story was unfolding.

"I understand you have new video coverage of the shooter. Don't you know what he looks like? How does a known perpetrator repeatedly escape police custody from a pinpointed location carrying a large rifle?"

"This shooter is crafty," Joe continued. "We have reason to believe that in at least one instance, he may have fired the rifle remotely. If anyone sees a suspicious person or any unattended weapon, please notify the department immediately."

Morrison leaned forward in his chair, focusing all of his attention on Joe, ignoring the Commissioner.

"What else should the public be looking for, Detective Bannon? You mentioned earlier that the department's made progress fleshing out the sniper's profile."

Joe parsed his words, remembering Lieutenant O'Neill's warning about not yet pointing to any one suspect.

"Our profile suggests the sniper may have been abandoned by his natural mother at an early age. He very likely moved between foster homes before eventually being adopted. We can't match his profile to anyone with a military record, so there's a good chance he developed his shooting acumen as a hunter. We also believe that the beards he's worn in the surveillance footage may be disguising some kind of facial deformity."

Morrison nodded, impressed with the new disclosures.

"That's a fair amount of new detail from the profile provided previously. May we share the video footage you've brought of his latest movements?"

"Absolutely."

The feed cut to blurry images of the sniper entering and exiting the Battery Park Ritz Carlton and the public housing complex opposite P.S. 132 in the Bronx.

"These videos aren't much clearer than the last footage," Morrison said. "The shooter seems to be aware of the camera position and keeps his head turned just enough so we don't get a clear shot of his face. Is there anything else you can share with our viewers to help them help you find and apprehend this killer?"

Joe paused for a moment.

"This shooter is a deeply disturbed individual. He scurries from one hiding place to another, killing innocent people from a safe distance. He's afraid to reveal himself in public with his facial deformity. He shouldn't be hard to pick out in a crowd. Anyone who sees someone matching his description should notify me or any branch of the police department immediately."

Joe peered directly into the camera lens.

"This man is a coward. Eventually, he will make a mistake, and we will find him. Then he will face justice commensurate with the pain he has inflicted upon others."

****

Ten miles away at his apartment in Flatbush, Todd Weir watched the live broadcast with intense interest. His eyes flashed when he heard Detective Bannon's cutting remarks. As he packed up his belongings, his next target suddenly became clear.

Chapter Twenty-Eight

Lieutenant O'Neill's office, 18th Precinct

July 12, 10:00 a.m.

Joe walked briskly through the detectives' workroom towards Lieutenant O'Neill's office. The detectives looked up from their desks, swiveling their chairs to follow his movement. Some smiled at him, while others simply nodded.

He was a few minutes late for his daily update meeting, already pushed back a couple of hours to accommodate his appearance on the Today Show. The Lieutenant didn't suffer latecomers lightly, and Joe didn't want any more enemies after an irate Mayor called following his TV interview. The Mayor was not pleased when he learned how Joe had put himself in the line of fire, saying it made the police force look unprofessional. He could still hear the Mayor's curse words ringing in his ears.

O'Neill's door was open, which was out of character for the Lieutenant. Normally, he closed his door at the start of every meeting to block out distractions and to single out anyone who showed up late. But this time, as he approached O'Neill's office he heard laughter emanating from the room. He could see Hannah and Kate chuckling about something with the Lieutenant.

Everyone suddenly made a straight face when he walked in.

"Detective Bannon," O'Neill said. "How nice of you to join us. Have you had a busy morning?"

"Um—yes. I was delayed a bit after my TV interview. The Mayor called. Apparently, he wasn't too impressed with my performance..."

"Yes, I heard all about it. The Mayor just contacted me a few minutes ago. You've become a media phenomenon. You've gone *viral*, as they say."

Joe's eyes widened.

"You mean beyond the millions of viewers who saw me put my foot in my mouth on live TV?"

O'Neill picked up a tabloid newspaper from his desk and held up the front page for Joe to see. The top headline in the New York Post read *Hero Cop Taunts Sniper*.

Joe groaned.

"Not only that," Hannah said. "You're tearing up Twitter. Your story is already a trending topic, with over a million tweets in the last hour. You've even got your own hashtag: #notyouraveragejoe."

"Are you going to make an appearance on the Tonight Show next?" Kate kidded.

"Apparently, not everybody thinks you bombed today," O'Neill said. "Though that was definitely a foolish stunt you pulled outside the coffee shop yesterday. Have a seat—we've got some work to catch up on."

Joe slumped into his chair and exhaled heavily. The last twenty-four hours had been a whirlwind, and he was exhausted.

"I'd sure like to know how the sniper traced Hannah and my steps and knew we'd be at that coffee shop when we were," he said.

"We've been working on that," O'Neill said. "I had your patrol car swept in the shop, and the technicians found a tracking bug inside the rear wheel well. Who knows how long this guy's been following you two. I'm assigning you a new car. We're keeping it in the garage to make sure no one tampers with it. And from now on, I want the two of you to wear your bulletproof vests at all times when you're on duty."

Joe frowned.

"That won't help much with a killer who aims for the head."

"Nevertheless, I want you taking every precaution. I think you should keep a low profile for the next few days. Try to limit any unnecessary outside exposure. At least until we know you're no longer being targeted. You didn't exactly endear yourself to this guy with your comments on TV this morning."

"You want me to hide indoors like everybody else who's afraid of this killer? Isn't that playing into his hands? Are you saying you don't want Hannah and me responding to any new attacks?"

O'Neill pushed an open hand towards Joe.

"Of course not. Carry on as you were. The two of you have been making good progress and have almost caught the shooter more than once. Just be careful out there and don't try any more stunts like the one yesterday."

Silence filled the room as everyone absorbed the Lieutenant's comments.

"Kate," O'Neill said. "What do you make of the sniper's actions yesterday? Do you agree with Joe that he didn't intend to kill him?"

"From his description of the events, yes. The sniper's been way too consistent up to this point for such a random break in his pattern. There's no way he could have missed by such a wide margin with two successive shots. Both landed just in front of Joe, halting his forward movement. I think this is the sniper's way of saying he still has total control and can stop anyone he wants."

"Why Joe and Hannah though? Until today, we didn't broadcast they were heading up the sniper investigation. And why wouldn't he kill them when he had a clear opportunity, as he did with the equestrian officer a few days ago?"

"He obviously has a powerful rifle scope if he can shoot someone between the eyes from such a long distance. He probably saw them respond to previous shootings, collecting evidence at the crime scene. He could have easily recorded their badge numbers and called to see which precinct they

143

were assigned to. Then it was just a matter of following their patrol car to monitor their movements and routine."

O'Neill looked at Joe and Hannah.

"Do you normally go to that coffee shop around the same time every day?"

"As a matter of fact, we do," Hannah said. "It's kind of our go-to place for lunch when we're on patrol."

"Well stop that, as of today. As a matter of fact, I'd like you two to become as unpredictable as possible. Be like the President—mix up your routine and travel routes as much as possible. If he doesn't know where you're going to be and when, he can't find you."

Joe and Hannah looked at one another and nodded.

O'Neill redirected his attention toward Kate.

"So why the warning shots, instead of taking them out?"

"That's a tougher one," Kate nodded. "He's looking like more of a control freak with each successive attack. Meticulous disguises, carefully scoping camera placements, the remote firing of the rifle. Like many serial killers, he thinks he's smarter than everyone else. He's probably starting to enjoy the cat and mouse aspect of the chase."

"He's clever all right," O'Neill said, looking directly at Joe. "What does the CCTV footage from yesterday show? You traced the shots to the Millenium Hotel, right? How did the sniper escape another locked down building while you were supposedly holding him in place?"

Joe was about to answer when Hannah stepped in.

"He didn't exit on the ground floor. That's why our team didn't find him. We locked all the exits and began sweeping the rooms as per protocol. The hotel's CCTV footage showed him going into a guest room on a lower floor than normal. We found a room with a broken window leading onto a utility terrace. We believe he rappelled onto an adjacent rooftop across the street then waited until things calmed down before leaving the area."

O'Neill couldn't believe what he was hearing.

"Did you check any street cams to confirm this?"

"Yes. We have footage of someone matching his appearance exiting a restaurant next door at 7:00 p.m."

O'Neill shook his head.

"So besides his superhuman firing accuracy, now he can swing from rooftops like Spiderman. What the fuck. Maybe he really is smarter than us after all. Who knows what other tricks this guy has up his sleeve?"

"We'll get him, Chief," Hannah said. "They always slip up eventually. It's only a matter of time."

"That's what I'm worried about. Time is not a luxury we can afford. I suspect this coffee house diversion yesterday was just a short intermission. I fully expect he'll strike again before another day is over. Unfortunately, his timing and locations are becoming increasingly unpredictable."

The Lieutenant sat back in his chair.

"Where are we in vetting Kate's profile list?"

"Almost done," Hannah said. "Our team has interviewed nearly a thousand adoptees in the New York City area. There's just a handful left. We haven't found anything suspicious or actionable yet."

"Except that guy in Flatbush," Joe said. "I still don't understand why the district attorney won't let us bring him in."

The lieutenant shook his head.

"We've been through this," O'Neill said. "I agree that on paper he looks suspicious. But we can't arrest someone just because he matches the general build of the suspect in our video footage or because he has a cleft lip. We don't have any eyewitnesses who can tie him to the scene of a crime and the videos don't show a clear shot of his face. Without a murder weapon or DNA evidence, we've got nothing."

"Can't we at least bring him into the station and lean on him a little?" Joe asked. "I think I could be pretty persuasive—"

"That's what I'm afraid of. This guy's gotten under your skin. It's too easy for you to cross the line. We're all under a microscope right now. The Commissioner says we have to go hands-off until we have more concrete evidence, so that's what we're going to do."

Joe turned his head and cracked his neck.

"What if we discreetly shadow him for a while?" he said. "We're running out of leads. At least we'd have a chance at stopping another killing if it does turn out to be him."

O'Neill turned his chair and looked out the window. He looked down at his desk and thumbed the sniper dossier. Then he glanced up at Kate. She raised her eyebrows and tilted her head, offering consent.

O'Neill turned back to Joe.

"Okay, but keep this under the radar. The Commissioner will have my badge if he finds out we're contravening his direct orders, not to mention the Mayor. Do not engage this guy under any circumstances unless you recognize a clear indication of intent to harm."

Joe felt his phone buzzing in his coat pocket. He pulled it out and looked at the screen.

"It's the Mayor," he said.

"I suppose you should take it," O'Neill said.

Joe held the phone up to his ear.

"Yes, Mr. Mayor," Joe said. "Thank you...Just doing my job, sir. Yes, I'll try to be more careful...If you insist, sir."

Joe tapped the screen to end the call and placed the phone back in his pocket.

"The Mayor says he wants me to go back on TV as soon as possible. Apparently, there's been a bunch of requests from media outlets and thousands of incoming tips since my appearance this morning. He thinks I'm a good face for the department."

"Well you do have a pretty face," Hannah kidded.

O'Neill smiled.

"Just try not to get it blown off, will you?"

146

Chapter Twenty-Nine

Cranberry Bog, Long Island

July 12, 4:00 p.m.

T odd Weir trudged through a wet marsh on the east end of Long Island with his dog by his side. He wore high rubber hip waders and a heavy pack on his back. His clothing was green camouflage from head to toe, including a spotted hunter's cap. He wasn't taking any chances he might be noticed or found in his new hideout.

He knew the police would soon be keeping a watch on him if they weren't already. But it didn't matter. He only needed another week or so to complete his business. Then he would pack up and move to another city to start over again. His skills were easily transferable. Every town needed a locksmith, and most customers were happy to pay cash. He could easily stay under the radar with a new trade name and pseudonym. Worst case, he could retreat back into the bush and lie low until the cops gave up the chase.

Weir was used to roughing it and living off the land. The one thing his adoptive father taught him that was useful was how to hunt and set up camp in the remotest of wilderness. He could kill and eat just about anything that flew, swam, or crawled. And he knew how to set up a blind to remain invisible to man and beast. This camp wouldn't require such elaborate arrangements. He was still close enough to civilization to run out for fast food if necessary.

Long Island was sparsely populated this far from the city. But the rich local residents with their country estates created a whole cottage industry of support businesses to cater to their needs. The bog was only a few miles from the Hamptons and would provide perfect cover. Heavily forested and surrounded by thick marsh, no civilians were likely to venture far off the hiking trails circling the area. Weir was more concerned for his black Lab, who'd grown accustomed to the creature comforts of city living.

Weir looked down and saw his dog breathing heavily as he paddled through the thick bog.

"Don't worry, buddy. We'll be on dry ground soon. It'll be just like the old days, when we hunted for game, upstate. Maybe you can help me catch a few ducks and we'll roast them up for dinner later. It'll just be for a little while. You know I always come back for you, right?"

Weir patted his dog's head.

"You're the only one who's worthy of respect. You don't judge me for how I look or where I came from. You're always faithful, not like the others who don't care who they hurt along the way. I've been abused and ridiculed since I was too young to fight back. Not any longer. The balance of power has shifted. We're the alpha males now."

Weir noticed an elevated patch of ground on a small island in the middle of the bog a hundred feet to his left. He waded to the island and pulled his dog onto the shore. The Lab shook himself dry then snorted noisily to expel the water from his nose.

"Come on boy, let's find a comfortable spot to set up camp."

Weir hacked his way through the thick brush at the edge of the island until he found a small clearing about thirty feet inland. He immediately set to building a shelter. He cut some saplings and arranged them in a rough cube shape, connected with baling twine. Then he covered the structure with leafy branches and moss until it blended in with its surroundings.

He placed his gear inside the burrow and retrieved two rubber frisbee-looking disks from the pack. He pulled their accordion sides up to form deep bowls then filled one with water and the other with two cups of dog food.

"There you go, buddy. This ought to get you through the next couple of hours. I've got a few things I need to take care of. I need you to be quiet and still until I get back, okay? We don't want to attract any unnecessary attention to our new home. There are some bad people out there who will take us away if they find us."

Weir attached a leash to the dog's collar then drove three inward-pointed stakes deep into the ground to secure the other end.

"Lie down and take a little nap until I return." He patted the dog down with a dry towel then rubbed his ears. "Good boy. I'll be back soon."

Weir covered the blind's entrance with some tree boughs then made his way back across the bog to where he parked his car. It was a two-hour ride back into the city, and he had one last bit of business to take care of while it was still light.

Chapter Thirty

Astoria, Queens

July 12, 8 p.m.

J oe sat on his living room couch with his feet propped on the coffee table and a glass of brandy in his hand. He'd taken the sniper file home to study the details and see if he could uncover any new clues. His shadowing of Weir's apartment with Hannah had shown no sign of any movement all day and the investigative trail had grown cold.

Fortunately, there'd been no new shootings during the day and dusk was rapidly approaching. He wondered if his comments on the Today Show had driven Weir underground. The whole city was on the lookout for the sniper, and they finally had something specific to watch out for. If it really was Weir, Joe thought, surely he'd want to lie low for a while?

Joe could hear his wife cleaning up in the kitchen after they'd shared their first home-cooked meal together in over a week. He'd been so preoccupied with chasing the sniper and working late vetting Kate's list of suspects, he'd barely given her any of his time. It felt good to spend some quality time with her and slow down over a glass of wine.

Jane rarely spoke of the incident so long ago that took their only child. She knew Joe carried a heavy burden of guilt for not being home to protect them. Neither of them wanted to relive the painful memories. They hadn't been able to conceive again after the horrible event; Joe wondered if Jane simply was too worried it could happen again. She kept herself busy by throwing herself into her work as the Communications Director for the Metropolitan Museum, but she never recovered the same zest for life she'd felt as a young mother.

"I hope you're not going to work on that sniper case all night again," Jane called over the clattering of pots. "You do realize you can't save the whole world singlehandedly, don't you?"

"Well somebody has to do it," Joe joked. "But now that I'm a big media star, I've got the whole city helping me. So maybe I can afford to put my feet up for a little while."

"That was quite a performance you put on today," Jane chuckled. "Even coming from a communications specialist, that was masterful. You had that pompous host eating out of your hands by the end of the interview. But I thought you weren't supposed to publicly talk about that suspect you've been so obsessed with these past few days."

"I didn't."

"Well not exactly by name. But you might as well have, by mentioning that whole facial deformity thing."

"I didn't specify what *kind* of facial deformity..."

"I sure hope you're right about this character," Jane said. "Because if you're not, whatever hang-ups he may have had about his appearance before this are going to be magnified by every suspicious New Yorker looking at him even more askance now."

"That's the idea. Hopefully, it'll be a little harder for him to sneak into his usual hiding places carrying that odd rifle case from now on. At the very least, we'll have a better chance of receiving a tip before he does any more damage."

Joe flipped through the case file slowly. He was looking for any pattern that might foretell where the sniper would strike next. The shooter's timing was no longer as predictable as it was when he started his reign of terror. The one-minute-after-noon pattern had stopped after the cab driver killing in Washington Square. Kate thought it might be a Biblical reference—the exact quote from Chapter 12, Verse 1 from the Book of Romans read:

I urge you, brothers and sisters, in view of God's mercy, to offer your bodies as a living sacrifice, holy and pleasing to God—this is your true and proper worship.

A living sacrifice—that fit, but why? Was Weir a religious fanatic trying to demonstrate how everybody should bow to God's will? Joe didn't see a profusion of religious artifacts when he searched Weir's apartment. Maybe the sniper simply chose the timing to coincide with the busy lunch hour when everybody headed outdoors for a midday meal? The initial regularity of the shootings certainly made the streets deserted around that time of day. Were the killings simply a power trip by someone who'd been taunted his whole life and never felt in control? Weir didn't exactly project an attitude of insecurity in the brief encounters he'd had with Joe.

Joe shook his head in frustration. He decided to get up and give his wife a little attention. She'd often shared useful insights on tough cases he'd worked on previously. He walked into the kitchen where Jane was washing dishes over the sink watching a light drizzle fall outside the window.

"Hon, can I ask your opinion about something? You've got a degree in psychology, so maybe you can help me fill in some holes in this suspect's profile..."

"If you remember, psychology was just my minor, but I suppose I know a few things about human behavior, so fire away. I mean, what else could we possibly be doing this rainy mid-summer evening?"

Joe leaned over and gave his wife a playful peck on her cheek. She snickered at his half-hearted romantic gesture.

"Well, I've been trying to get my head around the timing of these killings. You know how they all started around the same time? Just after noon each day."

"Yes—"

"And then suddenly they started happening at seemingly random times. Two at different times of the morning and one in the afternoon. I thought at first the shooter was firing at the same time during the lunchtime rush to scare everybody off the streets. Like he was on some kind of power trip or something. But that doesn't make sense now that he's mixing his timing up."

"Actually, it makes perfect sense. That's exactly how dog trainers shape animal behavior. They start by pairing the signal and response in very predictable timing patterns, like feeding a dog every time it performs a desired behavior like fetching or sitting. Once the dog understands the connection between the signal and response, the trainer gradually randomizes the delivery of the reward so the animal associates the signal such as a verbal command with the behavior instead of the reward. People are just like animals. They learn in much the same way."

"Holy crap," Joe said. "Do you really think the sniper is that smart? That he's consciously *training* people to be afraid of him firing at any time of the day?"

"You said yourself that he's exceptionally clever. The Today Show broadcast showed how New Yorkers are afraid to go outside now during daylight hours."

"Jesus," Joe muttered. "If you're right, I might need more of your professional services to decipher this guy's intentions. Can I put you on retainer?"

"I'm sure we can arrange some kind of trade for services."

Joe looked at the pile of dirty dishes stacked beside the sink.

"Do you want some help cleaning up?"

Jane shook her head.

"I've only got another five minutes or so to finish up. You go ahead and relax in the living room. I think you need the rest more than I do. But will you put all that sniper stuff aside for the rest of the night when I'm done? I wouldn't mind cuddling with you over a romantic movie before we turn in for the night."

"Of course, babe."

Joe gave his wife a warm hug and a proper kiss before heading back to the living room. He sat on the sofa and began to leaf through the sniper dossier again. Something else bothered him.

What about the victims? he thought. There was no rhyme or reason there either. A young pregnant woman, a middle-aged businessman, a cop, a cab driver, a ferry commuter, a schoolyard youngster, and a letter carrier. Could it be any more random than that? What was the connection between the victims—or was there no connection at all? Was this guy just one seriously fucked up individual who simply was angry at the world, as Kate suggested? Or did each one of the victims symbolize someone who'd wronged him in his earlier life?

Joe could see the possible connection with the pregnant woman. Weir was given up for adoption by his natural mother at a young age. He could be harboring anger towards mothers, especially those carrying an unborn child. The businessman might have represented all the comforts of life the sniper had been denied in his life. Weir ran what appeared to be a successful small business, but his living arrangements were far from luxurious. Could the police officer shooting have been over anger from possible mistreatment during a troubled youth? Maybe his locksmith skills were developed during hardscrabble years as a foster child, though there were no previous arrests on Weir's file. But why the cab driver, the letter carrier, and the young boy? What kind of grudge could he possibly have towards them?

Joe began to wonder if he was chasing the wrong suspect in Weir. He had an air-tight alibi for the ferry killing. But there were plenty of suspicious circumstances associated with that shooting. Like the powder residue on the roof of the Battery Park Ritz-Carlton hotel and the suspect matching Weir's description seen on the lobby cam. But the video footage was inconclusive, and the suspect's facial hair might have covered Weir's unusual lip deformity.

There was no way of connecting him directly to any of the crimes. No smoking gun, no eyewitnesses, and no DNA evidence. He had nothing on this guy other than a gut feel. What if he was wrong about Weir? What if the sniper was somebody else? What if Joe was wasting valuable time chasing the wrong suspect?

Joe threw the file down on the coffee table and leaned back on the sofa. He could hear the rain starting to come down harder as it pelted against the windows. A quiet movie with his wife was exactly what he needed to take his mind off everything.

"Almost done in there, hon?" Joe called out to Jane.

"Just one more minute. Drying the roasting pan then I'll be right there. Do you want to scan the listings to see if there's anything good on? No more of those shoot-em-up action flicks that you're always making me watch."

"No worries, babe. I've had quite enough shooting this week. A romantic movie it is."

Joe turned on the TV and thumbed through the on-screen listings with the remote. He found a movie that neither of them had seen before, starring two of their favorite actors. He selected the movie, queued it up, and hit the pause button."

"That's funny," Jane suddenly called from the kitchen.

"What? Are you going to make more fun of my television performance today?"

"No, I'm spying on the neighbors. You know that apartment building across the street? It's odd that people would open their windows on such a rainy night. Just about everybody is battened down. But there's this one apartment directly across the way with their window wide open. Their curtains will be getting wet—"

Joe nodded absentmindedly, thinking back to the sniper case. Then he suddenly leapt off the sofa.

"Jane!" he screamed at the top of lungs.

As he started running toward the kitchen, Joe heard a dull pop and the sound of broken glass, followed by the sickening thud of a body falling on the floor.

Chapter Thirty-One

Astoria, Queens

July 12, 8:30 p.m.

J oe raced out his front door, searching frantically for the open window in the apartment building across the street. The rain was pelting down on his face, and he ran his hand over his brow to clear his vision. He gave no thought to the possibility the sniper might still be watching and could pick him off in the glow of the streetlights. There was only one thing running through his mind—how he could stop the shooter before he got away.

Then he would tear him apart with his bare hands.

His vision darted from side to side up the face of the building until he saw some white curtains blowing against the dark brick wall. The open window was on the east end of the building. He counted the number of floors then sprinted toward the lobby. When he got to the glass door in the vestibule, he kicked it sending glass shards shattering to the floor.

He ducked under the door's cross-beam, darted into the main hall and saw the emergency exit sign on the east side. He ran to the exit door, flung it open and bounded up the stairway steps two at a time. The ten floors passed in a blur. Joe was so pumped full of adrenaline and rage that he could have scaled another twenty floors without slowing down.

When he got to the tenth floor, he swung open the door to the hallway and paused in front of the first apartment to his right. He pulled out his service pistol and pointed it at the door. His heart was racing a hundred miles an hour. Without giving a second thought, he raised his right knee and thrust the heel of his foot as hard as he could beside the door handle.

The door splintered open, and he rushed in toward the open window in the living room. His hands were locked together, pointing his Glock straight ahead. A naked young couple sat up on the living room sofa and looked at Joe in terror.

"Where is he?!" Joe screamed at the couple.

"Who?" the young man said, trying to cover himself and his partner up with a blanket. "It's just us—"

Joe glanced around the room looking for any sign of the sniper. He ran into the adjoining bedroom and bathroom. There was no sign of the shooter. He hurried back into the living room.

"Have you seen anyone with a rifle?" he asked. "Didn't you hear the gunshot?"

The young couple looked at Joe with their mouths agape.

"We heard something," the young man said. "We just thought it was a car backfiring."

Joe stared at the couple, wondering why they hadn't bothered to investigate or call 9-1-1. It had been over fifty years since Kitty Genovese was brutally murdered while her Queens neighbors blithely ignored her screams. Had nothing changed in New York City?

Joe looked at the young woman trembling in fear with the blanket pulled over her naked body. His chest was heaving from the ten story sprint. Rain from his soaked hair was streaming down his face. He peered through the window and saw his house across the street. The kitchen light radiated out into the black night.

Then the weight of what had just happened fell over him. He sunk to his knees and wept uncontrollably.

Chapter Thirty-Two

Union Square, Manhattan

July 13, 8:15 a.m.

Todd Weir sat at a sidewalk bistro table watching the morning rush hour unfold. He wasn't worried about being recognized with his hair and fake mustache dyed gray. He looked at least twenty years older than his real age. Besides, everyone seemed much more concerned in looking upwards for signs of trouble than at street level.

He was far more interested in the flow of pedestrian traffic emerging from the MTA subway station in the park across the street. Although it was noticeably thinner than usual for this time of day, Weir was surprised so many people were still braving the open streets to get to work.

I guess Maslow was right, he thought, referring to the famous psychologist's theory of human motivation. *Sustenance really is higher on the hierarchy of human needs than safety and security.*

He picked up a copy of the Daily News lying on his table and looked at the headline. *Cop's Wife Killed in Cold Blood*, it read in large type. Below the headline, there was a crude illustration of a sniper targeting a woman behind her kitchen window.

That ought to keep them guessing, he thought. *By foot, car, even in their own home—no one is safe. Not even cops and their families.*

Weir smiled as he thought about how easy it was to pick off anyone he wanted. It seemed strange to him that with so much advanced technology, modern man had been unable to protect himself from a simple bullet. Lower life forms had evolved all manner of natural defenses to protect themselves from their predators. Turtles had impregnable shells, chameleons changed color to blend in amongst their surroundings, and winged animals could fly to safety. But frail and thin-skinned humans had no natural protection other than their supposedly superior brains. Man-made laws had lulled them into a false sense of security, their wits dulled by the soft lifestyle of modern-day civilization.

The flock still needed herding, Weir thought, as he watched a new trainload of commuters emerge from the MTA rotunda. Too many people were defying his power.

Something has to be done about this.

He looked around the square to scope out a suitable location for his next hit. Preferably an older building, one with old-fashioned windows that still slid open. None of those modern curtain-wall towers with hermetically sealed air circulation systems. A rifle sticking out of one of them would be far too conspicuous. It had to be a tall building, at least fifteen to twenty stories. High enough to have a commanding view of the square, especially the Metro station entrance.

Weir panned around the square and stopped when he caught sight of a large limestone building about a block to the west. It took up almost the entire block along 14th Street on the north side between Union Square West and 5th Avenue. It abutted smaller structures on the north side with clear rooftop access between the buildings. And it had a tall, protective parapet on its roof.

Yes, he thought. *That one's perfect. That will keep the cops checking room to room while I make my retreat to the other side. My new disguise should allow me to slip away unchecked.*

Weir's gaze returned to street level. He glanced at the Best Buy building on the south side of the square. Three stories up its glass edifice shone the cryptic image of The Metronome, a digital art installation with fifteen large red numbers switching randomly like a broken bedside alarm clock. Most New Yorkers had no idea what the numbers symbolized, if anything. Some thought it was a kind of countdown clock or a real-time update of the national debt. It was actually nothing more than an elaborate clock, measuring the time in hours, minutes, seconds and tenths of a second. The first seven digits measured the time since the previous midnight, and the last seven digits measured it backward to the next midnight. It was the spinning digits in the middle that confused everybody.

Weir chuckled to himself at the irony of the image. Soon, it would represent a real doomsday clock, marking the exact time of his next killing in large, blood-red numerals.

****

Nine hours later, the peaceful quietude of Union Square Park was broken by the sharp crack of a rifle as afternoon commuters crammed into the narrow portico of the MTA entrance structure. One of the commuters fell to the ground, coating the granite steps in a thick pool of blood. A terrified shriek rose from the crowd as people suddenly stampeded over one another to get to the safety of the inner lobby.

Within a minute, the entire square was swarming with flashing police cars. Soon after, a black Emergency Services Unit van pulled up in front of the co-op building on 14th Avenue and ten heavily armed special operations officers poured into the front entrance.

Forty-five minutes later, an old man hobbling on crutches slipped out the side door of a walk-up building one block away. He made his way to the Astor Place MTA station nine blocks to the south. Then he took the subway to the Jamaica station in Brooklyn and transferred to the Long Island Rail Road where he took the train all the way to the east end of the island.

It was past someone's dinner time.

163

Chapter Thirty-Three

J oe walked through the detectives' workroom two days after his wife's killing with a changed attitude. Finding and capturing the sniper was no longer just part of his job. Now it was personal. He'd lost the two dearest people in the world to him through violent acts. Both times, he was in the service of protecting the public. But he was unable to save those who mattered the most to him. It was his job to find violent criminals before they could do more harm, but this one had gotten to him first. He was determined to put an end to this case and to this killer before he could take another life.

He felt the weight of the room bearing down as he approached the Lieutenant's office. None of his colleagues looked at him directly. Instead, they peered out of the corner of their eye, pretending to be buried in their work. Everybody knew how Joe felt and that he needed space to process what had happened.

The Lieutenant's door was closed. Joe walked right in without knocking.

"Joe," O'Neill said, looking up surprised.

"You shouldn't be here today. I wanted you to take a few days off. We can take care of this. You've got more important matters to attend to. Go home and be with your family in this time of loss."

"My family is gone," Joe said, taking his customary seat next to Hannah and Kate. "This is the most important thing I've got to do right now."

No one said a thing for a few long seconds as an awkward silence filled the room.

"Joe," Hannah said, reaching out to clasp his hand. "I'm so sorry. Whatever I can do to help you through this, please let me know."

"I'm sorry for your loss, Joe," Kate added. "I'd like to offer my help as well. I know how hard it is to make arrangements at a time like this."

"Thank you, everyone," Joe said.

He paused as he choked up with emotion.

"I appreciate your concern. I've spent the last twenty-four hours making the funeral arrangements. The service will be held tomorrow. I wanted to get back to work as soon as possible. I don't want to be home alone. This is where I belong."

O'Neill nodded solemnly.

"I understand. Are you sure you're ready to talk about the latest incident? This might be difficult—"

"I'm *fine*," Joe said. "I'd like to get on with it. We've all got a job to do. Let's review the latest evidence."

O'Neill looked at the sniper file on his desk and cleared his throat.

"We'll start with yesterday's incident," he said, flipping open the file. "The Union Square shooting. The location and time of day suggest he was targeting a random commuter. Same M.O. as before. Kate—what do you make of this?"

"It could be a possible reaction to the Today Show telecast two days ago. The interview with the stock trader showed that people were still commuting to work, albeit reluctantly. Maybe this was his way of closing the vice, to scare off the few people still braving the streets. This shooting may have been about consolidating his control."

Joe thought back to his wife's comments the night of the telecast, where she speculated about the shooter's motivation. The killings were looking more like a power trip with every shooting. He swallowed hard remembering their last tender moments together.

"And the other shooting..." O'Neill paused. "Joe, are you sure—"

Joe looked the Lieutenant square in the eyes and nodded.

"What could he possibly hope to gain by targeting a...cop's wife?" O'Neill asked.

Kate looked awkwardly in Joe's direction. She knew it would be impossible to offer her opinion without striking some raw nerves.

"The sniper obviously already knew Joe was working the case from the incident outside the coffee shop three days ago. I think that was his way of telling Joe to stop chasing him or at least that he was still in control. Joe's subsequent public appearance showing him leading the investigation and his comments about the shooter may have stoked his anger."

"His *anger*?" Joe interjected. "Isn't it high time we stopped focusing on this guy's feelings and focus instead on the facts? All this speculation on what's motivating him isn't getting us any closer to figuring out where he's going to strike next. I think we need to change tack."

O'Neill paused to give Joe a moment to calm down. He knew his detective was hurting and he didn't want to inflame the wound.

"What do you propose, Joe?"

"Kate's profile work has already uncovered a good suspect. I say we turn the screws on this guy. Let's bring him in and see what he knows. Everybody cracks under the right kind of pressure."

"Joe, you're asking me to contravene direct orders. From the Commissioner, no less. The District Attorney was very clear with his opinion. We don't have a legal basis to bring this suspect in based on the evidence. All we can do is put a tail on him, which is already stretching our jurisdiction—"

"He wasn't moving the last time we checked," Joe said, glancing at Hannah. "At least not that we could see. He put a tracking device on us—why can't we do the same with his vehicle?"

167

"Joe," O'Neill shook his head, "you know we can't do that."

"What about his phones then? If we could monitor his communications or movements more easily..."

"We'd need a warrant. Besides, the electronic devices we confiscated when we searched his apartment came up empty. He's obviously being very careful to cover his tracks. He's almost certainly using a prepaid cell phone to bypass any tracking efforts."

Joe slammed his fist on the armrest in frustration.

"How do you expect us to catch this fucker if our hands are tied at every turn?"

He was overstepping his bounds, but he didn't care any longer.

O'Neill swiveled his chair and looked out his window before he responded.

"Look, Joe, I understand how much you want to catch this sniper. We all do. I think you've gotten a little too close to the situation. We don't know that this suspect is really the shooter. We can't divert any more resources than we already are chasing a possible red herring."

Joe wasn't ready to concede the argument.

"If we can't find him ourselves, let's get the public working harder for us, then. We could release a police sketch of the suspect."

"You mean of *your* suspect?" O'Neill said.

Joe stared at the Lieutenant icily.

"He matches the height and build of the suspect on the videos. His face, as much as is visible, also fits. We have someone matching his appearance tracked to the time and place of multiple shootings. He only has a solid alibi for one of those shootings. And his profile fits Kate's construction like a glove. Isn't that suspect enough?"

"None of that is good enough for a conviction or even an arrest. Get me an eyewitness, a murder weapon, DNA evidence—even a clearer video—and you can bring him in.

168

Until then, we've got to explore all other avenues in this investigation. Let's start by talking about how we can do a better job cordoning the crime scene to prevent future escapes."

But Joe wasn't listening any longer.

He was already thinking about how he could bypass the legal system and take matters into his own hands.

Chapter Thirty-Four

St. Michael's Cemetery, Queens

July 15, 11:00 a.m.

On Thursday morning, a long line of flashing police cars traveled silently eastward along Astoria Boulevard. On its flanks, motorcycle cops escorted the procession toward its destination. When the black limousine at the front of the line reached 49th Street, it turned into St. Michael's Cemetery and began making its way to the rear of the burial grounds.

The hearse stopped opposite a tree-lined plot with an open grave. As the other cars in the procession slowly pulled up behind it, people exited their vehicles and walked up a small knoll toward the marked grave. Joe led the way with his and his wife's parents walking arm in arm. Behind him followed a huge contingent of police officers dressed in formal NYPD blues.

It seemed as if the entire force had come out to pay their respects. Even more so than with the cop who was killed a week earlier, there was something especially symbolic about this murder. The equestrian cop had been killed in the line of duty, which, as unacceptable as it was, wasn't nearly as horrifying as the cold-blooded assassination of a cop's wife. Even the Mayor had come to pay his respects in a show of support for Joe and the police force.

In view of the circumstances leading up to the event, security was boosted to an unprecedented level. The entire perimeter of the cemetery was monitored by beat cops spaced twenty feet apart while flashing cruisers patrolled the adjacent streets. ESU teams had cleared all non-essential buildings on the grounds and police sharpshooters lay positioned atop rooftops scanning every tall building within a mile radius of the cemetery. Lieutenant O'Neill didn't think the sniper would be brazen enough to attack during the ceremony, but he wasn't taking any chances. If the sniper tried anything, the full weight of the police force would bear down on him within seconds.

Joe tried to put the sniper out of his mind and think about his wife. As the pallbearers carried the casket up the hillside, he clenched his jaw fighting back tears. It was an almost impossible loss for him to bear after losing his only child so many years earlier. He had lost the two most important people in his life, and he had been responsible in one way or another for each loss.

He closed his eyes and bowed his head. He was not a deeply religious man, but he believed in a higher power and that a person's soul never truly died.

Lord, forgive my sins and watch over my family, he prayed. *I will bring justice to their memory and be with them soon.*

From the opposite side of the grave, Hannah watched her tormented partner with sadness. After serving almost ten years together, she knew him like family. She knew he'd be filled with intense and conflicting emotions at this agonizing moment. Grief, anger, guilt—and a crushing sense of revenge. If Joe could get his hands on the sniper at this moment, she knew he would strangle him with his own hands.

She looked around the gravesite. Hundreds of dedicated officers were on the lookout, but she still couldn't help feeling a sense of unease. With so many cops congregated in one location at one time, it would be a tempting target for a deranged killer so bent on flouting the law.

The Mayor was flanked at the gravesite by the Commissioner and the Police Chief. Lieutenant O'Neill and the entire 18th Precinct stood just behind them. Joe had wanted a private ceremony for his wife but had agreed to the police escort at the Lieutenant's suggestion. He knew the best way to ensure a peaceful ceremony was to cover the area with as many cops as possible. But he insisted on foregoing the trappings of a formal police funeral. This wasn't a line-of-duty killing, and his wife wouldn't want all the pomp and ceremony.

As the casket was placed on a platform over the open grave, the minister began his committal rites.

"Dearly beloved, we are gathered here today to lay to rest another departed soul..."

Joe's mind began to wander.

What kind of person could be so callous to take such a beautiful and innocent life? Whatever grudges the sniper may have harbored against him or the police, why take it out on his wife? How did she deserve any of this?

He clenched his fists tighter and tighter the more he thought about the sniper. He wasn't sure he'd found the right suspect, but he was damned if he'd let him slip through his fingers again.

This guy thinks he's above the law, Joe thought. *If the law can't contain or capture him, then let the law of the jungle prevail. The predator will become prey. He's not the only one who knows a little something about guerrilla warfare.*

As Hannah glanced at her partner across the grave, she could have sworn she saw a small smile form on Joe's lips.

Chapter Thirty-Five

728 E New York Avenue, East Flatbush, Brooklyn

July 15, 10:00 p.m.

J oe hid behind a thick tree in the park across the street from Weir's apartment building, looking for any sign of the sniper. At this time of night, in the shadow of its heavy canopy, he wouldn't attract much attention. He'd already noted the position of the street cams in the area and parked his car many blocks away to avoid possible detection. For what he was about to do, he didn't want to take any chance being placed at the scene.

He'd monitored Weir's apartment most of the evening and didn't see any movement. No lights had flashed on or off all evening, and there was no sign of Weir entering or exiting the building. Either he was out, or he was intentionally keeping a very low profile.

Joe grew weary of waiting and pulled his hoodie over his head. He walked across the street toward the entrance to the building's parking garage. Then he hid behind an abutment and waited for the automatic door to open. After a few minutes, the door began to roll up, and a car pulled out from the garage and turned onto the street. Joe ducked under the door before it closed and walked down the ramp with his head bowed.

He walked toward Weir's parking stall with a key dangling from his hand so as not to attract suspicion from any other building residents. If Weir could track his movements, he could just as easily track the sniper's. *Fuck the system,* Joe thought. This guy doesn't abide by the rules of civilized society, why should he? The sniper had been picking people off with impunity, and there was nothing Joe could do to stop him.

Until now.

It was time to stop following protocol and time to play by his own rules. Joe had a tracking device in his pocket, and he was prepared to attach it to Weir's vehicle. Then he could track Weir's movements directly and catch him in the act—or at least follow him to his murder weapon. If he picked up the sniper's trail, he'd take a couple of days off work. The Lieutenant would only think he was mourning his wife.

When he got to Weir's parking stall, it was empty. Joe looked around the garage to see if his locksmith truck was parked anywhere else. There was no sign of Weir or his vehicle.

Joe cursed under his breath.

There hadn't been another incident during the day, and it was too dark for another shooting. Was he out on a late-night locksmith call? Maybe he'd switched vehicles, Joe thought. Weir would have known that his locksmith truck could be traced back to him and might attract unnecessary attention. If he skipped town, it would be nearly impossible to track him. Joe had some business he needed to finish with the shooter. There was no way he was going to simply let the sniper slip away into obscurity.

Joe walked toward the underground lobby and entered the elevator area. He swung the door open to the stairwell and began making his way up to the seventeenth floor. If he couldn't track Weir's outside movements then he would catch him when he returned home. At least Weir had a dog that he seemed to care about. He'd have to return home every few hours or so to feed it and take it out.

When Joe got to the seventeenth floor, he opened the stairwell door to the hall and peered through the crack. The hallway was clear. He walked toward unit 1708 and reached into his pocket. As he neared the unit's front door, he slowed down and walked on the balls of his feet to make as little noise as possible. When he got to the door, he placed his back against the wall so as not to cast a shadow under the threshold. If Weir were inside, he didn't want to provide any warning.

He held his ear to the wall and listened. There was no sign of activity. No footsteps, no television, not even the sound of the dog breathing or snoring. Joe crouched down to the base of the door and placed the object in his hand near the bottom corner. It was a strip of bacon. He blew over the bacon to send the scent wafting into the room. If the dog were present, surely it would smell the food and move toward the door.

Nothing.

Joe looked up and down the hall to make sure no one was coming then got on his hands and knees and peered under the door jamb. The apartment was dark except for a digital clock on the stove projecting a pale glow into the living room. From what he could see, everything seemed to be in the same position he remembered it when he searched the apartment a few days ago. The furniture was still there, and Weir's knick-knacks still lay undisturbed on the bookshelf.

Joe breathed a sigh of relief. At least Weir hadn't moved out.

He got up and walked to the end of the hall. He opened the stairwell door and sat down on one of the steps. Then he took two black leather gloves from his pocket and pulled them slowly onto his hands.

When Weir came home, Joe would be ready. It didn't matter how long it took. The sniper's reign of terror would end tonight. Weir was going to disappear, never to be heard from again.

But not before Joe took one last measure of the man.

Chapter Thirty-Six

The Standard Hotel, Meatpacking District

July 15, 11:30 p.m.

T en days after the sniper's rampage had begun, New York
City had fallen ghostly silent. Few people dared to step
outside in daylight hours for fear of being caught in the
shooter's sights. He'd demonstrated a willingness to target
any person from any walk of life, across all five boroughs.
Nobody wanted to tempt fate. Even within their own homes,
drapes had been pulled and blinds drawn to prevent prying
eyes catching its residents off guard.

The only time New Yorkers were comfortable venturing
outside was after dark. The one unifying theme among the
killings was that almost all of them were executed outside in
broad daylight. The exception with Detective Bannon's wife
was viewed as a personal vendetta. As long as they stayed
indoors during the day and kept their blinds drawn at night,
most people felt they were safe from the sniper.

But it was a different story after dusk in New York's
dance clubs. The restricted social contact from people staying
locked in their homes had created a cabin fever that needed
an outlet. Just as the 9/11 bombings a generation ago had
snapped New Yorkers' apathy and stimulated an outpouring
of love, so it was in the current crisis. Young people poured
into nightclubs and partied as if there was no tomorrow.

One of the hottest nightclubs was Le Bain at the top of
the Standard Hotel in the Meatpacking District. Raised on
stilts over the Highline elevated park along the West Side, it
offered spectacular views of Lower Manhattan from its 18th-
floor rooftop setting. One of its biggest attractions was a

179

sunken hot tub pool where scantily clad partygoers danced and frolicked to pounding music.

On this late Thursday evening, the club was busier than ever. The dance floor was crammed with gyrating bodies, and the pool was overflowing with half-naked people cavorting as other patrons looked on. Late at night and this high above street level, no one felt threatened.

Security in the main floor lobby and at the club entrance was extraordinarily tight. Everyone had to pass through metal detectors and have their bags checked. The club overlooked the Hudson River, and there were no other buildings as tall as the Standard for almost a mile in any direction. There was no safer place in New York to hold a party and let your hair down.

What the partygoers didn't realize was that the flashing strobe lights atop the hotel late at night acted like a beacon for other types of wayward souls. And not everyone was in a party mood tonight. Six blocks away, from the water tower atop the luxury co-op building at 627 Hudson Street, someone else was watching the merrymaking through his Smith & Bender rifle scope.

And he was not impressed.

Although the sniper was viewing the building at an oblique angle more than a half a mile away, the two-story high windows surrounding the 18th floor of the Standard Hotel provided a clear view of the activity inside the club. The hotel made no effort to block the view of the Manhattan skyline for its patrons, and the flashing lights of the interior illuminated the club like a bright stage in a darkened theater.

The sniper panned the room with his scope. Everyone was laughing and reveling as if they didn't have a care in the world. He sneered and exhaled slowly.

This was no way for frightened children to behave. Didn't they know the big bad wolf was still watching? Another disciplinary lesson needs to be administered to teach them to respect authority.

He swung his scope along the length of the floor toward the southwest side of the building. At the corner overlooking the Hudson River sat a large hot tub illuminated from below. Inside, scores of semi-nude bathers were dancing to the music in the bubbling waist-high water. On the walls surrounding the hot tub, red neon lights flashed faux flames toward the ceiling. He zoomed in closer. Two attractive young women were rubbing their naked breasts together as they danced, their lips locked in a passionate kiss while their hips gyrated to the music.

The sniper lifted his hand to the front of his scope and turned the magnification dial to maximum. He watched the women's erect nipples flexing as they rubbed against one another. The pace of his breathing increased, but it was not from sexual arousal as much as anger. He flashed back to his high school years when pretty girls would make fun of his appearance and reject his awkward advances. He remembered the taunts and whispers of his classmates as they ridiculed him.

There's that Weirdo guy. He's so ugly. How could anybody kiss him? I'd be sick to my stomach if he ever touched me.

Watching the women laughing behind the nightclub window, he suddenly heard the giggles of his tormenters from years ago. He moved the crosshairs of his scope upwards and focused on the forehead of the topless blond girl.

This will teach them, he thought. *Only God can judge who's worthy. I hope you've said your prayers. Otherwise, you'll be going to a different kind of loud and fiery place.*

A second later, the window in front of the hot tub shattered and the blond woman dropped into the water. At first, the noise and flashing lights distracted the partygoers from what had just happened in the pool. But as horrified bathers scampered out of the tub and screamed at what they saw, a stampede of clubgoers began retreating to the exit.

In the pool, the blond girl lay floating face down, her hair spread out on the surface, surrounded by a pink halo in the frothing water.

Chapter Thirty-Seven

The Mayor's Office, City Hall

July 16, 9:30 a.m.

C ommissioner Pope sat in the anteroom to the Mayor's office waiting to be invited in to his scheduled nine a.m. meeting. The Mayor was already a half hour late, and Pope did not take kindly to being held up. The two men had a contentious relationship, not least because both had oversize egos.

Neither one liked sharing authority on important police matters. Pope had a distinguished history with the NYPD, working his way up through the ranks since graduating from the police academy thirty years ago. He had the respect of the rank and file and until recently, the admiration of the public. He was widely credited for bringing the crime rate down in the city during his tenure as Commissioner.

For his part, the Mayor was relatively new to the job, elected to the office just under a year ago. New York had a celebrated history of larger-than-life Mayors. Fiorello La Guardia, who presided during the Great Depression, unified the city's transit system and had the airport named after him. Rudy Giuliani, the powerful former District Attorney for New York, rallied the city after the World Trade Center attack and made a run for President. Michael Bloomberg, the billionaire industrialist, restored fiscal order to the city after the Internet bubble burst in the late '90s. The incumbent mayor felt he had much to prove to leave his own mark on the city.

Unfortunately, the recent slew of sniper shootings dominated the political headlines. The Mayor's switchboard lit up with frightened and angry citizens demanding action. He knew if he didn't take decisive action soon that his chances for a second term in office would evaporate, not to mention his larger political ambitions. He huddled with his advisors for over an hour before the meeting with the Commissioner, discussing how they could best handle the situation.

The door to the anteroom swung open.

"Carl," the Mayor said. "Come in. Sorry to keep you waiting. It's been a crazy couple of days."

The Commissioner followed the Mayor into his office.

"It's been a crazy couple of *weeks*," Pope sighed.

The Mayor offered the Commissioner a cup of coffee then sat behind his large desk flanked by U.S. flags.

"That's what I wanted to see you about this morning. Something has to be done about the sniper situation. This shooter has taken over the city. People are afraid to venture outdoors, and businesses are closing their doors. The tourism trade is normally at the height of the season, but it's completely shut down. The Union Square shooting was the last straw. Now everyone's afraid to go to work. We've lost control of our city."

Pope found it interesting that the Mayor never mentioned any loss of life. His concerns related only to commercial and political interests. Unlike the Commissioner's main priority, which was keeping the streets of New York safe.

"The ancillary damage has been...unfortunate," Pope responded. "But we've lost nine lives since this started, and I'm far more concerned about what we can do to prevent more lives being stolen."

The Mayor paused for a moment, realizing how insensitive he'd been.

"Yes—sorry about your man Bannon. It's a shame about his wife. Such a brutal and senseless killing. Do you think this will compromise his role as our media spokesman? The public will view him as even more of a hero after this."

The Commissioner could hardly believe his ears. Instead of empathizing with the Detective's loss, it sounded like the

Mayor was looking to capitalize on the tragedy. It was another example of the Mayor using other people as a scapegoat and not leading from the front.

He breathed in and out slowly to calm himself down before replying.

"I can't imagine he'll want to be back in the spotlight for a while. The man just lost his wife. I suspect he'll need a little time to process his loss."

Pope had grown accustomed to being the public face of the police force during his tenure as Commissioner. He'd become comfortable in front of the camera and felt a little blindsided when the Mayor asked Detective Bannon to handle the media.

"I'll be happy to take the lead on the public outreach again," he said.

The Mayor looked at the Commissioner blankly. Before the meeting, his advisors had told him of the enormous political opportunity this case presented. Like Mayor Rudy Giuliani had done after the 9/11 bombings, they thought the people were primed for a charismatic leader to rally the public. In times of great crisis, they said, the people always unite behind a strong leader. Mayor Braxton felt this was his chance to establish his legacy.

"I've been thinking about that, Carl," he said. "I think it's time I actually addressed the people. They're obviously frightened and looking for leadership at a time like this. I'd like to make a public statement."

The Commissioner paused, taken aback. Perhaps he'd misjudged the Mayor.

"What kind of statement? Were you thinking of a televised address?"

"I want it to be bigger than that," the Mayor said. "I want to get out among the people and show them we won't be cowed by this sniper. I'd like to make a speech at the site of the last shooting in Union Square. Of course, it will also be televised by all the major networks."

The Commissioner's brow furrowed.

"Are you sure that's a good idea, Mr. Mayor? That's a wide-open and very public place. After you alert the media, it may attract the attention of the sniper. He's already shown how easy it is to pick someone off in the Square. I can't guarantee I'll be able to assure your safety."

The Mayor nodded and smiled.

"Actually, I don't have any intention of alerting the media until the last possible moment. Only you and a select group of officers will have advance notification of the timing and place of my address. If the sniper doesn't know where I'll be, he can't shoot me, right? But before I put this plan into action I need to be certain it's safe. If we keep this low-key, will your people be able to protect me?"

Pope thought about the Mayor's plan for a long time. There were many variables and risks to consider. Traffic would have to be routed around the event to avoid accidents. The perimeter would have to be secured from gawkers. Media personnel would need to be pre-cleared. And police sharpshooters would need to be positioned on high ground to keep a lookout for the sniper.

"This is a bigger operation than you might imagine, sir. We'll need to mobilize a few hundred officers at least, plus the ESU team. But if we can keep this contained until the time of your address—yes, I think we can protect you."

"A few hundred officers?" the Mayor said. "Isn't that about the size of one of your precincts? What if we only notify Lieutenant O'Neill and have his team secure the site. I'd like to have Detective Bannon beside me. Like it or not, he's become the public face of this campaign."

The Mayor paused as he looked at his Commissioner.

"What do you say, Carl?"

Pope shook his head and sighed.

"It's a hell of a plan, Mr. Mayor. I think we can make it work. I'll check with O'Neill and begin making the arrangements. When were you thinking of making your address?"

"Tomorrow at noon. In front of the statue of Washington, in the middle of the Square. That ought to set the tone and project the right amount of confidence. Make it happen."

Chapter Thirty-Eight

Lieutenant O'Neill's Office, 18th Precinct.

July 16, 9:00 a.m.

B rady O'Neill sat behind his desk flipping through the latest notes in the sniper file. Joe, Hannah, and Kate sipped their coffee while they waited for the Lieutenant to start the meeting. After a few minutes, O'Neill closed the heavy file and exhaled deeply.

"Looks to me like the sniper's shifting his M.O.," he said, peering up at the detectives. "I'm concerned about this new pattern of indoor shootings. Previously, the shooter was focused on outdoor targets. Kate—can you make any sense of this?"

Kate shook her head.

"Honestly, Lieutenant, I'm at a bit of a loss to explain this one. The location, the timing, the victim—none of it fits the previous pattern."

"Perhaps he's getting bored?" Joe interjected. "Maybe he just gets off killing people who are enjoying themselves."

It was obvious to everyone that Joe was venting. No one wanted to check him, knowing the pain he was still feeling so soon after losing his wife.

"He's running out of easy targets," Hannah suggested. "It's getting pretty quiet out there on the streets. Shooting fish in a barrel isn't quite as simple when they're all hiding below the surface."

"And this latest fish wasn't exactly well camouflaged," Joe snipped.

O'Neill looked at Joe and raised his eyebrows.

"Joe, let's keep this professional. I know you're still hurting—"

"I was simply pointing out that the latest victim presented a highly visible target..."

"As visible as one can be eighteen stories above the street," O'Neill said. He looked at Kate. "Why a nightclub, and why this particular one?"

"Le Bain is one of the city's most popular clubs. The sniper may be tracking people's interior movements more closely with the streets emptying out. The flashing lights on top of the Standard Hotel late at night would attract attention from anybody in the vicinity. Joe might not have been so far off. Maybe the sniper was angry people were in a partying mood and that he still hadn't created enough fear—"

"What's his end game?" O'Neill said. "Is he simply shooting people who piss him off, or do you think he has a plan for some kind of escalation? Can we detect a pattern that might give us a clue to where he might strike next?"

Kate looked at the Lieutenant blankly. O'Neill turned to Joe and Hannah.

"What about the sniper's vantage point this time? There aren't many tall buildings in that part of the city. The shooter would have to be at a high elevation to see through the windows that far above street level."

"We're still in the process of reviewing CCTV footage from other high-rises within a mile radius of the hotel," Hannah said.

"No eyewitnesses pinpointed the sound of a rifle this time?" O'Neill asked.

"There's not many people outside who would hear suspicious noises, especially at that time of night."

O'Neill leaned back in his chair and placed his hands on his head. He closed his eyes while he considered his next step. His thoughts were suddenly interrupted by the sound of his cell phone buzzing on his desk. It was an incoming call from the Commissioner.

O'Neill picked up the phone and held it to his ear.

"Lieutenant O'Neill," he said. "Yes, Commissioner...I understand. That soon? I'll mobilize the department...Yes sir, I'll inform him."

O'Neill hung up the phone and looked straight at Joe.

"That was the Commissioner. The Mayor wants to make a public address. Tomorrow. And he wants you by his side when he makes the announcement."

Joe squinted his eyes in surprise.

"Did he say what it's about? Where is he planning to make this announcement?"

"Union Square. At noon."

"Holy shit," Joe exclaimed. "Is he crazy? That's where the sniper hit two days ago. How can we possibly protect him?"

"That's what we need to figure out. He's placed our department in charge of arranging security. He's not going to announce his plans until just before he makes the address. He thinks the sniper can't hurt him if he doesn't know when or where this will be happening."

O'Neill looked at the three officers in turn.

"This needs to stay on a strictly need-to-know basis. I don't want this information going outside this precinct. I'll arrange a meeting with our patrol team within the hour. I need you three to stay the course in collecting Intel. If you come across anything at all that looks actionable, let me know immediately. The best case scenario is to have our suspect locked up ahead of time to avoid any more surprises. This one's on me—we can't afford to screw this one up."

Hannah peered at Joe then turned to the Lieutenant.

"With all due respect sir," she said, "I think there will be a fair amount of exposure for someone else too. The Mayor won't be the *only* one in the line of fire tomorrow."

"You two just watch your backs and make sure you're not followed," O'Neill said. "Let me take care of your other flank."

Chapter Thirty-Nine

Time-Warner Center, Columbus Circle

July 16, noon

J oe rested his elbow on the escalator handrail as it moved upward from the lobby toward the third floor of the Time Warner Center. Normally, the mall would be packed at this time of day with lunchtime diners and shoppers sampling its upscale fare. Located on the southwest corner of Central Park at the junction of three subway lines, its brand name boutiques and Michelin-starred restaurants were a popular destination for tourists and midtown residents.

He peered down at the large bronze statues of Fernando Botero's Adam and Eve standing in the lobby. The nude sculptures were a magnet for visitors to the Center, who would often have their picture taken next to the rotund figures. So many people had fondled Adam's genitals while taking a selfie that his buffed penis had grown a brassy shine.

But today the mall was eerily quiet. A few lone shoppers walked from the underground subway entrance to their target destination, scurrying through the lobby with its exposed three-story-high windows. After the two recent indoor sniper shootings, nobody wanted to tempt fate being caught in the sniper's crosshairs. But Joe didn't give it a second thought. He'd been careful to monitor his tracks after the sniper attack outside the coffee shop. Besides, his own safety was the last thing on his mind.

He turned his body to take in the midday sunshine streaming through the lobby's tall windows. The view of Central Park was spectacular as he approached the third floor, with the tall statue of Christopher Columbus in the middle of the traffic circle outside the front entrance dominating the picture. He closed his eyes and thought about his wife.

They would often meet at the mall's famous French bakery for a quick bite then take a walk in the park whenever Joe had a break in his routine. She loved the taste of the pastel macarons stacked behind the bakery's glass showcase. Jane would tease Joe that he should order a donut to maintain the public's image of the lazy cop.

But Joe was in no mirthful mood today. His wife's murder was still fresh in his mind, and he was seething at his continued inability to catch the sniper. His surveillance of Weir's apartment the previous evening had come up blank and the sniper's trail had gone cold. He didn't want any more distractions from his single-minded pursuit, but a cryptic message late yesterday from Miles Lundberg piqued his interest.

Have some information of interest, Miles' text read. *Lunch tomorrow?*

Sure, Joe replied.

Meet me at Bouchon Bakery, TW Center, at noon. Keep your chin up.

As Joe stepped off the escalator, he peered toward the cafe in the mezzanine, looking for the Medical Examiner. He saw Miles waving by the railing overlooking the lobby. As he approached Miles' table, the M.E. stood up and held out his hand.

"Good to see you, Joe," Miles said, clasping Joe's hand warmly. "How've you been holding up?"

"As good as can be expected."

Miles looked into Joe's eyes, feeling his pain.

"I'm so sorry, Joe. Jane will be missed by everybody."

"Thanks, Miles."

It was awkward speaking with the Medical Examiner knowing that just a few days prior he was examining his wife's body. Joe peered out the window toward the park to deflect the subject.

"Interesting choice for a rendezvous," he said.

"I know you have a soft spot for this place. Besides, something tells me you're watching your back pretty carefully these days."

"You got that right."

Joe didn't waste any time getting to the point.

"What's up? You said you found something new?"

"It's not so much a find as an *idea*. After the ferry killing, I was racking my brain about the disappearance of the rifle from the hotel rooftop where you tracked the sniper's movement the night before. I've got a crazy idea, but one you should be able to check out fairly quickly. If you can confirm it, you might have enough evidence to bring your suspect in."

Joe rested his arms on the table and leaned forward.

"I'm all ears, Miles. At this point, I'm willing to do just about anything to bring this guy to justice."

Miles couldn't have known how literally Joe meant what he said.

"Okay. I have this quirky hobby—building and flying drones. The technology has gotten pretty sophisticated over the last couple of years. Their payload capacity has increased quite a bit, and you can maneuver them fairly easily from your smartphone. You said your suspect appeared to bring the rifle into the building then left without it. What if he *flew* it off the building instead of carrying it out?"

Joe blinked at Miles and paused to process what he said.

"But it would still have to *land* somewhere, right? Wouldn't it be obvious to just about anyone who saw a strange rifle flying through the air?"

"Not if it took off high enough above the ground and landed in a remote location. The roof of the Ritz-Carlton is forty floors above the street. You confirmed the suspect's location at the time of the shooting in Liberty State Park across the Hudson. A rifle flying five hundred feet above the river might just look like a large bird. If it landed in a park that early in the morning, it could easily go unnoticed."

Joe paused for a few seconds then he began to nod.

"Okay, let's say there's something to this crazy idea of yours. We'd still need video proof or an eyewitness to place him at the scene. If nobody saw the rifle do its bird trick, there's an equally good chance nobody noticed the sniper retrieve it."

Miles smiled.

"You've got video of him entering a store in the Liberty State Park area around the time of the ferry shooting, right? Maybe some of the store's customers or their staff saw a strange object landing in the area around the same time. Another CCTV in the vicinity might have captured it on video. The last time you were there you were only looking to confirm your suspect's alibi. Now you've got something else to look for."

Joe looked out the tall glass windows of the atrium toward the park. Something still didn't add up.

"So what if somebody can corroborate this story? The sniper obviously got away with the rifle. How do I track it to him?"

"You don't need to. You just need to prove that he was present when and where the gun landed. That should be enough to issue an arrest warrant. Then you can search his known hangouts to locate the weapon. He might have hidden it, but at least you'll have him locked up while you build your case."

Joe's mind was already racing ahead.

If he could place the sniper at the scene of the murder weapon, he could release his photo and place him at other crime scenes while enlisting the public in locating the murder weapon.

Or he could simply take matters into his own hands. No one would miss the sniper if he just disappeared.

Joe stood up and kicked his chair back.

"Miles, if this pans out, I'll pick up the tab for a more expensive meal of your choosing next time. I hope you don't mind if I skip out on lunch while I follow up on this. Every second matters with this madman on the loose."

Miles nodded.

"Do your thing, Joe. Nothing would make me happier than to have you put me out of business for a little while. Good luck—check back soon."

****

Three hours later, Joe raced out of the 7-11 store near Liberty State Park with a smartphone in his hand. One of the store's customers had heard the drone's engine around the time of the ferry shooting and taken video footage of the strange UFO. It clearly showed a rifle-shaped object landing in a wooded section of the park where Weir was placed on the morning of the Ferry shooting.

Maybe Joe wouldn't have to bypass the law after all.

Chapter Forty

7 New York Avenue, East Flatbush, Brooklyn

July 16, 9:00 p.m.

Joe and Hannah stood on opposite sides of Todd Weir's apartment door and listened for any sign of movement. Surrounding them were ten heavily armed Emergency Services cops with assault rifles. With arrest warrant in hand, Joe wasn't taking any chances being blindsided by the cornered sniper. The detectives had monitored the building for the last three hours to watch for any sign of the shooter. Weir's truck wasn't in the underground garage or within a mile radius of the building. They'd hoped to make a clean arrest, but it seemed nothing the sniper did was simple.

With dusk rapidly approaching, it was time to act. Either Weir was quietly holed up in his apartment, or he was hiding out in an unknown location. This time the NYPD would tear the place apart and take everything they found back to the station for forensic testing. If Weir wasn't here, Joe would post a twenty-four-hour guard to catch him when he returned.

Joe crouched to the bottom of the door and snaked a cable cam under the sill. The apartment was pitch black. Everyone's eyes were glued on the connected monitor, washed in fluorescent green from the infrared sensor on the cam. Joe twisted the cable in his fingers and turned the cam to pan the room. There was no sign of Weir or his dog. He turned the audio sensor to maximum and listened for any sounds.

A door opened two units down, and a noisy couple stepped into the hall. One of them looked in the direction of the ESU team poised outside Weir's door and froze. The ESU team leader held up his hand and placed his finger on his lips then hastily motioned for them to go back inside.

Joe looked up at Hannah and shook his head. He pulled the cam back from under the door and placed it beside him on the floor. Then he motioned to the two ESU cops who were standing in front of the door with a steel battering ram. He held up his index finger and made a knocking motion with his knuckles in the air. The ESU cops nodded and prepared to ram the door.

Joe reached out and rapped three times on the door.

"Mr. Weir!" he called out. "Todd Weir! This is Detective Bannon with the NYPD. We have a warrant for your arrest. Open the door immediately."

Joe only waited five seconds before he gave the ESU officers his signal. The cops holding the ram swung it back then slammed it against the door with all their strength. Joe and Hannah pulled out their pistols and prepared to follow the ESU team into the unit.

A gigantic explosion suddenly blew out into the hall as the door flew open. The ESU officers in front of the door were thrown onto the opposite wall, rendered unconscious from the blast. Joe and Hannah were blown in opposite directions and crumpled to the ground. The last thing Joe remembered before he blacked out was how the sniper had outwitted him again.

As a wailing alarm filled the empty hall, a dozen bloodied officers lay still outside Weir's apartment unit.

Chapter Forty-One

New York Methodist Hospital, Brooklyn

July 17, 8:00 a.m.

Hannah woke up with an excruciating headache the morning after the Weir apartment raid. Her ears were ringing, and she felt sick to her stomach. She turned her head and saw her husband Ryan sitting in a chair beside her bed. He stood up when he saw she was awake and came to her side.

"Hey, baby," he said, reaching out to hold her hand. "How are you feeling?"

Hannah grimaced in pain.

"Uh...I've felt better. Where am I? What happened?"

"You're at Methodist Hospital in Brooklyn. There was an explosion at your suspect's apartment last night. Apparently, it was a set-up. Joe's outside with your folks and the kids. He can fill you in on the details."

"An explosion? That explains why my head is spinning." Hannah forced a smile. "Am I going to live?"

Ryan chuckled.

"The doctor said it's just a bad concussion. You may need a few days to recover, but it could have been a lot worse. One of your fellow officers was killed."

Hannah's head snapped toward her husband.

"Is Joe okay?"

"He was knocked unconscious, but the doctors have cleared him. They want you to stay under observation for another day."

Ryan squeezed Hannah's hand gently.

"Maybe this rest will give you an opportunity to think about that career change we've been talking about."

"And miss all this excitement? I'd be bored to death as a prosecutor."

"At least it would be a slow and predictable one, unlike with this job. You'd still be putting bad guys away. You know how I worry when you strap on that gun and walk out the door every day."

Hannah looked at her husband and crinkled her eyes.

"We'll talk about it later. For now, there's a case I need to close. Can I have a few minutes with Joe before the kids come in? I'd like to get filled in on the incident last night."

Hannah's husband shook his head.

"I was hoping this shock might knock a little sense into you. But I see you're just as hardheaded as ever. I'll fetch Joe. Just promise me you won't go knocking down any more doors for a while."

As her husband retreated into the hall, Hannah looked around the room. There was an assortment of flower bouquets arranged on tables on either side of the bed. The sickly aroma made her gag.

God, I hate hospitals, she muttered.

Joe entered the room carrying a bouquet.

"Hey, beautiful. I know you hate these things, but someone left this for you at the desk."

Hannah motioned for Joe to place in on the bedside table.

"Place it over there with all the other memorials," she sighed. Her expression suddenly turned serious. "What happened, Joe? The last thing I remember was the battering ram..."

"Me too. That bastard had it all set up. It was a dirty bomb. Fertilizer and gasoline, loaded with nails and ball bearings. He meant to inflict as much physical harm as possible."

"Ryan said one of our guys didn't make it?"

Joe nodded solemnly.

"Bruno, from the ESU unit. One of the nails penetrated his carotid and he bled out before the medical team arrived."

"But how—"

Joe read his partner's mind.

"There was a tripwire attached to the door. Forensics found it over the top rail. Which is why the cable cam didn't see it..."

Joe's eyes trailed off to the bedside window, and Hannah placed her hand on his arm.

"Don't blame yourself for this. You did everything you could. No one could have predicted—"

"I'm beginning to think we can't predict much of anything with this killer. And now he's disappeared. How the hell are we supposed to stop this guy, Han?"

Hannah sat up in her bed and looked at Joe resolutely.

"They always screw up eventually. Don't worry, Joe. We'll find him."

"It's the eventually part that bothers me. We're losing somebody new every day. Now the Mayor's putting himself in the line of fire."

Hannah turned her wrist to look at her watch.

"I almost forgot. That's only four hours from now." She swung her legs to get out of bed. "I'm not letting you do this alone."

Joe grabbed her arm and pressed her back onto her pillow.

"Hold up, girl. The doctors say you need a few more days to recover. I'll be fine. No one else knows about this besides us and a few television producers. Besides, you've already seen that the sniper's bullets can't touch me."

Hannah rolled her eyes.

"Okay, Superman. Just make sure our spotters keep an eye on the rooftops. That way at least you'll know when to throw your body in front to the Mayor if the shooter shows up."

Joe smiled and leaned over to kiss Hannah on the forehead.

"Don't worry, partner. I'll come back later today with an update. In the meantime, feel free to watch the live address on the local news. Thankfully, the Mayor will be the talking head this time."

"Just make sure he *keeps* his head—and yours—will you?"

"Not to worry," Joe said. "Catch you later."

As Joe left the room, Hannah reached over to read the cards from her well-wishers. Two minutes later, her children bounded into the room to greet their mother and she suddenly felt the need to throw up.

Chapter Forty-Two

Union Square

July 17, 11:30 a.m.

J oe paced nervously over the plaza of Union Square looking for anything unusual. Lieutenant O'Neill had appointed him the point person in charge of coordinating final security arrangements for the Mayor's public address. With only thirty minutes until the speech was scheduled to begin, the Detective was feeling increasing concern about the exposure of the site.

The Mayor's speaking platform was installed in front of the George Washington Statue in the south section of the park. In front of the platform was two hundred feet of open courtyard with an unobstructed view from three sides. All around the plaza rose high-rise buildings from which anybody carrying so much as a peashooter could rain down fire.

Joe looked up at the tall buildings on each side of the Square. He knew police spotters and sharpshooters were in position scanning the rooftops of every structure having a clear sightline to the platform. He pulled out his two-way radio and pressed the talk button.

"Spotter-South—report," he said.

"All clear," his radio returned.

"Spotter-East?"

"All clear on the east side."

"West?"

"Just a couple of nude sunbathers soaking up some rays in their rooftop garden."

Joe was in no mood for playful banter.

"What about the windows?" he said.

"We've scanned the open ones. We'll be on the lookout for any new openings in the next half hour."

Joe nodded, satisfied that the obvious sniper nests had been checked. But he still wanted to take every precaution.

"Powder residue from earlier shootings indicates that the barrel doesn't necessarily protrude from the face of the building. Be sure to search inside open windows also."

"Copy that," the East side acknowledged.

"Will do, Joe," said the West side.

"Ten-four," reported the South.

Joe placed the radio in his pocket and began walking the perimeter of the one-square-block park. Barricades had been erected on the sidewalk lining the Square and patrol cops stood in ten-foot intervals to prevent anyone entering the grounds.

Not that they were needed, Joe thought, looking around the Square.

There was a scattering of young people scurrying in and out of cafes along the edge of the park. A lone customer of the Best Buy store at the corner of Broadway and 14th Street tripped over a homeless person camped outside its entrance. An old man on crutches walked out of the MTA station and disappeared into a building on the west side of the Square. Joe wondered how the Mayor hoped to build public confidence with a virtual ghost town as his backdrop.

By the time he'd circumnavigated the Square, a convoy of trucks with tall antennae and network television logos emblazoned on their sides had taken up position on the south edge of the park. Cameramen with big boxes on their shoulders were already recording soundbites from reporters holding microphones. Joe recognized one of the reporters as the correspondent from the Today Show who'd interviewed the stock trader during Joe's television appearance a few days ago.

"This is Elizabeth Porter, reporting from Union Square," she spoke into the camera. "We're expecting an important announcement at noon today. There are no further details, but judging by the extraordinary security in the park, we're expecting it to be a prominent public official."

The cameraman panned around the plaza then zoomed in on one of the patrol officers talking into his shoulder radio. Joe checked the other reporters and camera operators. The sniper had shown a preference for shooting from above, but the Detective wasn't taking any chances. The throng of television crew with their heavy equipment and cables could easily disguise a man with a gun in the crowd.

At least they don't yet know the Mayor will be speaking, he thought. *Maybe we can avoid a disaster in this circus after all.*

Someone tapped Joe on his shoulder, and he swung around. It was Lieutenant O'Neill.

"Whoa, Joe," O'Neill said. "No need to be so jumpy. Everything looks secure from my vantage point. Have you noticed anything out of place?"

Joe exhaled slowly and shook his head.

"Just the usual hipsters and a few old folks. I guess the only ones showing their faces in public these days are those who think they're invincible or those who don't care anymore."

"And those with big egos," the Lieutenant said, seeing the Mayor approach them with the Commissioner at his side.

"Good Morning, Mr. Mayor," O'Neill said. He nodded toward the Commissioner. "Commissioner."

"Is everything in order, Lieutenant?" the Commissioner asked.

"Yes, sir. We've secured the perimeter and have men stationed around the Square to prevent any unauthorized personnel entering the grounds."

"What about the high ground?"

"We have sharpshooters on the rooftops looking for suspicious movement on all three sides. It's all clear so far."

The Mayor looked at the barricades and the wall of uniformed cops lining the park.

"It looks like a war zone out here, Lieutenant. Not exactly confidence-inspiring."

O'Neill glanced at the Commissioner before addressing the Mayor.

"We were asked to do everything within our power to ensure your safety, Your Honor. I believe you're as safe as one can possibly be under the circumstances."

O'Neill motioned to the armada of cameras taking up position in front of the platform. The statue of George Washington riding his horse with his hand elevated in triumph appeared prominently above the stage.

"It looks like all the cameras will be pointed toward you. I think you'll have a suitably inspiring backdrop for your speech."

The Mayor nodded then turned to Joe.

"Detective Bannon. Good to see you back on the job. Are you set to take the podium with me?"

"Yes, sir." Joe paused. "Will you need me to make any comments?"

"No, I'll be controlling the narrative today. My team will position you to my side and slightly to my rear. I'll make a few comments about your heroism and your help tracking the sniper. I just need you to look brave and confident."

"I'll try my best, sir."

The Mayor and his entourage walked to the platform and ascended the steps onto the stage. After a few minutes conferring with the Lieutenant and the Commissioner, Joe followed suit and took his place beside the Mayor.

****

At precisely twelve noon, a sea of red lights popped up on the array of video cameras as the Mayor stepped toward the microphone stand.

"Fellow citizens of New York," he began. "I've come to Union Square today to make an important announcement. I know many of you are concerned about what's been happening on the streets of our fair city these past two weeks."

Some of the reporters nodded and whispered among themselves.

"It's true, there is a killer in our midst who has cowardly taken many innocent lives. But he is one man among a city of eight million. We have forty thousand dedicated New York City police officers focused on finding and capturing this individual."

The Mayor turned and motioned toward Joe.

"Such as Detective Joe Bannon, who lost those dearest to him in the service of his country and his city."

Joe clenched his jaw, trying to remain calm. He couldn't believe the Mayor was using his personal tragedy to score political points.

The Mayor turned and pointed toward the cameras.

"But you can help too. We're releasing a composite sketch of the suspect who we believe is responsible for these killings. If you encounter anyone with his likeness or see any other suspicious activity, please call 9-1-1 immediately."

The Mayor paused while one of his aides unveiled a picture of Todd Weir on a large easel on the other side of the stage. The cameras focused on the image for a few seconds then turned back to the Mayor.

"But there is something else you can do," he continued. "You can begin to go about your everyday lives and not be bullied into submission by this criminal. Staying away from your jobs and off the streets only feeds this behavior. We must not let him win the day. I implore you to return to your jobs and your normal routine as soon as you can."

Joe glanced at Lieutenant O'Neill standing below the stage and saw him grimace. Apparently, Joe wasn't the only one thinking the Mayor's guidance was ill-advised. The Commissioner stood ram-straight and expressionless beside the Lieutenant.

Had the Mayor even bothered to consult with any front-line cops before approving his speech? Joe wondered.

"Our boys in blue are closing the net on the killer and will have him in custody soon," the Mayor said.

Joe's mind wandered back to his earlier surveillance of the Square. There was something about the scene that didn't fit, but he couldn't place it. He peered over at the portrait of Todd Weir and wrinkled his forehead.

The Mayor spread his arms as he looked around the Square.

"This beautiful park and public square needs to be reclaimed by those who rightfully own it—the citizens of New York City."

Joe racked his brain trying to make the connection to what he'd seen earlier.

The hipsters, the hobo, the old man.

There was something about the old man and the way he walked. His gait was vaguely familiar. Plus his crutches looked odd, like they were made out of some high-tech metal.

The Mayor turned to look at the statue of Washington and raised his hand in salute.

"Our founding fathers refused to submit to those who would restrict our freedoms, and neither will we. Citizens of New York, return from your homes, return to your jobs, and return to the streets of our beautiful city. Show the world that we are not afraid—"

Oh my God, Joe thought. *The old man! It was the sniper in disguise!*

Just as Joe set to run to protect the Mayor, he felt a wet blob hit his face and he heard a loud bang echoing from three sides of the Square. Instinctively, he reached up to his face and looked at his hands. They were coated with blood. He looked toward the Mayor, who crumpled to the ground like a collapsed marionette.

Joe rushed toward the stricken Mayor and called into his radio.

"Secure the perimeter! Secure the perimeter! Look for an elderly man on crutches. Lock down the block and don't let anyone pass outside a four-block radius."

Joe kneeled over the Mayor, but he could see that it was already too late. He held his fingers over Braxton's carotid artery and felt no pulse.

The Mayor looked up at Joe with vacant eyes. In the middle of his forehead was a gaping red hole.

Chapter Forty-Three

Union Square

July 17, 12:15 p.m.

Seconds after the Mayor was shot, pandemonium erupted on the south side of Union Square. Hundreds of flashing cruisers and emergency vehicles converged on the area. Every television reporter picked up a microphone and began reporting what they had just seen. The Mayor's assassination was replayed on a closed loop for millions of horrified viewers.

As soon as Joe recognized that the Mayor couldn't be helped, he pulled out his radio. His first call was to spotters on the west side, where he'd seen the old man on crutches go earlier.

"Spotter-West," he blurted into the radio. "Any sign of the shooter?"

"We heard the rifle, but haven't been able to place the source. It seemed to come from all three sides. We're still scanning, but haven't seen any sign of the shooter."

That's strange, Joe thought. Witnesses at the scene of previous sniper killings had been able to pinpoint the general angle from which the shot was fired. Were the tall buildings surrounding the park creating an echo that made it sound like the gunshot came from all sides?

"Spotters-South and East—what have you seen?"

"Nothing here, Joe. We heard a loud bang on our side too."

"Ditto on the East. It sounded like the gun was fired right on top of us. But we haven't seen any suspicious activity on the rooftops or from any open windows."

Joe shook his head and stopped to think.

How could the sniper have fired from three directions at the same time? Had he set up another remote-firing rifle in multiple locations? Had he planted a device to mimic a gunshot simultaneously from three different sources?

It didn't matter. The sniper had created a diversion to distract attention from his location, but Joe already knew which building the old man in the crutches went.

He lifted his radio and pressed the talk button.

"The suspect entered the large white building on the north side of 14th Street between Union Square West and 5th Avenue. I need all spotters to keep a lookout for an old man on crutches on any side of that block. I'm taking a team to lock down the building. If you see anyone matching that description, fire a warning shot then shoot to kill."

An ambulance came screeching to a halt in front of the platform as Lieutenant O'Neill and the Commissioner scrambled onto the stage.

"Joe," O'Neill said, seeing the blood on Joe's face. "Are you all right?"

"I'm fine, it's just splatter."

Joe pointed toward the building across the street.

"We need to lock down the block. I saw the shooter enter the white building just before the Mayor was shot. We're looking for an old man on crutches."

O'Neill pulled out his two-way radio.

"All officers from the 18th Precinct," he ordered, "encircle and lock down the block on the west side of Union Square. Apprehend anyone carrying crutches. K-9 team, follow Detective Bannon to search the building."

Commissioner Pope looked at the fallen Mayor, dumbfounded. It had been a long time since he'd been in an operational role and he was unsure what to do.

"Brady," he said to Lieutenant O'Neill, "what can I do to help?"

"Coordinate other units to lock down traffic on a four-block radius around the park. Have them search every vehicle trying to exit the area. Tell them what to look for."

The Commissioner pulled out his phone and turned aside to call the Chief of Police.

Within seconds, three officers holding German Shepherd dogs on leashes came up beside Joe. They were holding soiled clothing found in Weir's apartment to the dogs' noses.

"Which direction, Joe?" one of the K-9 officers asked.

"Follow me."

Joe began running toward the tall building across the street on the west side of the square. Twenty other patrol cops followed in pursuit.

Five minutes later, Joe flung open the door leading onto the rooftop of The Victoria co-op building at 7 East 14th Street. The dogs were pulling on their chains, following the scent.

Joe stepped out the door with his sidearm drawn and pivoted in both directions. There was no sign of the sniper. He walked slowly out onto the flat rooftop, followed by the K-9 crew and the patrol cops. The dogs' noses were glued to the ground following a trail.

"They've definitely got something, Joe," the K-9 officer said.

Joe turned around the corner of an elevator shaft holding his pistol close to his face. He knew if the sniper were nearby, he might only have milliseconds to respond.

The dogs zeroed in on a spot near the base of the elevator shaft and sniffed furiously.

"This is where the trail ends," the K-9 officer said.

Joe looked toward Union Square. The view to the platform was blocked by the overhang of the roof fifty feet east of the elevator shaft.

"He didn't have a view of the stage from this vantage point," Joe said.

Then he looked up toward the top of the shaft. It was four stories to the crown.

"But he would from up there."

Joe pulled on the steel door to the mechanical room. It was locked.

He pulled a card out of his pocket and retrieved his phone. Then he tapped a few buttons and held the phone to his ear.

"The building manager will have a key—"

A voice suddenly spoke on Joe's police radio.

"Joe, it's Lieutenant O'Neill. We've apprehended a suspect matching your description. Can you come down and confirm?"

Joe looked at the rest of his crew.

"I need to check this out. See if the dogs can pick up the scent anywhere else on the rooftop. The shooter may have rappelled over the side. The rest of you, secure the crime scene for a forensics sweep."

Joe opened the rooftop exit door and disappeared back into the building.

Five seconds later, Todd Weir opened the lid to the building's water tank on top of the elevator shaft and quietly slipped inside.

Chapter Forty-Four

Victoria Co-op building, 7 East 14th Street

July 17, 12:45 p.m.

In less than ten minutes, Joe was back on the rooftop.

"Did the dogs pick up the scent anywhere else?" he asked the K-9 crew.

The officers shook their heads.

"Just here on the north side of the mechanical building and around the exit door," one of them said.

Joe pulled a key from his pocket.

"The sniper hasn't been identified. He may still be inside this tower. Exercise extreme caution. The K-9 team will lead the way."

The officers withdrew their sidearms and Joe unlocked the door leading from the rooftop into the mechanical room. The dogs immediately picked up the scent and pulled their handlers up the three flights of stairs to the water tank room. Joe flung open the door at the top of the landing. Sunlight streamed in from above. The room was about twenty feet square with a ten foot diameter water tank resting in the open air about one foot inside the east wall.

The dogs barked loudly and sniffed at the base of the tank. Joe motioned to two officers. He made a slow circular motion with his left hand, indicating he wanted them to walk clockwise around the tank. He crept slowly in the other direction around the outside of the cistern, keeping his body close to the side. If the sniper was still in the room, he'd soon be cornered by cops approaching from opposite sides.

It took about thirty seconds for the two teams to join on the other side of the tank. Joe dropped his gun and looked around the room. There were no other places to hide in the small enclosed space.

"Looks like we missed him," one of the officers said. "Maybe we can pick up his scent outside the building."

Joe paused and thought for a moment. Then he looked up toward the top of the water tank. The only clear sightline to the Square below from the windowless room was from the top of the tower.

He pulled out his two-way radio and pressed the talk button.

"Spotters, this is Joe. Can you focus on the water tower on the top of the limestone building on the north side of 14th Street? Do you see anything?"

There was a pause for a few seconds.

"We see it, Joe. But there's no sign of the shooter. Just the clear canopy on top of the tank."

Joe looked at the tank and rapped the side of it with his fist. It was made of eight inch wide cedar wood planks fitted tightly together to form a ten foot high drum. At the top of the tank, wooden joists radiated over the sidewalls to support a large conical wooden lid.

The officers looked at the Detective, perplexed.

"Joe, he'll be getting away—" one of the K-9 officers said.

Joe held up his hand.

"I want to check something. It will only take a minute."

He saw an aluminum ladder lying against the far wall of the room. As he approached it, he noticed fresh footprints on the dust-covered rungs. He propped the ladder vertically against the tank and began climbing the rungs. When he got to the top, he inspected the canopy. There was no sign of scuffing or smudging from someone climbing on top. Then he turned and looked at the near brick wall. He could see two small circular marks about six inches apart embedded in the soot covering the top edge. He recognized the pattern immediately.

Bipod legs.

Clever, Joe thought. The perfect sniper position. The overhang of the tank lid provided cover for this section of the wall. It would be hard for the spotters to see someone lurking in the shadows. The sniper probably scoped the platform manually then rested his rifle at the last second.

He looked back toward the tank and squinted his eyes.

Could he...?

Joe holstered his gun and pushed up hard on the edge of the lid. It was heavy but it moved up a few inches. He was able to push it a couple of feet to the side and peer inside. The waterline was about one foot below the top of the tank. He turned to the team peering up from below.

"Can someone hand me a flashlight?"

One of the officers scampered up the ladder and passed Joe his tactical flashlight. Joe turned it on and ran it over the surface of the water. It was clear and still. He pointed it upwards and scanned the support joists. Nothing. If Weir had managed to get himself inside this thing, Joe thought, the only place to hide would be under water.

Joe knew that most people's limit for holding their breath was about three minutes. He pointed the light beam beneath the surface. His flashlight only penetrated a few feet into the murky water. He moved it slowly around the inside edge of the tank then ran a couple of cross patterns through the middle. He couldn't see anything other than dark emptiness. He scanned for another three or four minutes then pulled the lid closed and descended the ladder.

"There's nothing there," Joe said to the team. "Let's see if we can pick up his scent outside the building."

As the team moved down the stairs, Joe looked up at the water tank one last time. The sniper had eluded his grasp yet again.

Chapter Forty-Five

Adirondack Wilderness Area, Upstate New York

Twelve years earlier

Twelve-year-old Todd Weir lay next to his adoptive father in a hunting blind in the Adirondack Mountains. He'd spent most of the morning building the structure from materials harvested from the forest. Under close direction from his father, he chopped small trees and vines to construct the shell of the burrow then painstakingly covered it with twisted branches, moss, and dead leaves. In the dense autumn foliage of New York State, the improvised hut was difficult to distinguish from the natural landscape, even to a practiced eye.

Which was entirely the point, since they were using the lair to hide from the experienced eyes of mature whitetail deer. Other hunters were content to erect ready-made camouflaged tents from which to spy upon wild game. But Weir's father insisted on following the purest rules in teaching his son the way of the wild. He viewed animals as sacred creatures, provided by God for the sustenance of man.

Man will have dominion over the fish of the sea and the birds of the heavens and over every creeping thing on the earth, he quoted from the Book of Genesis.

Everything they killed was harvested and eaten at the kill site or cleaned and packed to be consumed later. Virtually no part of the animal was wasted. Muscle and entrails were cooked up as main courses. Bones and cartilage were chopped to make soup broth. Hides were skinned for use as rugs, blankets, and knapsacks. Animal heads were stuffed and mounted as decorative trophies.

Weir's father had initiated the boy into the rites of butchering captured game at an early age. A wild deer begins to deteriorate the minute it dies, he instructed his young son. It needs to be dealt with immediately. If the animal doesn't die of suffocation from blood choking its lungs with a properly placed bullet, a hammer blow to the back of the head will quickly put it out of its misery.

Heat is meat's worst enemy, he explained. A felled animal had to be disemboweled and hung to dry in the shade as soon as possible. As soon as it was dead, the beast should be placed on its back and its abdomen sliced open from its breastbone to its anus. The vital organs should be removed and bagged. Then the carcass should be hung by its hind legs from a branch to cool and drain before removing the meat. Todd wasn't spared any aspect of the procedure. His father would stand over the boy watching him gut the carcass until the entire animal was harvested.

Whoever kills an animal shall make it good.

Young Weir had his baptism in blood, literally.

From their blind's vantage point on top of the escarpment, father and son had a commanding view of the river valley below. The river drained into a quiet lake, which was a favorite respite for deer, moose, and black bear. The hunters looked through the scopes of their Winchester M70 rifles and scanned the valley. The big prize was a mature whitetailed buck. Although moose and bear were larger, venison meat tasted better.

Deer were also smarter and fleeter. There wasn't much sport dropping a big dumb moose or a foraging black bear. Deer were far more skittish and aware of their surroundings. Perhaps they'd learned the dangers of human predators who felled so many of their kind every hunting season.

The bigger and more mature the deer, the more prized the kill. Male deer were easy to age, based on the number of points on their antlers. Since antlers never stopped growing, the more branches on its stem, the older and wiser the animal had proven itself in avoiding predation.

"See anything?" Weir senior asked, as they scanned the valley.

The boy shook his head.

"Just rabbits and squirrels."

Normally, this rite of passage would be a great bonding opportunity for father and son. But there had been an uneasy tension between the two from the earliest days of Todd's adoption. The boy never felt comfortable being alone or in close quarters with his adoptive father.

"That will hardly get us through the night," the father said.

His general rule was that they would remain out on the camping trip until they captured the targeted game. That often meant sleeping overnight together in their makeshift shelter.

"We'll need a bigger meal than that to fill our gullets," Weir continued. Then he looked at Todd and smiled. "There'll be a special treat for you tonight if you bag an eight-pointer or better."

Todd grimaced. He knew exactly what his father meant. The old man always took advantage of these excursions away from prying eyes to take his measure of the boy. That involved more than just butchering wild game.

Todd looked through his rifle scope and scanned the valley to quell the pit in his stomach. After a few minutes, he saw another hunter weaving among large boulders along the river bank. The man stopped for a moment and crouched behind a large rock. He lifted his rifle from the sling behind his back and pointed it at something further down the bank. About five hundred yards away, a large whitetailed buck lowered its rack to the water for a drink.

"Do you see that?" Weir whispered excitedly to his son. "He's a beauty. I count at least ten points."

The old man panned the bank to see if there were more deer in the vicinity and noticed the other huntsman.

"There's another hunter closing in from upstream," he said to his son. "But you've got the cleaner shot. Take him while you've got the chance!"

Todd swung his rifle sight between the hunter and the deer.

"Don't be a pussy!" his father said. "Forget the other guy. Take the shot."

Weir had gotten reports from his son about being bullied at school. He'd hoped that teaching him to hunt would make a man out of him and teach him to stand up for himself.

"Kill that buck, or you'll be the one stuck like a pig tonight," he snapped.

Todd breathed heavily as he tried to purge the vision from his mind. He saw the hunter creeping closer to the buck using the cover of the boulders. When he was about three hundred yards away, the hunter knelt beside a rock and rested his barrel, taking direct aim at the animal.

Weir thumped his son in the chest with his fist.

"You're always letting someone else take advantage of your weakness. Kill or be killed, boy."

Todd clenched his teeth and took aim at the deer, pointing toward the center of its chest. At least it will be a humane kill, he thought. He paused for a moment.

Every moving thing that lives shall be food for you, his father often said.

Suddenly the boy swung his rifle twenty degrees to his right, took aim and fired. The hunter's head snapped backward and he crumpled to the ground. At the sound of the rifle report, the deer bolted upright and darted into the woods.

Weir turned to look at his son, dumbfounded.

"What have you done?!" he screamed.

"You said not to let others take advantage of me," Todd replied.

Weir looked at the boy with his mouth agape. Then he hurried out of the blind and scanned the camp. The last thing he wanted was cops digging around asking what they did on their hunting trips.

"Gather your gear!" Weir snapped. "We've got to get out of here before anyone figures out what happened."

He grabbed a can of kerosene and poured it over the blind then lit a match and threw it at the dry tinder. It lit up like a bonfire within seconds.

"Come on," Weir said, grabbing his son's arm. "We'll double back around the back of the mountain to cover our tracks. Neither one of us can afford to be connected to this."

As the two scrambled towards the north, Todd's lip curled into a grin. He'd finally found his source of power over his oppressors.

Chapter Forty-Six

Lieutenant O'Neill's Office, 18th Precinct

July 18, 8:00 a.m.

L ieutenant O'Neill entered his office carrying a cup of
coffee and closed the door behind him. He sat down and
stared into the cup for a long time, stirring the contents
silently. Joe, Kate, and Hannah watched him without saying
a word.

The events of the previous day had placed everyone at a
new level of tension. Every media outlet across the country
was replaying the Mayor's assassination, with pundits
criticizing the NYPD for gross neglect and incompetence.
The embattled new Mayor had fired Commissioner Pope and
appointed a retired U.S. Army general in his place. In
consultation with the Governor, a state of emergency had
been declared, and the National Guard was called up. The
streets of New York were patrolled by heavily armed soldiers
wearing full battle gear carrying M-16 assault rifles.

O'Neill looked up from his desk and noticed Hannah
shifting uncomfortably in her chair.

"You look a little green, Detective Trimble. Are you
sure you're ready to return to duty?"

"Yes, sir. I'm just feeling a little queasy about what
happened to the Mayor and Bruno."

O'Neill nodded.

"You two were the lucky ones. Unfortunately, there'll be
another funeral tomorrow for one of our fallen. Officer
Moretti served with distinction."

The three officers nodded solemnly in recognition of the
slain ESU officer from the Weir apartment raid.

"Let's review where we stand," O'Neill said. "We've got twelve dead citizens, including a Mayor who placed his life in our hands. And a suspect we're no closer to catching, who always seems to be one step ahead of us."

An awkward silence filled the room.

"What I'd *really* like to know is how the sniper managed to find out where the Mayor was going to be ahead of time. There's no way he just happened to find himself in the same place at the same time."

"He must have been tipped by somebody," Joe said.

"I agree, but from whom? The only people that knew about this were the Mayor, the Commissioner, and this precinct. Even the press wasn't notified until a couple of hours before the announcement. That would hardly be enough time for the sniper to get to the site and set up. And how the hell did he escape yet again?"

"The dogs tracked him the top of the building on the west side of the square," Joe said. "But the trail goes cold a few feet from the rear entrance."

"Which suggests he had wheels. I'm assuming you've checked all the street and commercial cams in the vicinity?"

Joe nodded.

"The building's CCTV shows an old man on crutches entering via a back door a half hour before the shooting. But there's no record of his leaving the building."

"Are you a hundred percent sure this old man was the sniper?"

"It took me a while to make the connection, but yes. Among all the other cops in the square that morning, he only looked at me when he exited the MTA station. And those were no ordinary crutches."

"Is it possible he could still be hiding inside the building?"

Joe shook his head.

"We searched every nook and cranny and checked every unit. He simply disappeared."

O'Neill slammed his fist on his desk.

"What is it with this guy? How is he always one step ahead of us? I'm starting to believe the media might be right, that he really is smarter than us."

O'Neill buried his head in his hands and massaged his temples. Then he looked up at Joe and Hannah.

"Sorry. I know you're doing everything you can and have made tremendous sacrifices. I'm just frustrated, as I know you are."

The Lieutenant leaned back in his chair and took a deep breath.

"So what's our next play?"

"We've been monitoring the suspect's apartment building," Hannah said. "It looks like he's gone into hiding. There's been no sign of him for over forty-eight hours."

"What about his family? He's adopted, right? Have you checked with the parents?"

"That's next on our plan," Joe said. "I'm sure he knows we'll be checking the obvious places. Still, maybe they can provide some clues to his whereabouts."

O'Neill turned to Kate.

"Kate, have you got any ideas based on his profile where else we should look?"

"Now that his picture's being circulated around the country, it won't be easy for him to rent another apartment. Plus, he has a dog to care for. My guess is he'll find some place off the grid to pitch a tent. We might have to wait for someone to recognize him when he surfaces to replenish supplies. Or catch him when he strikes next."

"Any clues who or where that might be?" O'Neill asked. He looked outside his office window. "The only people roaming the streets are heavily armed soldiers and cops. Who can he go after next—the governor?"

Kate cocked her head and shrugged.

"He's definitely escalating his targets. First Joe's wife, then the explosion at his apartment, and now the Mayor. I think with each new success, he's becoming more confident. The higher the profile, the more press he gets to feed his ego. I wouldn't put it past him to target another public figure."

O'Neill stopped to take a sip of his coffee.

"I don't think the new Mayor or the Governor would be dumb enough to try another trick like Mayor Braxton pulled. Nobody wants to have their brains blown out on national TV for the whole world to see."

He looked out his window as a National Guard truck rumbled by.

"At least we now know who we're looking for. Joe and Hannah, keep me advised if you uncover any useful Intel from Weir's parents. Kate, can you notify your agents across the country to keep an eye out for our suspect? If he's set up camp outside the city, we'll need every law enforcement resource at our disposal to find him."

"Already on it," Kate said.

O'Neill stood up and placed his hands on his hips.

"Assuming we all still have our jobs tomorrow, we'll reconvene here for our usual update at nine a.m. Watch your heads out there."

As Kate and Hannah exited O'Neill's office, they glanced at one another. Hannah raised her eyebrows and forced a smile.

"Good luck with that."

Chapter Forty-Seven

Cranberry Bog, Long Island

July 18, 8:00 a.m.

T odd Weir woke up to the sound of splashing water in the shallow marsh surrounding his island. It wasn't unusual for him to hear the occasional splash of a mallard or a loon as it dove underwater to catch a morning meal. But this was a sustained sloshing sound, and much louder. And it was approaching his camp.

He peered through a crack in his shelter and saw someone wading through the bog in his direction. The man was wearing hip waders, a dark green uniform, and a trooper hat. He was walking purposefully toward Weir's outcropping. When he reached the edge of the island and emerged from the water, Weir saw the holster on his hip.

Shit, Weir cursed under his breath. *A ranger. What does he want?*

Weir had camouflaged his shelter and placed it far enough away from the water so as not to be visible to stray hikers or birdwatchers. And he'd been careful to enter and exit the camp under cover of darkness. But he also knew if the ranger was aware who was on the island, he would have brought more support.

He threw on some cargo pants, pulled a baseball cap over his head, and stuffed his hunting knife in his side pocket. The ranger turned his head from side to side. He was definitely looking for something. Weir slipped his rifle inside his sleeping bag. Then he picked up his Browning pistol and stuffed it under the belt of his trousers behind his back. He wouldn't give the ranger any reason to suspect foul play, but he'd be ready in any case.

For a few moments, Weir thought the ranger might not notice his shelter. But he obviously had experience tracking poachers. His head stopped as he looked at Weir's blind. He squinted for a moment then began walking directly toward the shelter.

Damn, Weir thought.

Weir's dog stood up at the sound of footsteps approaching their hut and began barking. Weir snapped on a leash and pulled him out of the blind. He stretched and feigned surprise when he saw the ranger.

"Good day, officer. What brings you to this patch of wilderness so early in the morning?"

Weir's dog pulled on its leash, snarling at the man.

"These wetlands are part of a nature preserve. I'm an Environmental Conservation Officer with Suffolk County. We received a complaint about a barking dog. Pets aren't allowed within the preserve other than on marked trails."

The officer looked behind Weir toward his shelter.

"Neither is overnight camping, for that matter."

Weir spread his arms in supplication.

"I had no idea, officer. My dog and I were just trying to enjoy some solitude. There aren't many places this close to the city where you can find this kind of peace."

The officer scanned Weir's camp. Fifty feet away, he noticed a fire pit and two dead rabbits hanging from a tree branch.

"How long have you been camping here? It looks like you were planning to settle in for a while. An experienced hunter such as yourself should be better informed of the local regulations, especially this close to civilization."

"We've only been here a couple of days. We weren't planning on staying much longer. I'll be happy to pack up and move on."

The ranger looked at Weir suspiciously. He hadn't yet recognized him as the sniper. He wasn't sure if the camper was just an avid outdoorsman or a homeless person.

"You'll have to disassemble your shelter and remove the dead animals. This is a nature preserve, not a hunting range. And I'll need to see some ID."

"Of course..."

As Weir reached around to his back pocket, he let go of the dog's leash. The animal lunged toward the conservation officer. With only a few feet between them, the officer didn't have time to pull out his sidearm, and he turned defensively to the side. Weir swiftly extracted his hunting knife and closed the distance.

He stabbed the knife deep into the officer's back just above the kidney and grabbed his mouth to muffle his cries. Then he pulled the knife out and made three more hard uppercut jabs into the man's abdomen just below his ribcage. The officer went limp, and Weir lowered him to the ground. He sputtered a few times then rolled his eyes, drowning in his own blood.

Weir's dog barked loudly. Weir grabbed it by the back of the neck to make it heel.

"Shhh, boy," he said in a quiet voice. "It's okay. You did good. I need you to be quiet now like we do after we capture deer. Be still while I prepare the kill."

Weir went into his shelter and came out with some nylon rope. Then he went to the edge of the water and retrieved four large flat rocks from the shore. He wound the rope between his elbow and his hand a few times to measure the length and cut four ten foot sections. Then he laid the rope in parallel lines on the ground and placed one rock over each section.

He wrapped the rope sections in a cross pattern over each rock, then flipped them over and tied a secure knot. He placed one rock on top the officer's chest and turned his body over and wrapped the rope tightly around his torso a couple of times to bind them together. Then he placed another rock on the officer's thighs and repeated the procedure with the two other rocks, tying them to his back.

Weir threw his dog a bone to keep it busy then dragged the officer's lifeless body to a secluded side of the island. He submerged the body in four feet of water until it rested on the floor of the marsh. When he returned to his camp, his dog was still gnawing on the bone. He went into the blind, packed his gear, and came out with a stuffed duffel bag.

"Come on boy," he said. "We need to find a camp further away from prying eyes. I think I know just the spot."

Chapter Forty-Eight

Jackson Heights, Queens

July 18, 9:00 a.m.

J oe and Hannah stood on the porch of a red brick row house in Queens waiting for the occupants to answer the door. Joe looked through the windows for any sign of movement. He knew it was unlikely that Weir would return to his childhood home, but he wanted to be ready if their paths crossed.

Hannah's right hand rested nervously over her holster.

"Are you sure we shouldn't be covering the back exit?" she asked her partner.

Joe shook his head.

"He wouldn't be stupid enough to come to such an obvious place. Besides, he disowned his namesake, remember? I'll be surprised if his adoptive parents have any clue about his whereabouts."

A woman in her mid-fifties opened the door.

"May I help you?"

Joe flipped open his wallet and showed his badge.

"Detectives Bannon and Trimble, Ma'am. Are you Mabel Weir?"

The woman's face fell. It was obvious she'd been anticipating the call.

"Yes…"

"May we have a few minutes of your time?"

The woman opened the door, and the detectives followed her into the living room.

"May I get you some tea?" she said.

Joe welcomed the opportunity to have a few minutes to look about the room alone.

"That would be lovely, thank you."

As the woman retreated to the kitchen, he and Hannah scoped the lower level. There were no tracks in the hall or dishes on the table. Joe ran his finger over the top edge of the wainscoting lining the walls. The house was impeccably clean and ghostly quiet. There was no visible sign of habitation other than the middle-aged woman.

Joe noticed some oval-shaped faded patches on the living room walls. He picked up a picture frame resting on a side table. The image showed a man and a preadolescent boy sitting beside a dead deer. The man wore a broad smile, but the boy's face was expressionless. Joe recognized the flat upper lip immediately.

"I suppose this is about my boy," the woman said, placing two cups of steaming tea on the coffee table.

"Yes," Joe said, taking a seat opposite the woman. "Are you Todd Weir's mother?"

"His adoptive mother. He came to us when he was seven."

Joe opened his notepad and scribbled some notes.

"Is your husband here as well?"

"He passed away a couple of years ago of a heart attack," the woman said, betraying no emotion in her voice.

"I'm sorry for your loss, Ma'am."

"There's no need to be. He wasn't a kind man. It's much quieter around here now."

"Are you aware of the purpose for our call?"

The woman nodded.

"My son's face is all over the news. But I can't imagine he could ever..."

Joe picked up the hunting photo.

"Can you share some insights into his childhood?"

The woman paused for a long moment as she looked at the picture.

"My husband used to take Todd hunting frequently. I think he thought it would take his mind off his troubles at school."

"What kind of troubles?"

"He was bullied a lot because of his appearance. It's unfortunate because he was such a good boy. Nobody deserves to be treated like an animal."

Joe peered down at the picture of the dead deer.

"Did your son enjoy these hunting expeditions with his father?"

"At first, I think he enjoyed being treated like a big boy. You know, being able to hold and fire a rifle. Men are attracted to these things, aren't they? I could never understand why some people enjoy killing helpless creatures."

The muscles in Joe's jaw clenched as he remembered how his wife had died.

"The boy looks distracted in this photo," he said.

"I think there was more going on in those hunting excursions than just hunting. My husband had certain...predilections. I sometimes heard him sneaking into Todd's room when he thought I was asleep. I'm afraid he used these hunting trips as an excuse to feed his urges..."

The woman's voice trailed off as she choked up.

"Did you notify the authorities about your concerns?" Hannah asked.

"My husband was a violent man. He would beat me at the slightest provocation. I'm sorry, but I feared for own safety as much as my son's. I was glad when Todd was finally old enough to leave our home."

"At what age was that?"

"Seventeen. He took a job as a locksmith's apprentice in Greenpoint, a few miles from here. We didn't hear from him much after that. I think he was happy to have his own space and control over his life. He was always a bit of a loner."

"Did you ever see him exhibit violent behavior?" Joe asked.

The woman shook her head.

"No. He was always the submissive one. Until something happened around the age of twelve."

"What happened then?" Joe asked.

"There was a noticeable change in both my son and my husband after they returned from one of their hunting trips. Normally, Otto would gloat about how he and Todd stalked and killed another large deer. They were always bringing home the spoils of their hunt. I didn't mind eating the meat, but the trophy heads were too much. I threw them all out as soon as my husband died."

"Do you know what happened on that trip?" Joe asked. "How did they behave differently?"

The woman's mind wandered back a few years.

"They returned home much later than usual that night. Normally, if they couldn't make it home before dusk, they'd stay another night at the camp and return the following morning. Plus, they didn't bring home any game meat or trophies."

She paused to take a sip of her tea.

"They were strangely quiet the following day. Nobody wanted to talk about what happened up there. But it must have been something awful. Otto's relationship with Todd was completely different after that. He became very distant and unaffectionate. Thankfully, I never again caught him sneaking into Todd's room. They never hunted together again."

"Did your son's mood change as well?" Hannah asked.

"He remained detached, like he'd always been. I think that was his way of coping with being shuttled around so many foster homes before settling with us. But I never heard any more complaints about him being bullied at school. I think those hunting expeditions saved him in some way."

Joe and Hannah glanced at each other awkwardly.

"When was the last time you heard from your son?" Joe asked.

"It's been a couple of years. I tried to reach out to him, but he never wanted to come back into this house. Painful memories, I suppose."

"Do you have any idea where he might be now?" Hannah asked.

"The last time we spoke, he said he'd taken an apartment in Flatbush. He apparently started up his own locksmith business. You might be able to contact him that way."

"I'm afraid he's gone into hiding," Joe said. "Do you know of any favorite hangouts or places he liked to go?"

The woman looked outside her living room window.

"He didn't have any friends that I know of. But he would often go out on his bike for long periods when he wasn't away hunting with his father. When I'd ask him about it, he said he liked to go out to Jones Beach and just watch the ocean. How he got that far on his bike is a mystery. He didn't have much money..."

The woman's eyes suddenly welled up as she looked at Joe and Hannah beseechingly.

"How could he have gotten to this point? Are you sure he's connected to all these killings?"

"We aren't certain yet, Mrs. Weir," Hannah said. "That's why we're trying to find your son. We'd like to confirm some of the details. We're just trying to keep everyone safe, including your son."

The woman peered down at the photo of her son and nodded sadly.

"Thank you for your time, Ma'am," Joe said, standing up.

He handed the woman his card.

"If you do happen to hear from your son, please notify us immediately. We'll let you know when we have more information."

The woman walked Joe and Hannah to the door and closed it quietly behind them. The detectives looked at one another for a long moment on the porch. Hannah had a pained expression on her face.

"Don't even think it," Joe said. "A monster is no less a monster just because of a troubled past."

Joe descended the steps and walked toward their squad car parked across the street.

"Let's check out this Long Island connection."

Chapter Forty-Nine

Jones Beach, Long Island

July 18, 11:30 a.m.

J oe and Hannah strolled along Jones Beach, watching the surf break fifty yards off shore. They'd driven to the resort town on Long Island to see if they could find any clues to the sniper's whereabouts. But the entire village was deserted. Even the usually bustling ice cream shops lining the boardwalk were closed from lack of customers.

Hannah sidestepped a syringe lying in the sand.

"Looks like the only dangerous things we're going to find out here are some used condoms and hermit crabs."

Joe kicked a dead sea anemone back into the water.

"And some other spineless creatures."

"At least we got some fresh air," Hannah said. "I don't think you've gotten more than ten minutes of sunshine since..."

"Since my wife's funeral?"

"Sorry. I just meant—"

"Don't worry about me. I'll be fine."

Joe stopped by a dune and sat down in the sand.

"What about you, Hannah? I think that's the second sentence you've spoken all day."

Hannah sat down beside Joe and stared off to the horizon.

"It's just all the crazy stuff that's been going on the last couple of days. Jane, the Weir apartment blast, the Mayor. It makes you more aware of the risks..."

"We knew what we were signing on for when we took this job. Don't go soft on me now."

"It's not me I'm worried about so much as my family. Now the sniper's targeting children and people close to us."

Joe placed his hand on Hannah's arm and squeezed it gently.

"So far, he seems to be taking out his frustrations mostly on me. I don't think you've got too much to worry about. With the TV appearance and all, he sees me as the ringleader."

Hannah looked at Joe and raised an eyebrow.

"Which you basically are. I'm surprised he didn't try to take you out with the Mayor when he had another chance. You might not want to stand out in the open again like that for a while."

Joe snorted.

"If he wanted me dead, he's had ample opportunity. I think he's enjoying this little battle of wits as much as he is offing innocent people. Not that there's been much sign of intelligence on *this* side of the equation. So far, he's outsmarted us every step of the way."

Joe picked up a handful of sand and let it fall between his fingers.

"At least we ID'd him," Hannah said. "Out of the millions of people in New York City, that was a good piece of detective work. And you were the one who kept the focus on Weir until we were able to connect him to the crime."

"But it's all circumstantial. We still haven't actually found the smoking gun."

"We find him, we'll find the murder weapon."

Joe shook his head skeptically.

"Now that he's gone into hiding, we're going to have to wait for someone else to be shot to have our chance."

Joe's radio crackled.

All units, code 246. Suspected sniper shooting. Eighty Riverside Boulevard, Upper West Side.

"You were saying?" Hannah said.

Joe suddenly jumped up and sprinted toward his squad car.

Chapter Fifty

80 Riverside Boulevard, Unit 22D

July 18, 12:30 p.m.

F orty-five minutes later, Joe and Hannah stepped through the open door of a luxury condominium unit on the Upper West Side. The hall entrance was crawling with uniformed and forensic cops. A young woman wearing a robe sat sobbing on the sofa. Her blond hair had a dark red stain on the left side. A man in his late twenties lay at the base of the near wall, thick blood oozing from the back of his head onto the hardwood floor.

Joe saw one of the patrol cops from his precinct and walked over to speak with him.

"Looks like another sniper victim," the cop said, recognizing the Detective.

He pointed to the far window.

"Clean shot right through the glass. Lots of high-rises to shoot from in the vicinity. The woman said it happened almost an hour ago. The shooter's probably long gone by now."

Joe looked at the bullet hole in the window then turned around to trace the path of the incoming bullet. There was a large blood stain at eye level on the adjacent wall, with a small circular hole in the middle.

Joe kneeled down and turned the dead man over. There was no entry or exit wound on the front side of his head.

He looked up and saw the surprised look on Hannah's face.

"That's a departure," she said.

He walked over to the sofa and showed the distraught woman his badge.

"I'm sorry ma'am. I'm Detective Bannon, with the NYPD. I just need a few moments of your time."

Joe noticed the wedding ring on the woman's finger.

"Can you tell me what you and your husband were doing when the shot was fired?"

"We were…making love." The woman pointed toward the blood-stained wall. "Right there, next to the kitchen."

Joe hesitated.

"Were the two of you standing up at the time?"

"Yes." The woman's shoulders shook as she sobbed. "What kind of person shoots someone when they're—"

"How many shots did you hear?" Joe asked.

"Just one. I hid behind the kitchen island right after it happened."

The Detective pushed the woman's bloody hair gently to the side.

"Are you injured? Do you need medical attention?"

"No, I think this is Dean's blood." She peered at her husband lying on the floor and whimpered. "Oh baby…"

Joe looked at the stricken man then at the stain on the wall. He turned to see the perfect round bullet hole in the living room window.

"Ma'am, do you have some binoculars in your apartment?"

The woman looked up at Joe, confused.

"What? Yes." She pointed to the top of a bookcase near the window. "Over there…"

Joe got up and pulled the binoculars off the shelf. He walked to the bloodstain on the wall, centered his head over the bullet hole then turned around with his back to the wall. Then he pointed the field glasses toward the hole in the pane and lifted his hand to twist the knob on top. He paused for a moment then lowered the binoculars and walked to the edge of the window. He made a mental note of a landmark on the high-rise tower across the street then looked down and counted the number of floors up from the street.

"Let's go," he said, turning to Hannah. "Looks like our sniper might not be so clever after all."

****

A few minutes later, the detectives stood outside the door of another condominium in direct line of sight to the crime scene. They paused with their handguns drawn.

"What's your plan?" Hannah whispered.

"Knock once, then kick the door in," Joe said.

"That didn't work so well for us last time."

"He was expecting us last time. This time he won't."

Hannah hesitated.

"Shouldn't we get a warrant? The Lieutenant—"

"How many times have we lost this guy because we gave him time to slip away? I'm not taking any more chances this time."

Hannah nodded and raised her pistol. Joe banged his fist three times on the door.

"Police! Open the door."

Joe listened for movement inside. He heard some shuffling sounds and footsteps quickly moving from one room to another. The footfalls returned and approached the door slowly. The detectives braced themselves, cocking their pistols.

An unfamiliar man answered the door. He looked disheveled and nervous.

"What's this all about?" he said with a shaking voice.

"We have reason to believe a gun was fired from this location. May we come in?"

The man hesitated for a moment considering his options.

"Yes, I suppose. But I've been here all day and didn't hear any gun shots."

Joe motioned to Hannah to keep a close watch on the man as the Detective walked toward the living room window. Half way up the glass was a sill with a sliding pane. He opened the window and looked down at the sill. There was some black powder in the trough. He ran his index finger over the powder then raised the finger to his nose.

Joe swung around and leveled his pistol at the man.

"Where is it?" Joe said.

"Where's what? I don't know what you're talking about."

Joe looked around the room. He moved to the sofa and flipped up each cushion. Then he motioned to Hannah to keep the man covered while he ran into the bedroom. He lifted the mattress and saw a rifle resting on the box spring. He placed his hand over the barrel. It was still warm.

Joe returned to the living room and pulled the man's arms behind his back, cuffing his wrists.

"You're under arrest for murder."

As Joe read the man his rights, Hannah took out her police radio and called the forensics team.

Joe looked at Hannah and shook his head. It was a new sniper.

"I guess it's true what they say. Copies are never as sharp as the original."

Chapter Fifty-One

Broadcast Studio, The Today Show

July 21, 8:00 a.m.

In the days that followed the west side killing, more copycat shootings emerged in New York City and began to spread to other cities across the country. The live assassination of Mayor Braxton on TV screens across America seemed to ignite a visceral reaction among a large swath of disenfranchised citizens. Whether it was anger directed against the government or toward other symbols of their hatred, the cockroaches had come out of the woodwork to feast on the spoils.

The escalation of random violence was ravenously covered by the media, with the major networks and newspapers sensationalizing every new killing. The Today Show, broadcast from the center of the action, was no exception. After repeated requests, Detective Bannon had been persuaded back into the studio to provide an update on the latest killings. As much as he hated the spotlight, Joe felt he should take advantage of its large audience to help capture his wife's killer.

Doug Morrison made idle conversation with Joe while makeup technicians applied final touch-up. When the go-live countdown began, the host's expression suddenly turned serious and he turned to the camera.

"Another day is dawning across America," he said as the red light lit, "and the wave of random sniper violence shows no sign of abating. Yesterday, there were eight more shootings in cities and towns across the country. Every new killing seems to embolden another person to take up arms and begin executing random citizens. The high rate of violent crime in this country has taken a new turn, with lone gunmen taking potshots at whoever crosses them the wrong way.

"Detective Joe Bannon, who's led the search for the original sniper, is back in our studio to share his thoughts on this disturbing trend. But first, we'd like to hear from another law enforcement expert—Dr. Nathan Chandler, Professor of Forensic Psychology at George Washington University."

The camera cut to show a middle-aged man in a suit and bow tie looking into the lens.

"Professor Chandler, what do you make of this alarming new trend in violent crime? Are these simply copycat killings, or are they representative of some kind of built-up collective anger?"

The professor paused to consider his answer.

"I think it's a bit of both. The New York City sniper who started all this presented a new prototype of a cold, calculated killer. He showed that anybody can be killed from a safe distance with the right tools and planning. The fact that he's gotten away with it so many times seems to have encouraged other like-minded people to take out their frustrations in a similar manner."

"What kind of frustrations are you referring to?" Morrison asked. "What causes someone to randomly kill innocent victims?"

"Sometimes the victims simply represent the emblems of their frustrations. The Son of Sam killer targeted amorous young couples who represented his own failure developing close relationships. Jack the Ripper targeted sex trade workers who represented the corruption of morals he ascribed to."

"But the New York City sniper has targeted people across a wide range of ages, genders, and demographics. How can he have a grievance with pregnant women, letter carriers, and young children at the same time?"

"There may be other forces at work. His situation appears to be a classic example of operant conditioning.

250

When he behaves a certain way, something happens to him. If the response to his action is perceived as beneficial and if it's repeated enough times, the behavior becomes conditioned, or habitual. The probable outcome of his aiming a gun at a stranger and pulling the trigger is the immediate and very public death of that person. A somewhat delayed, but just as reliable, outcome is all media attention his act attracts and his seeing his name in the paper. For a previously obscure or marginalized individual, this kind of power and attention can be very addictive."

The camera cut to Morrison as he turned to address Detective Bannon.

"Detective Bannon, first I'd like to offer my condolences for the recent passing of your wife. I know the entire nation admires your courage and sacrifice in attempting to bring this killer to justice."

Joe nodded his head silently.

"You've followed the New York City sniper from the beginning and have developed your own profile of the killer. Does the Professor's description of the killer's motivation align with yours?"

Joe paused for a moment.

"I agree that the need for power drives many of these criminals. It's easy to shoot an unarmed and ill-prepared person in broad daylight from a safe distance. I think this killer and others like him are fundamentally weak individuals who lack the courage or fortitude to stand up to their challenges and tackle them like a man."

"Are you characterizing their behavior as cowardly?"

"Anyone who takes an innocent person's life without risk of consequence is a coward."

Morrison paused to let his viewers soak up the sound bite.

"The Professor has suggested that avoidance of consequence is feeding this behavior. You've had considerable difficulty capturing the original sniper. Can you give us an update on your search for the killer?"

"The suspect has been identified. Todd Weir is on the run and the entire country now knows what he looks like. Just like his victims, he will need to come out in the open eventually. When he does, we'll be ready for him."

"What about the copycat killings? Dr. Chandler thinks the New York City sniper has become something of a role model for a new generation of killers. Do you think his capture will stop the spread of these killings?"

"Our experience in New York City has been that the copycat killers have been far sloppier and less careful in their planning. They've been much easier to track and capture. We've apprehended three new snipers in the last few days. I believe good police work and the rule of law will always triumph over a rogue wolf."

Morrison turned back to the camera.

"Judging by the amount of traffic in the streets, I'm not sure the citizens of New York share your confidence. Our correspondent Elizabeth Porter is standing by to sample the latest mood."

The camera cut to the correspondent standing in a department store next to a middle-aged man.

"Elizabeth," Morrison said, "what is the prevailing sentiment among the citizens?"

"Doug, I'm standing inside one of New York City's busiest transportation hubs at Grand Central Station. As you can see, there are a few shoppers milling about the underground stores, but outside in the streets it's still ghostly quiet. Most people traveling outside their homes are sticking to the underground corridors connecting the shopping malls with subway terminals. Few people are feeling confident enough to venture onto the streets."

The correspondent pointed her microphone toward the man.

"Sir, can you tell me how you're feeling venturing out in public?"

"I'm keeping my head down and under cover," the man said. "The rooftop sniper is still out there. I'm not taking any chances showing my face in public until he's locked away. If he can take out the Mayor, he can take out anyone."

"Now that his image has been widely circulated, how will you react if you see him?"

The man pulled his coat aside to reveal a pistol stuffed in the front of his trousers.

"I'm carrying my own protection now. If I catch him unaware, I'll give him some of his own medicine. The cops can't seem to catch him, so it's up to every person to protect himself."

"Are you saying you'd shoot him on sight?"

"I'd lay my sights into him, that's for sure. One twitch and I wouldn't hesitate to blow him away. Let's just say he might not be the same man when the cops come to cart him away."

The correspondent turned to face the camera.

"There you have it, Doug. It appears the citizens of New York have had enough. Some of them are literally taking the law into their own hands."

The camera cut back to the host in the studio. Morrison turned to address Joe.

"I'm pretty sure I can guess how you feel about this, Detective Bannon."

Joe remained expressionless for a moment then looked coldly into the camera.

"I believe our founding fathers implemented the Second Amendment for a reason. The citizens have every right to protect themselves. But we will uphold the law. Anyone who takes the life of someone else, unprovoked, will be held to account."

Morrison looked into the camera.

"You heard it folks. The sheriff has spoken. It's looking more and more like the Wild West out there every day."

Chapter Fifty-Two

Oval Office, The White House

July 21, 8:30 a.m.

T he President shook his head as he watched the Today Show. The wave of recent sniper shootings in New York City and the slaying of the Mayor had captured his attention as it had the rest of the nation. Until recently, he'd been content to allow local law enforcement agencies to manage the situation. But the rapid and escalating rise of similar shootings across the country had kindled his desire to take personal action.

He'd summoned the Secretary of Homeland Security, Otto Kellerman, to his office to discuss appropriate responses. Although domestic violence technically fell under the responsibility of the FBI, the Secret Service came under the umbrella of the Department of Homeland Security. And the President had an idea that would require the utmost secrecy and personal security.

He felt a certain affinity for the beleaguered New York City cop at the center of the fray. The President knew what it felt like to have his family under constant threat and to be looking over his shoulder for hidden assassins. When the Today Show cut to commercial after Detective Bannon's final comment, the President flicked off the monitor and turned to his Secretary.

"Sometimes I wonder if our founding fathers ever considered the possibility that arming the people might create more problems than it was intended to solve."

The Secretary nodded.

"It doesn't help when a peace officer encourages others to take the law into their own hands."

"Maybe not, Otto, but I understand where he's coming from. I know what it feels like to always be in the crosshairs. With snipers popping up all over the country, citizens are feeling besieged. Something has to be done."

"I don't know what else we can do beyond supporting the local law enforcement agencies in tracking down the killers. We've seen this pattern before, with school and nightclub shootings. It only takes one nut job to create a whole new cottage industry of domestic violence."

"That's precisely my concern. If we don't stop this in its incipient stage, we'll have an epidemic that can't be stopped."

"Did you have something in mind, Mr. President?"

"Like the psychologist said, if people see they can get away with it, they'll be encouraged to do more of it. We need to stop them getting away with it."

"But how can we stop killers in multiple locations across the country any more effectively than local law enforcement?"

"I don't think we need to stop them all. We just need to stop one. The one who started it all—the New York City sniper that everybody else is using as a role model. If we can capture him and put him away, we'll send a strong message that nobody is above the law."

"What do you propose, sir?"

"I'd like to set a trap."

"A trap? You mean some kind of decoy?"

"I suppose you could say that. Though I don't think I've ever been called that before."

The Secretary's eyes opened wide.

"Sir? You're suggesting putting yourself in the line of fire to draw him out?"

The President nodded.

"He seems to have a penchant for shooting authority figures. What better target than the President of the United States?"

Kellerman's jaw slackened. He couldn't believe what the President was saying.

"Mr. President, the best defense of the Secret Service has always been the cloak of uncertainty. Not knowing where you'll be and when is our secret weapon. Are you proposing to broadcast your public appearance ahead of time?"

"Exactly. We'll let the whole country know where I'll be and when. I was thinking Central Park, around noon. That's one of the sniper's favorite times and places, right?"

The Secretary looked at the President, aghast.

"Sir, you know I can't let you do this. It would be impossible to ensure your safety."

"Come on, Otto, your guys are supposed to be the best. People are always trying to take potshots at me. So far, you've done a pretty good job holding them at bay."

"Yes, but that's always been under *our* rules of engagement. You're throwing the rules out the window. Short of putting you in a bulletproof cage, I don't see how we can stop a determined assassin who'll have plenty of time to prepare. The New York City sniper has proven to be very resourceful and Central Park is surrounded by high-rises. We'll have no way of knowing where he'll be, or be able to stop a bullet fired from up to a mile away."

The President shook his head.

"I don't want any barriers or walls. I want to make a statement that everybody should be free to go about their business without reservation. Besides, if you make it look impossible to kill me, no one's going to want to even try."

The Secretary paused for a long moment.

"Just to be clear, Mr. President, you want to make a public address in broad daylight with virtually no protection and tell every would-be assassin in America exactly where you'll be and when?"

"Precisely. Of course, this plan will only work if I don't get shot. Your job is to make sure I don't get shot."

"Sir, you know our agents would take a bullet for you. But it's impossible to step in front of a ballistic projectile traveling faster than the speed of sound when you don't know where it's coming from."

"This is the United States of America. We figured out how to cloak a ten-ton bomber and shoot down intercontinental missiles. Surely you can figure out how to misdirect one little bullet."

Kellerman shook his head and sighed.

"How much time have I got?"

The President paused.

"Every day we're losing more innocent lives and encouraging new would-be snipers. I'll give you forty-eight hours."

Chapter Fifty-Three

The Bellagio Hotel, Las Vegas

July 22, 9:00 a.m.

L ance Britten rubbed his tired eyes as he tapped the door of the penthouse suite at the Bellagio Hotel. His magic act at the Mirage went late into the night and he normally didn't drag himself out of bed before noon. But he'd gotten a cryptic message from an unusual source that was too intriguing to ignore. Besides, anyone who could afford the twenty thousand dollars per night penthouse suite at one of the strip's most luxurious hotels was an opportunity worth exploring.

A tall middle-aged man with a crew cut answered the door. His broad shoulders and stiff posture gave him the bearing of a military man.

"I'm here to see Mr. Richardson," Britten said.

"You must be Lance Britten. Please come in."

The man stepped aside and waved Lance into the room. He extended his hand to introduce himself.

"James Richardson, Director—Secret Service. Thanks for coming so early in the morning. I know you Vegas performers keep late hours."

Britten looked about the room. There were no other occupants, which seemed odd for such a large and sumptuous suite.

"How could I pass up an invitation from the Secret Service? Though I can't imagine what business you'd want with me. I'm just a magician."

"That's exactly what we're looking for."

The man led Britten onto a large terrace overlooking the famous Bellagio fountain. A large brunch spread was laid out on a table next to the window.

"Please, have a seat. Help yourself to the buffet."

Britten glanced at the dancing water sprays in the pool below. He grabbed a tea biscuit from the buffet table and sat down.

"How can I help you, Mr. Richardson?"

"As you probably know, the Secret Service is tasked with protecting the President. We've been studying your impressive portfolio. We need you to perform a special trick."

"Do you want me to make the President disappear?" Britten joked.

"In a manner of speaking. Can you make him vanish with a bullet flying toward him?"

Britten choked on his biscuit.

"A *real* bullet? You realize I work with illusions? I make things disappear through misdirection and sleight of hand."

"I think you're being unduly humble. You make elephants disappear and shoot people with flaming arrows. How hard can it be to make one man disappear or misdirect a little bullet?"

Britten looked at the Secret Service doubtfully.

"Is this for real? I thought you guys had all kinds of fancy technology to protect the President. What makes you think a magician can help you?"

"That technology is good for *preventing* people taking shots at the President. We go out of our way to keep his itinerary and movements a secret so the bad guys don't know where to find him. But this time the President wants to make a public address and announce his plans in advance."

"Why would he want to do that?"

"To catch a bad guy who's proven to be very evasive. Someone who's taken out plenty of other important people."

260

Britten nodded. He'd read about the recent spread of sniper shootings and seen the Mayor's assassination on the newsreel.

"So this is some kind of setup? You're trying to draw someone out then use artifice to misdirect his focus. That's something I might actually be able to help you with. If I control the setting and the terms of engagement, just about anything is possible."

"That's what I was hoping you'd say."

"What's the venue and how much time do we have to prepare?"

"Central Park. Two days."

Britten's eyes widened.

"That complicates things. I usually work in a darkened theater with plenty of props at my disposal. Will the President be delivering his address outside?"

"Yes. And he's insisting on a minimum of visible walls and barriers. He wants to show that it's safe to go out in public. While at the same time making it look as easy as possible for someone to shoot him."

"Isn't that an oxymoron?"

"That's why we're calling a magician. You're a master at making the impossible look possible."

"Let me get this straight. You're asking me to move the President after a bullet has already been fired at him?"

"Either the President, or the bullet, yes. We'd rather the two not meet."

Britten smiled.

"How far away and from which direction will the bullet be fired?"

"We have no idea. The sniper could set up virtually anywhere in a three hundred and sixty degree radius from the President's position. There are high-rise buildings surrounding Central Park on all sides. The shooter normally fires from a fair distance away—up to a mile off."

"Great. With a high-powered rifle, that gives us almost exactly one whole second to move the President out of harm's way."

Richardson snapped his head toward Britten.

"You have ballistics experience?"

"Just at the local gun range. It's kind of a hobby. I find it therapeutic to shoot real objects once in a while after spending all week making them miss in my shows."

"That could be helpful," Richardson nodded. "Now that you understand what the terms of engagement are, do you think this is possible?"

Britten paused for a moment to think.

"It's harder to misdirect a bullet than the object it's directed toward. But it's possible. A bullet's momentum is controlled by the medium it passes through. If you could sufficiently change the air conditions between the shooter and its target, you could theoretically bend the bullet's path."

"How might you propose to do that?"

Britten reflected back to his physics course in college. His unusual experiments in thermodynamics had attracted the admiration of his classmates and led to his interest in magic.

"You could slow it down either by increasing humidity or making the air colder. If you really wanted to be imaginative, you could flood the field with a super-dense transparent gas, such as xenon or tungsten hexafluoride. Of course, you'd have to do all this without the shooter realizing what you're doing. A good sharpshooter with a sophisticated weapon would know how to compensate for ambient changes."

Richardson shook his head.

"That would necessitate a large-scale engineering effort. I'm not sure we have that kind of time. What about the President? Can't you move him instead of the bullet before it gets to him?"

Britten reached for a danish on the buffet and chuckled.

"That's ninety-nine percent of what magic is all about. Moving the target somewhere the audience can't see while making it appear to stay in one place. It's easy when the audience is in a fixed and known location. It's usually done with mirrors and curtains. But in your case, we won't know where the viewer will be, so we won't know how to position the mirrors to properly shift the location of the President."

"David Copperfield moved the Statue of Liberty. How hard can it be to move one man?"

"He didn't actually move the *statue*," Britten huffed. "He moved the stage the audience was sitting on without them realizing it, so when he pulled the curtain back they were looking somewhere else. We're not going to have the luxury of knowing where our subject will be viewing from. You're asking me to move a fixed object in plain sight in the blink of an eye."

Richardson crossed his legs and leaned back in his chair.

"Yes, I suppose that's exactly what I'm asking you to do. I was told you're the best. I've got appointments with three of your contemporaries lined up later this morning. Maybe they can figure it out."

Britten took a glass of Mimosa off the buffet and swished it around in his mouth. He gazed off at the fountain while he pondered the challenge. He knew this was a once-in-a-lifetime opportunity he couldn't pass up. If he could pull this stunt off, he might be able to leverage the trick for his Vegas act. When the final burst of water shot up from the fountain, he smiled.

"There might be a way," he said. "But it will require some careful planning and it won't be cheap."

"You'll have the full resources of the United States government at your disposal."

Britten paused.

"If it works, can I have exclusive rights to use the technique in my own show?"

"Mr. Britten, if it works, the President himself might agree to perform in your next act."

Chapter Fifty-Four

18th Precinct, Lieutenant O'Neill's office

July 23, 8:00 a.m.

Joe, Hannah, and Kate walked into Lieutenant O'Neill's office holding steaming cups of coffee. O'Neill motioned for them to sit down.

"You might want to have a seat before you take another sip," O'Neill said. "I wouldn't want you to spill it when you hear the latest news."

"How can it possibly get any more exciting than it already is?" Hannah joked.

"Unless we're being fired for neglect of duty," Joe suggested. "I wouldn't blame the Commissioner, under the circumstances. Our failure to stop the original sniper seems to have drawn out a whole new raft of hit men."

O'Neill cocked his eyebrow.

"That, and every redneck vigilante this side of the Mason Dixon line. Thanks to your enthusiastic endorsement on live TV."

Kate noticed Joe shifting uncomfortably in his chair.

"With respect, Lieutenant," she said, "I'm not sure these people needed extra encouragement to begin acting irrationally. Insecure and angry people eventually find an outlet for their emotions. Some people kick their dog. Unfortunately, this group is taking out their anger on innocent civilians."

O'Neill leaned back in his chair and took a sip of his coffee.

"Well we've got a new civilian to be concerned about as of this morning," he said. "The President of the United States."

The three officers' eyes suddenly widened.

"How is *he* getting mixed up in all of this?" Joe asked.

"I just got off the line with the Commissioner. The President wants to make a public address here in New York in two days."

Hannah's brow creased.

"Wasn't the assassination of the Mayor a strong enough signal to discourage politicians from making public appearances for a while?"

"Apparently not. The President's concerned about the spread of shootings across the country and he wants to assure the citizens the situation is under control."

"Sounds familiar," Joe said.

"Exactly how does he propose to do that?" Hannah asked.

"By setting an elaborate trap," O'Neill said.

"What makes him think he'll be any more successful than the Mayor keeping the plan secret?" Joe asked.

"He's not going to. He'll be making it public later today. He plans to deliver a public address on the Great Lawn of Central Park this Saturday."

"You've got to be kidding me!" Hannah said. "Could he possibly pick a more exposed spot anywhere in the city? How does he expect us to protect him? Every two-bit sniper with a peashooter will have his choice of nests to shoot from overlooking the park."

"That's exactly the President's plan. Apparently, he wants to make it easy to lay sights on him. The Secret Service has some master plan for ensuring he doesn't get shot."

"Like jumping in front of the bullet?" Joe said.

"Something like that," O'Neill grunted. "They're not telling us. I guess that's why they call it the Secret Service."

"So how are we supposed to help?" Hannah asked.

"Our mission is two-fold. First, do everything in our power to locate the sniper before he fires to neutralize the threat ahead of time. Second, be prepared to close in quickly once the President's detail pinpoints the sniper's location after he takes the shot."

"Exactly how are they going to do that?" Joe said.

"Again, that's strictly need-to-know. But we'll be sharing the same radio frequency with the Secret Service throughout the address, so we'll be able to coordinate our efforts."

"If you call sharing half the available Intel a coordinated effort," Joe said.

"Let's not worry about what's already been decided. As crazy as this sounds, this might be our best chance to capture the killer for a long time."

"Or killers," Hannah said. "Who knows how many other closet anarchists will jump at this opportunity to take down the President."

"That may be so," O'Neill said, "but no other shooters have demonstrated the original sniper's pinpoint accuracy or evasive ability. Whatever the Secret Service has up their sleeve, something tells me the window of opportunity will be very tight. Plus, this time we'll have the entire New York City police force mobilized for the effort, along with the feds. If ever we'll have a perfect chance to snare our suspect, this is it."

Joe, Kate, Hannah looked at the Lieutenant doubtfully.

"Of course," the Lieutenant added, "we could become heroes and bypass the whole production if we find the shooter before the President's address. Kate—has the FBI uncovered any suspicious activity for us to follow up on?"

"We've contacted every government agency to watch and listen for unusual activity. There's been nothing suspicious reported other than the disappearance of a conservation officer recently on Long Island."

Joe suddenly sat up on his chair.

"*Where* exactly on Long Island?" he said.

"Suffolk County, on the northern tip. The officer disappeared after investigating a noise complaint concerning a dog on a remote preserve—"

Joe stood up, throwing his chair against the back wall.

"Kate, can you text me the details? We've got to follow up on this right away."

O'Neill looked at Joe, perplexed.

"What makes you think this has anything to do with the sniper?"

"His mother mentioned Long Island was one of his favorite getaway spots. The dog, the remote setting this close to the city, it all fits. Maybe we'll get lucky and save the President having to put his head on the block."

As Hannah and Joe rushed out of the office, O'Neill looked at Kate and cocked his head.

"Not to mention a few other heads," he said.

Chapter Fifty-Five

Stony Brook, Long Island

July 24, 11:00 a.m.

J oe tapped his foot impatiently as he and Hannah waited in the lobby of the Environmental Conservation Office for Suffolk County. They'd called ahead for an urgent meeting with the captain of the regional office, and Joe was eager to discuss their latest finding. Ten minutes later, a gray-haired man in a green uniform emerged from his office and walked toward the detectives.

"Tom Milburn," he said, extending his hand. "I'm in charge of the Long Island office. How can I help you?"

Joe and Hannah showed their badges.

"Detectives Bannon and Trimble. NYPD, 18th Precinct," Joe said.

"What brings you out to the big island, detectives?"

"We understand one of your officers disappeared recently," Joe said.

"Yes. Officer Chris Hanley, four days ago. I was already worried, now all the more so. What's your interest in the matter?"

Joe chose his words so as not to alarm the captain any more than necessary.

"It's a longshot, but we have reason to believe your man may have had contact with one of our suspects, Todd Weir."

Milburn recognized the name immediately from the FBI Most Wanted poster hanging in his office.

"The sniper who killed the Mayor? Do you think Officer Hanley may have been shot?"

"More likely a chance crossing of paths," Joe said. "We understand your officer was investigating a noise complaint when you last heard from him?"

"Yes, in Cranberry Bog, near Riverhead on the north side of the island. We've searched the area to no avail. If you have additional pertinent details, I'm all ears."

"We'd like to examine the area to see if we can find any clues."

"Of course," Milburn said. "If you can help find our man, my department is at your disposal."

Joe looked at some charts hanging on the Captain's office wall.

"Do you have a map of the preserve?"

Milburn walked over to one of the frames and pointed toward it.

"This is the one. It's mostly wetland. Doesn't get many visitors. There's a rarely used hiking path around the perimeter."

Joe and Hannah looked at the maze of topographical symbols.

"Did Officer Hanley indicate where on the preserve the noise complaint was reported coming from?" Hannah asked.

Milburn drew a square outline over the glass with the back of his pen.

"No, but this is the boundary of the preserve. It's fairly small—less than a square mile."

Joe studied the map and pointed to one of the features.

"Those green hash marks. Does that indicate a marsh?"

"Technically, it's a bog. A miniature version of the Everglades. It's very dense with marine plants. The preserve used to be a cranberry plantation many years ago."

Joe noticed a solid green circle in the middle of the light blue area.

"Is that an island?"

"A small one. It's surrounded on all sides by the bog."

"I'm assuming your people have already searched the area?"

"Yes, although we had no reason to suspect foul play before. Under the circumstances, I think we need to undertake a more thorough search now."

"Do you mind if we tag along? It's possible our suspect may still be hiding there."

"I'll put together a team immediately. If your man is still there, I don't want to take any chances. Give me ten minutes—you're welcome to join us."

****

Forty-five minutes later, Joe and Hannah waded through the hip-deep bog as Captain Milburn and ten other DEC officers converged on the small island at the center of the preserve. Joe held his firearm above the surface as he scanned the horizon in all directions for any sign of movement.

"Isn't this a bit of an unusual spot for your sniper to hang out?" Milburn asked the detectives following behind.

"His profile indicates he's an experienced hunter and that he frequently came to Long Island," Joe said. "The proximity to the city would make this an ideal hideout for someone with a bounty on his head."

"The sniper's picture was prominently displayed in our office," the Captain said, clenching his jaw. "If Hanley recognized him, it could have turned violent quickly."

"That's what I'm afraid may have happened," Joe said.

Milburn squinted toward the island.

"We found evidence of recent camping on the island. The fire pit appeared to have been used a few days ago. And there was a rather elaborate homemade shelter. Whoever was here looked like he had plenty of woodland experience."

271

When they got to the edge of the island, Joe stepped onto the shore and noticed footprints in the mud.

"Someone's definitely been here recently," he said.

"Those may be from the search team I sent out three days ago."

Joe raised his pistol and looked through the dense brush toward the center of the island.

"Can you point me toward the shelter?"

Milburn escorted the detectives about one hundred feet inland. He crept to the side of a small clearing and motioned to a tangle of vines and branches. His officers raised their sidearms and pointed to the mound while the Captain pulled some of the branches aside. Inside was an empty hollow the size of a small closet.

"It's not much," he said. "But it's large enough to sleep one person and a dog."

Joe shook his head at how well the shelter was camouflaged.

"I wouldn't have noticed this if you hadn't pointed it out to me," he said.

"Someone went to a lot of trouble to blend into the landscape," Millburn said.

"Someone like a hunter," Joe nodded. He motioned inside the burrow. "Do you mind if I take a look?"

"Knock yourself out. We found a few rabbit carcasses and some empty water bottles. Whoever built this thing appears to have made a hasty exit."

Joe pushed the vines aside and ducked into the shelter with his partner. Hannah winced at the smell of decaying meat and swatted some flies from her face.

"Not the most comfortable accommodations on Long Island," she said.

"This is probably as close to nirvana as it gets for a hunter looking to be invisible to man and beast," Joe said.

Hannah tapped one of the rabbit carcasses with the toe of her shoe.

"If you say so. What are you hoping to find here?"

"Anything that connects us to the sniper or where he may have gone."

The detectives got down on their knees and slowly crawled around the small enclosure. Joe stopped suddenly and pushed aside some loose material on the ground.

"Found something?" Hannah asked.

He lifted a piece of torn paper from among the twigs and looked at it carefully. He blew some dirt off it and held it up for Hannah to see. It was a hand-drawn sketch showing a rectangle with some notes and symbols placed on it.

"What do you think it is?" Hannah said.

Joe studied the sketch for a minute then looked up.

"I think it's a drawing of Union Square." He pointed to a circle near the base of the rectangle with the notation GW inside it. "That probably represents the Washington statue on the south side of the park."

Hannah looked at the drawing and pointed to some notations on the outside of the rectangle.

"What are those blocks?"

Joe paused to examine the map more closely.

"I think they're marking the position of the tallest buildings on each side of the square. The one marked BB on the narrow side of the rectangle is likely the Best Buy building on the south side. The two small boxes on the left side signify the twin towers on the east side of the square. And this long rectangle with a 'V' on the right side conforms to the shape of the Victoria co-op building on the west side of the square."

Joe nodded more excitedly the longer he looked at the sketch.

"We heard a gunshot sound simultaneously from three sides of the square when the Mayor was shot. I think the sniper planted some kind of audio device on top of these towers to misdirect his location."

"What are those two small circles on the Victoria building? The one closest to the Square has an 'X' in it."

Joe stopped a moment. Then he pumped his head angrily.

"Son of a bitch. Those are the twin water towers on the rooftop. The K-9 unit traced the sniper's scent to the one nearest the park. I knew that's where he fired from."

Hannah looked at Joe then pointed to a notation directly in front of the statue.

"I guess we know what this 'M' symbol represents."

Joe folded the paper and placed it inside a specimen bag, then stepped out of the burrow.

"Our man was definitely here," he nodded to Captain Milburn. "I think we should search the property thoroughly. If your officer surprised the sniper, it could have ended badly."

Milburn motioned for his men to fan out and begin searching the island. Joe turned his body slowly in each direction then stopped as he faced east.

"What do you see?" Hannah said.

"If you were the sniper and you needed to dispose of a body, where would you hide it?"

"Somewhere hard to find, as far from prying eyes as possible."

"Remember the hiking path we saw on the map? That side of the island is furthest away and would be the most protected from pedestrian traffic."

"Let's check it out."

Joe began hacking through some dense brush at the side of the clearing. Within ten feet he noticed a path of broken branches and trampled brush lying on the forest floor. The detectives followed the path until it stopped at the water's edge. Joe and Hannah looked up at one another and nodded.

They stepped into the water and waded out in forty-five degree opposite angles, dragging their feet along the bottom to feel anything unusual lying in the water. About twenty feet from shore, Joe bumped into something heavy. He reached under the surface and pulled the object toward the surface. When it emerged, he motioned for the Captain who had followed their trail and was standing on the shore.

"Captain," Joe said. "I'm afraid I have some bad news."

Chapter Fifty-Six

Three Hundred Central Park West, Upper West Side

July 24, 1:00 p.m.

T odd Weir peered through his rifle scope toward the Great Lawn of Central Park from the thirty-eighth floor of the Eldorado building. The iconic twin towers on the west side of Central Park had been a familiar Manhattan landmark since they were built during the Great Depression. Home to artists, celebrities, and famous socialites, virtually everyone who lived there was well known in Manhattan society.

Weir had little difficulty bypassing the building's security system. Entering via an emergency exit door after dark, he'd easily picked the old-style tumbler lock then taken the elevator to the upper floors. After watching the movement of residents from the stairwell, he'd targeted a frail older woman who appeared to live alone. Waiting until she was asleep after midnight, he picked her door lock and cut the security chain with a bolt cutter. Then he crept into her bedroom and quietly suffocated her. It would take forty-eight hours before the smell of the decaying body began to spread outside her unit, but Weir planned to be gone long before then.

Peering outside her living room window, he saw the platform upon which the President planned to deliver his address being constructed on the south side of the meadow. It seemed almost inconceivable to Weir that the President would take this kind of risk after the recent shooting of the Mayor. But he knew the Secret Service had additional tools at their disposal and that they would go to extraordinary lengths to protect the President.

The stage was about fifty feet square and was enclosed in a transparent glass cube with only the front side open. Weir suspected the panes would be bulletproof, cutting off the line of attack from an incoming bullet. Depending on how deep inside the enclosure the President stood, the angle of opportunity would be as little as fifteen degrees in each direction. This cut off most of the possible shooting positions from either side of the park and also eliminated the possibility of shooting from high above the platform. That left the only effective angle of attack either directly in front of the platform or hundreds of yards away from an elevated position.

Weir nodded in admiration. The President's security detail had done their homework. For a wide open venue, they had designed the logistics to minimize the size of the kill zone and maximize their chance of closing in on the shooter quickly.

A small lake lay directly in front of the platform. The Jacqueline Kennedy Onassis Reservoir covered almost the entire width of the park, extending a third of a mile toward the north end. Weir swung his scope to the north section. A wall of buildings ran along the narrow length of 110th Street at the top edge of the park. It had the most direct sighting to the stage and was far enough back to reach the President at a low angle.

But it was also a mile and a half away and would be the obvious location from which to take a shot. Although it was within the firing range of his high-powered rifle, Weir knew this section of the park would be closely monitored. The New York City police department and every security agency of the United States government would be scanning any building within shooting range of the President. Satellite cameras would be looking at every rooftop and sharpshooters would be peering through every open window searching for the sniper.

Weir also knew his echo trick that he'd used to distract spotters for the Mayor's killing wasn't likely to work twice. The Secret Service had special technology to filter extraneous noise and hone in on the real shot. This time, Weir would have only seconds to make his escape instead of minutes. He'd have to find a less likely firing position—one from which he could make a quick retreat.

He traced a line from 110th Street toward the President's platform. The northern section of the park called The Loch was heavily forested. Between The Loch and the reservoir was an open meadow dotted with baseball diamonds and playing fields. If he could find a tall enough tree, he might be able to get up high enough to find a clear line of sight to the President.

The Secret Service would most likely concentrate their search for the sniper among the tall buildings lining the far edge of the park. But Weir knew they were also likely to use tracking dogs to scour the interior of the park. If he was going to have any chance at avoiding detection and making a safe getaway, he'd have to find a way to hide his scent and outrun the cops if they pinpointed his location.

Weir scanned the bike paths and walking trails running through the northern section of the park. A cyclist was winding along the trails, weaving past the military monuments and sparse pedestrian traffic. The sniper looked up from his scope, paused for a moment, then smiled.

He packed up his rifle then calmly walked to the ensuite bathroom and turned on the bathtub faucet. While the tub was filling, he walked over to the dead woman's bed and picked up two black and white picture frames from her nightstand. They showed the woman performing a Broadway solo many years ago and standing next to the President and his wife backstage.

When the tub was full, Weir took off his clothes and submerged himself in the water. He picked up a loofah lying at the side of the tub and scrubbed his head and body vigorously for two minutes. Then he went to the kitchen, looked under the sink and pulled out a plastic bucket. He carried the bucket to the bathtub and skimmed it across the surface of the water, filling it near the top.

Ten minutes later, he walked out the front door of the luxury apartment. He took one last look at the old woman lying on her bed, surrounded by pictures of her famous friends. Soon, he thought, she'd be remembered in the company of Presidents for another reason.

Not long after, the few pedestrians walking on the west side of Central Park paid little mind to an old man riding a wobbly bicycle along the sidewalk. No one noticed that the pail perched at the side of his bike had a slow leak and was leaving a trail of water drops all the way around the perimeter of the park.

Chapter Fifty-Seven

The Loch, Northern Central Park

July 25, 11:00 a.m.

L ate Saturday morning, a long motorcade of black SUVs made its way down 5th Avenue along the east side of Central Park. In the middle of the pack were two black limousines. Four flashing NYPD motorcycles and a marked squad car led the procession. Every intersection south of the Robert F. Kennedy Bridge leading from LaGuardia Airport was blocked to allow unrestricted access to the convoy's final destination.

When the caravan reached 85th Street, it turned into the park just north of the Metropolitan Museum and wound its way to the Great Lawn. Scores of gray-suited Secret Service agents wearing dark sunglasses stood about the meadow craning their heads like owls looking for prey. Many more uniformed NYPD officers patrolled the northern section of the grounds and along the streets lining the edges of the park. On the rooftops of the tallest buildings on each side of the park, Secret Service sharpshooters scanned every building with a clear line of sight to the Presidential platform.

Eighteen hundred yards away, Todd Weir lay face down on a tall branch of an oak tree at the south end of The Loch. From his position near the edge of the North Meadow, he had a clear view of the Presidential platform across the open playing field and the large reservoir.

He'd climbed the tree using ropes and carabiners to avoid touching the trunk. His entire body was covered in camouflage clothing, making him virtually invisible in the thick canopy of the deciduous tree. His exposed skin was coated with camouflage paint, as much to prevent dead skin cells falling onto the ground below as to blend in amongst the dense foliage. On the branch below rested a small green bicycle, which he'd stolen the night before to pedal to the tree without setting foot on the ground.

He scanned the nearest trail leading from his tree to the west side of the park. It was lightly traveled by parkgoers enjoying the afternoon sunshine. The President's appearance had drawn out just enough curious gawkers to help cover the sniper's retreat. Weir knew everybody would be looking up for signs of the shooter. He had the element of surprise to his advantage. Before anyone would be able to place his position, he'd be racing off the grounds on his bike toward his escape route. If the security detail did happen to identify him, they'd be reluctant to shoot with so many civilians nearby.

Weir turned his scope to the motorcade coming to a stop beside a stand of trees next to the Great Lawn. He zeroed in on the limousines and watched for the President to emerge. A man and woman matching the height and build of the First Couple got out of one of the cars and moved to a covered shelter near the stage, with their backs to his position.

No matter, Weir thought. In less than thirty minutes, he'd have a clear shot at the President's head on the raised platform. The pretty backdrop of Central Park visible through the clear transparent panes of the stage would soon be painted in more vibrant colors.

Chapter Fifty-Eight

Central Park West, Upper West Side

July 25, 11:30 a.m.

T he bloodhound tugged his handler forward as it sniffed the sidewalk next to the luxury co-op buildings lining the west side of Central Park. Joe and Hannah followed closely behind with their pistols at their side, looking for any sign of the sniper. The dog had picked up Weir's scent next to the Metropolitan Museum on 5th Avenue and led the team almost two miles half way around the park.

Joe looked at the handler and shook his head in frustration.

"What the hell, Lou? We're being led in circles."

The handler stopped and instructed the dog to heel.

"I've seen this before. Fugitives sometimes double back over their trail and trace a circle to confuse the animal. It's hard to pinpoint where they stopped when it's a continuous pattern. But this is highly unusual for an urban environment. There's a lot of traffic on these sidewalks. Dogs usually have difficulty picking up the scent."

Hannah watched the dog sniff the pavement and pull in the direction of the south end of the park.

"This one sure seems to know where he's going."

Lou nodded.

"The scent's been uninterrupted for many blocks, and it's particularly strong." He resumed walking with the dog. "It's almost as if the sniper *wanted* us to find it."

"As a diversionary tactic?" Hannah asked.

"Possibly," Lou said. "But there's something else that's unusual. Normally the trail meanders, following the target's normally jerky movements. This one goes in a perfectly straight line."

"Isn't that because the streets and sidewalks along the sides of the park are also perfectly straight?" Joe said.

"Partly. But dogs usually sniff the ground in a zigzag pattern matching the footsteps of the target. This trail is one solid line. It's almost like it was *painted* on the ground."

"He has to stop somewhere along the way, right?" Hannah said. She looked down the sidewalk at the uninterrupted wall of luxury co-op apartments. "There's virtually nowhere to hide at street level. Will the dog be able to sense if the target veered off the path?"

"It should, assuming he's still walking. But this pattern almost seems like he's floating."

Joe looked at the pedestrian traffic moving along the sidewalk on the park side of the street.

"The only other method of conveyance would be on a bicycle or a stroller," Joe said.

"City by-laws prohibit riding bicycles on sidewalks," Hannah said. "The wealthy residents living in these co-ops would quickly shoo an itinerant rider onto the street."

"There aren't many people walking the lanes of Manhattan these days. I can't imagine many people would complain. Plus, the Guardsmen wouldn't recognize it as unusual."

Joe turned to the dog handler.

"What do you make of it, Lou?"

"A bicycle wouldn't leave much of a scent trail—only where the rider touched his body to the ground when he stopped. This is a strong and continuous trail. If the sniper was riding a bike, he'd have to drag a piece of his clothing behind him to duplicate this pattern."

"He's leading us somewhere," Hannah said.

"Probably in the wrong direction," Joe mused.

The dog suddenly stopped at a gate leading to an alleyway between two large buildings.

"Got something?" Joe asked Lou.

The handler nodded.

"Yes. Your man definitely went in here."

Joe raised his pistol and swung the gate open slowly.

"Watch for him to the sides and above. Lou, be prepared to release the dog if you see the suspect. We may only have a few seconds to react."

The dog stopped by a metal door leading into one of the buildings.

"This is where the trail stops," Lou said.

Joe pulled on the door. It was locked tight. He bent down and examined the lock.

"Weir wouldn't have much difficulty picking this. Let's go in the front and see if we can pick up his scent on the other side of the door."

The team backtracked and entered the lobby. The dog quickly found the sniper's scent and traced it to the main elevator. They rode the elevator to the top floor then Joe pushed the buttons for the descending floors. Three floors from the top, the dog picked up the scent and led them to unit 2912.

Joe pulled out his Glock and nodded to Lou and Hannah. Hannah leaned in toward Joe's ear.

"Shouldn't we call for backup?" she said. "What if he has the place booby-trapped again?"

Joe looked at his watch. It was ten minutes before noon.

"The President is scheduled to begin speaking in just a few minutes," he whispered. "We haven't got time."

He pointed two fingers at his eyes then turned them toward Lou and Hannah. He separated his two index fingers indicating he wanted them to cover his flanks. Then he reared back and kicked the door as hard as he could. It didn't budge. He tried again. It didn't crack. He lifted his pistol and pointed it at the door jam where the latch crossed and fired three times.

As the door flew open, Joe rushed into the apartment. The entrance foyer and living room were empty. There was no sign of habitation. Joe glanced to his sides then moved into the living room while Lou and Hannah searched in the other directions.

"Joe," Hannah called a few seconds later. "I've found something."

Joe hurried to the end of the hall and entered the master bedroom where Hannah was standing. An old woman lay still on her bed with her eyes open. Joe walked over to the bed. The woman was deathly pale and her skin was cold. She'd been dead for hours.

Hannah went into the ensuite washroom to make sure it was clear.

"That's odd," she called.

Joe and Lou followed behind and looked at the tub full of water.

"The woman still had her nightgown on," Hannah said. "Why would she leave the tub full?"

"Unless somebody *else* was taking a bath," Joe said.

"You're suggesting the sniper killed the woman in cold blood then calmly took a bath?" Lou said. "That's cold."

Joe dipped his hand in the water then rubbed his fingers together and held them up to his nose.

"No oil and no soap. That's not the kind of bath I've ever known a woman to take."

"Maybe the sniper was trying to wash off his scent?" Hannah said.

"Or trying to *concentrate* his scent," Joe said. "Lou, how do dogs normally track someone's scent? I mean—do they smell his breath, the smell of his shoes, or something else?"

"Actually, it's mostly dead skin cells. Our bodies slough off millions of dead cells every day. Every person's skin has a unique scent, like a fingerprint. Dogs track the path of dead cells left on the ground like a trail of breadcrumbs."

Joe picked up the loofah floating on top of the water and ran his fingers over it.

"Looks like our sniper sloughed off a lot of dead skin cells."

He ran to the bedroom window and threw back the curtains. The Central Park reservoir was directly across the street and the President's platform two hundred yards to the south.

Joe lifted his hand and turned his wrist. It was five to twelve.

"Hannah," he said. "Give me your binoculars."

Hannah pulled a pair of field glasses from a pouch at her side and handed them to Joe.

"Do you see something?"

"Not yet," Joe said. "But I think I know where to look."

He swung the binoculars to his left as he panned the north section of the park through the window.

"Weir went to a lot of trouble to create a false trail around the park," Joe said as he searched through the glasses. "This is the only building he entered. I don't think he plans to fire from a tower at all. He knows we're going to be watching every high perch with a clear shot at the platform. With this many cops covering the area, he wouldn't have enough time to get out. I think he's going to fire from the park."

"How?" Hannah said. "Wouldn't the dogs pick up his trail?"

"Not if he entered the grounds on wheels."

Joe moved the binoculars slowly up and down as he scanned the width of the park in the area above the reservoir. The only protected area was the thicket of trees above the North Meadow. He lowered his glasses and scanned a straight line from the stage. The area across the reservoir and the north field was completely open to the stand of trees.

He lifted the binoculars and adjusted the knob on top of the lens. Then he moved the glasses in a small circle and stopped.

287

"What the..."

Through the thin canopy at the top of one of the trees, Joe saw a small red reflection in the overhead sun. It almost looked like—.

"A bicycle!" he said out loud.

"A what?" Hannah said, looking where he pointed. "There's a lot of bicycles in the park today. How can you be sure this one belongs to the sniper?"

"Because this one's sitting in a tree."

Joe dropped the binoculars and ran out the front door of the apartment with Hannah and Lou in rapid pursuit. As he tapped the elevator button, he looked at his watch.

The President was scheduled to begin speaking in less than a minute.

Part 3: All In

Chapter Fifty-Nine

The Loch, Central Park

July 25, 11:50 a.m.

E veryone's looking up.
I suppose that makes sense. I'm the rooftop sniper after all. The one who shoots defenseless citizens from the safety of a hotel room or high-rise tower. The anonymous coward who likes to blow faces off faceless people.

How about now?

It's Todd Weir versus the President of the United States. The most powerful man in the world against Public Enemy Number One. Hardly anonymous, or *safe*. I'm mingling with the people now. In the most popular outdoor space in the busiest city in the world. Could I make it any easier?

I see you, Secret Service. Can your sharpshooters see me? You're looking in the wrong places. The best-trained eyes in the world can only find targets in plain sight. And there are too many people in the park for your satellite cams to distinguish my heat signature. Congratulations, Mr. President. You've drawn the people out of their hiding places. You'll soon be a victim of your own success.

I don't see my favorite detective yet. Did you find my latest stooge? She's right where you'd expect. I see her curtains are pulled back. Was that you, Joe? I practically led you right to her. Seemed like a nice old lady, but she had a good long life. It was her time.

You must be pissed. So close, yet again. The killer who keeps slipping through your fingers. I saw the venom in your eyes as you stood beside the Mayor. Sorry about your wife. So pretty and so vulnerable. But what were you thinking? I tried to warn you at the nightclub. Everybody's fair game. Nobody can hide from me.

Shouldn't you be down here protecting the President with all of his men? It's such an impressive security detail. New York's Finest, the National Guard, and the best of the best—the Secret Service. If they can't find one man, I don't know who can.

Maybe the hounds can. If this were the jungle, they'd probably have caught me by now. Lucky for me, we keep them on leashes in the concrete jungle. But a chain is only as strong as its weakest link. And their handlers are so predictable. Follow your nose. It's as plain as the one on your face.

Did you like the trail I left for you? The park is so pretty this time of year. You must have seen quite a bit of it. I'd have shown you more, but I thought you should get to the old woman before she stinks up such a nice building.

I see some trackers are moving about the park's interior. Smart move, you can never be too careful. Some of those copycat killers might try to take a shot at the President from behind a tree.

The dogs seem distracted, though. Too many scents to keep track of, I suppose. Must be confusing for the poor critters. One's right below me. He senses something. The scent's in the air, but the wind is playing tricks. Keep looking, little buddy. You'll find my trail soon enough.

Three minutes to twelve. How nice of the President to choose my favorite time of day to make his appearance. Offering his body as sacrifice. Judgment is about to be passed.

The glass stage is shining in the sunlight. Like an unspoiled vessel, cupped in God's hands. Visible to the heavens, for the rapture to begin. The stage is darkening. Perhaps the chosen won't be going into the light after all. That's no regular glass, but I suppose we knew that already, didn't we, Mr. President?

No matter, I only need one open window. You wanted to look accessible. You wanted the people to be accessible. That's why you chose this venue. Protect the freedom of speech and freedom of assembly in America, and all that. You wanted to make a statement.

You're about to make a more powerful statement than you imagined. I see you, Mr. President. Step up to the podium. Your public awaits. You look very Presidential— defying the enemy, putting on a brave face.

I can hear your echo as you speak. I'm a little too far away to make out what you're saying. But I'm sure it's very impressive. Even more than the Mayor's speech. Assure the people, Mr. President. America is great. It will never be intimidated. It has prevailed over greater threats.

The time is nigh. Goodbye, Mr. President. Your fate is in the wind.

Poof.

What? You're still talking. That's not possible. I never miss. And you didn't even flinch.

Ahh... Very clever, Mr. President. You're not even there, are you? I didn't foresee that.

Who's the coward now?

Very tricky. A double glass pane. Your team is lining up the holes. Now they're pointing lasers toward me, telling your men to converge. It's time to leave the roost.

I'll see you another day, Mr. President. Keep your head about you. You won't have it for long.

Chapter Sixty

Northern Central Park

July 24, 12:05 p.m.

S econds after Weir fired at the President, hundreds of NYPD cops and Secret Service agents rushed toward his position. Weir cut his bike loose and quickly rappelled down the tree. Then he jumped on his bike and began pedaling furiously toward the nearest exit on the west side of the park.

He knew he'd have only seconds to escape the dragnet. But if he could make it out of the park, he'd have a good chance evading the pursuit in the maze of midtown Manhattan buildings. Most of the cops would be pursuing on foot and by car. He'd planned his escape route to make maximum use of narrow lanes, stairs, and other obstacles. His bike could outrun any person and go places other vehicles wouldn't be able to follow.

His biggest threat was the dogs. They'd soon pick up his scent from under the tree and connect it to the bike. His only chance was to get to the river before their handlers could catch up with him. Then he could hide under water just as he did at the water tower and let the strong current carry him downriver out of harm's way.

When he emerged from the thicket of trees in The Loch, parkgoers were surprised by the camouflaged cyclist racing past them. They'd heard the crack of a rifle but could still hear the President speaking from the platform. Nobody expected the sniper to be lying among them. But the President's security detail knew otherwise. They'd quickly pinpointed his location by lining up the holes in the dual panes of glass behind the President. The laser pointed directly at Weir's perch in the tree, and his position was radioed to every cop in the vicinity.

Weir stayed close to the treeline, zigzagging along the trails to evade the sharpshooters tracing his path from above. He heard the ping-ping sound as bullets struck the pavement beside him. Once he made it onto the side streets, he knew he'd have the protection of the tall buildings and narrow lanes to provide cover.

He just needed to get out of the park.

As he turned onto the bridal path, an equestrian cop noticed him and took up the chase. Weir looked over his shoulder and saw the horse quickly closing the gap. He veered back into the thicket and ducked under some branches. The horse struggled to follow the cyclist's path as it stumbled through the dense brush.

Bullets slammed into the trees beside Weir, sending splinters of bark into the air. The cop was shooting indiscriminately, looking for payback for his fallen comrade. Weir saw a large oak tree and pedaled directly toward it. At the last second, he ducked under a large branch and glanced back. The cop lined Weir in his pistol's sight and was just about to fire when he slammed into the overhanging branch and fell backwards off the horse.

The cyclist turned onto the park's main boulevard and pumped his legs as fast as he could. A uniformed cop saw him coming straight toward him and raised his gun. Weir swerved toward the main exit. A bullet whooshed past his ear. He pulled up on the handlebars and thrust his weight forward to jump over a tripline. The cop who was following behind flew forward, slamming his face into the ground.

As he raced toward the park exit at 100th Street, Weir suddenly saw Detectives Bannon and Trimble turn onto the path from Central Park West. Joe spread his legs and raised his pistol, drawing a bead on the sniper. Weir crouched down to lower his profile and raced straight toward the Detective. Two bullets flew over his head. He swerved to the side and kicked out his leg, striking Joe in his stomach. Joe went down on one knee and aimed at Weir's back as he crossed the intersection leading away from the park. A bullet slammed into Weir's bulletproof vest, thrusting him forward. He flinched in pain and wobbled for a moment, then sped away down 100th Street.

Joe caught his breath and saw another cyclist pedaling down Central Park West. He ran up to the rider and yanked him off the bike.

"Police! I need to borrow your bike," he said.

He hopped on the bicycle and began racing after Weir down 100th Street.

"Follow me in the car," he yelled to Hannah over his shoulder. "I'll radio where to cut him off."

Chapter Sixty-One

Manhattan, Upper West Side

July 24, 12:10 p.m.

W eir sped westward along 100th Street, weaving between oncoming traffic. He glanced over his shoulder, and when he saw Joe following only a block behind, he disappeared into a lane between two buildings. Joe pulled his police radio out of his pocket and struggled to support it on the handlebars as he pressed the call button.

"Sniper between Columbus and Amsterdam, just south of 100 Street," he said. "Watch for a cyclist wearing camouflage clothing."

Joe turned into the lane and saw Weir crouched over his bike racing southbound. The Detective stood up on his pedals and pumped his legs furiously. He was beginning to close the gap when he suddenly felt a sting in his chest and was wrenched backwards, slamming onto the pavement. His bike coasted forward about thirty feet then crashed into the side of a building. As he lay on the ground with his head spinning, Joe looked up and saw a transparent fishing line quivering in the air four feet above him.

He looked down the lane and saw Hannah's car pull up, blocking the exit. The only way out of the alley was past either of the detectives.

Finally, Joe thought. *He's got nowhere to go.*

Hannah got out of her car and took aim at the cyclist. He zigzagged erratically, making it hard for her to get a direct line. She hesitated when she saw Joe fifty feet behind the cyclist. If she missed the sniper, she could hit her partner. She waited until the rider got close enough to fill her field of vision. Then she fired two rounds directly at him. But it was too late. Weir pulled up on his handlebars and hopped his bike over the hood of her car then sped westward along 97th Street.

Joe rose to his feet and looked at his partner incredulously.

How could she miss from that distance?

He picked up his bike and hurried down the alley in Hannah's direction. As he raced past her patrol car, he glanced at his partner with a confused expression. Hannah just stared at him blankly.

Joe looked ahead and saw Weir two blocks away.

"All units," he called into his radio. "Sniper heading west on 97th towards Broadway. Block all outbound routes."

Within seconds, a wall of flashing police cruisers appeared at the corner of Broadway and 97th Street. Weir veered to his left and disappeared into another alley beside a church. Joe followed him into the laneway but lost sight of the sniper. He slowed down and removed his pistol from its holster. Sensing another trap, he looked up warily and to the sides for any sign of Weir.

Nothing.

Suddenly, Weir stepped out of an alcove thirty feet ahead and pointed his pistol at the Detective. Joe instinctively flung his bicycle forward, holding the handlebars. The bike swung up ninety degrees, providing a modicum of cover. Two bullets pinged off the metal frame. Joe returned fire and Weir retreated into the alcove.

Joe knew he was exposed in the narrow alley. The flimsy bike wasn't likely to block another hail of bullets. He pointed his gun at the edge of the wall waiting for Weir to show any part of his body. If he could keep him cornered for just another minute, reinforcements would soon arrive and block any chance at his escape.

Just as he reached into his coat pocket to radio in the sniper's position, Weir raced out of the alcove, crouched over his handlebars. He turned away from Joe and sped down the lane. Joe fired four shots in rapid succession. Weir flinched as one clipped him in the right shoulder. But it wasn't enough to disable him. At the back of the church, Weir turned to the left and out of sight.

Joe raised his radio.

"Sniper between 97 and 96 Street, just west of Amsterdam."

He could hear the wail of police sirens moving toward his position. A little further behind, the excited barking of tracking dogs closed in from the east.

Joe looked up at the cross atop the church steeple.

A little help? he pleaded. *Don't let this guy get away again.*

Two seconds later, he heard shots on the other side of the church.

Not yet, he cursed. *Save him for me.*

Joe raced to the corner of the church. There was a throng of flashing police cruisers but no sign of the sniper. He saw Hannah standing beside her car and raced up to her.

"Where is he?" Joe panted.

"We got here within seconds of your call," Hannah said. "No one's seen him."

Joe shook his head and cursed.

"What?" he said. "He can't get away this time."

Joe looked down at the pavement and a saw a trail of red spots. They led into a maze of buildings across 96th Street. An NYPD supervisor's car suddenly skidded to a halt beside the detectives and Lieutenant O'Neill stepped out.

Joe wasted no time in enlisting O'Neill's support.

"Lieutenant," he demanded, "we need to close off the block. Hannah, circle around in the car. The sniper's injured and leaving a blood trail. Don't let anyone out on either side. I'll check the courtyard."

Joe hopped on his bike and followed the trail between two buildings. He knew the sniper would have the advantage as long as he remained hidden. The Detective was an easy target moving through the narrow lane. But if Weir was going to make a stand, he would have done so already. Nothing about this guy was random. Holing up in a surrounded block didn't fit his profile.

Joe pedaled just fast enough to follow the blur of red dots on the pavement. The spots were coming more quickly now and in larger sizes. If the sniper was still riding, he'd soon start to lose energy. The odds were now in Joe's favor. If Weir stopped, the dogs would find him. If he kept moving, he'd bleed out and soon lose consciousness.

He only had a matter of minutes left.

Joe wove slowly through the courtyard, holding the bicycle's handlebar in his left hand and his pistol in his right hand. The blood trail merged onto 95th Street and crossed the avenue between two police cruisers.

Joe cursed again. Weir was staying just ahead of the dragnet.

He heard the familiar chop-chop sound of rotor blades and looked up. A police helicopter appeared over the 95th Street block, shining a high-powered light into the darkened alleys. A ring of news helicopters fluttered a half mile away on the periphery.

Good, Joe thought. *The more eyes looking for this guy, the better.*

He pulled out his radio and pressed the button.

"Suspect moving south of 95th street between Amsterdam and Broadway. I think he's trying to get to the river. Block all exits to the west."

Chapter Sixty-Two

Manhattan, Upper West Side

July 24, 12:30 p.m.

J oe pedaled his bike slowly through the courtyard looking for the camouflaged rider. Against the gray and red residential buildings of the Upper West Side, the sniper's mottled green clothing was no longer an advantage. Far from blending in with his surroundings, he appeared just as he was—a jackal among lambs.

The Detective's eyes darted from side to side, skipping from the ground to the rooftops of the tall buildings surrounding him. With Weir now injured, he knew the sniper would be even more unpredictable. Joe couldn't afford to be blindsided by another booby trap or ambush. And his suddenly fainthearted partner could no longer be counted on to have his back. There was something he saw in her eyes when she lined the sniper up at the end of the lane that he'd never seen before. Aided by the speed and maneuverability of his bicycle, the sniper was staying one step ahead of the tracking dogs and the police cruisers. Joe was the only tenuous link keeping a connection with the target.

The blood trail wove erratically between the buildings in the courtyard. Overhead, the police helicopter followed the Detective's path through the labyrinthine maze of lanes. Its spotlight danced ahead of him, searching for the rider. Joe knew Weir wasn't likely to abandon his bicycle and flee on foot. His only slim chance at escaping the dragnet closing in on all sides was to keep moving in the shadows.

The spotlight suddenly stopped when it caught the outline of someone lurking in an alcove. Weir hesitated for a moment then darted out of the niche and banked his bike south onto Broadway. Joe pumped his legs and followed him onto the main boulevard. One hundred feet ahead, Weir was racing down the street against oncoming traffic.

Two blocks away, a train of flashing patrol cars raced toward the rider. The patrol car at the front of the line skidded sideways to block Weir's forward movement. Weir banked onto the grassy median separating the northbound and southbound lanes and resumed his pace on the opposite side of the street.

Joe hopped the median and picked up the chase. The roar of the helicopter above his head was deafening as it swooped low, skimming over the trees lining the median. The Detective lifted his pistol and tried to get a bead on the sniper. He was weaving too quickly between the cars moving in the same direction on the busy avenue.

Even in the middle of a life-and-death police chase, Joe thought, *New York drivers still refused to yield.*

Weir swerved off Broadway onto 91st Street, heading west. Joe shook his head as he saw the treeline of Riverside Park rapidly approaching.

I can't let him get to the park, he thought. *There's too much cover. The river's only three blocks away...*

Joe raised his pistol to take aim at the rider. Traffic was thin on the side street, and he finally had a clear shot. But just as he was about to fire, a strange thing happened. People began pouring out of cafes and buildings lining the sides of the street, and they converged on the rider. They'd somehow been informed of Weir's movement, and a mob mentality had taken hold. Recognizing the sniper was finally on the run, they'd abandoned their fear and begun to turn the tables.

The predator had become prey. The shadowy guerrilla was no longer taking people out on his terms. The battle was now in the open, and the odds had changed.

It was eight million to one in the people's favor.

Chapter Sixty-Three

F ive hundred feet above the unfolding street drama, a swarm of helicopters monitored the chase scene with intense interest. Like locusts swarming over a ripe cornfield, they moved in tandem, soaking up the action as it moved westward. The sniper killings was the biggest story in the country, and the capture of the New York rooftop sniper was a coup no news organization wanted to miss.

The NBC local affiliate was no exception. Elizabeth Porter, the street correspondent for the Today Show, was reporting live from one of the helicopters. Her cameraman zoomed in on the sniper with the detective in hot pursuit and was broadcasting the chase on millions of televisions and portable electronic devices across America. The whole country was glued to their screens, transfixed by the drama taking place on the streets of Manhattan.

Doug Morrison and NBC news anchor Robert Raynes provided running commentary as the two cyclists snaked a serpentine trail through the Upper West Side.

"The New York sniper is desperately trying to evade police pursuit on a bicycle," the anchorman reported. "We have reports that the cyclist following close behind is Detective Joe Bannon from the NYPD. Bannon has been trying to catch the rooftop sniper since his first killing almost three weeks ago. This is the closest anyone has gotten to capturing the mysterious killer.

"Doug, I understand that shots were fired as the President was speaking in Central Park. Can you give us an update on the situation?"

The camera cut to the Today Show host in the Rockefeller studio.

"Bob, all we know is that a single shot was fired in the vicinity of the Great Lawn as the President was giving his address. He continued speaking while his security detail closed in on the suspect."

"That's highly irregular," the anchorman said. "In similar incidents, the President has always been hustled away into a waiting vehicle and rushed out of harm's way."

Morrison nodded.

"It's definitely unusual. It's almost as if his security people were anticipating the attack and somehow knew the President couldn't be harmed."

"We're following the sniper on the live cam," Raynes said. "Can you tell us where he is right now?"

Morrison turned to his monitor.

"Elizabeth Porter is following the chase from our helicopter flying over the action. Liz, what are you seeing?"

The camera cut to the correspondent, wearing a headset. The roar of the helicopter engine above her cab forced her to shout into the mic.

"Doug, the sniper is moving westward toward Riverside Park along 94th Street, just past West End Avenue. Another cyclist, who we believe is Detective Bannon, is following closely behind. Hordes of people have begun pouring out of buildings all around the area, taking up the chase."

"Are they security personnel or ordinary citizens?" Morrison asked.

"From what we can tell, they appear to be average New Yorkers. The live coverage of the chase seems to have awoken a primal urge for revenge. People are no longer afraid to move openly onto the streets of Manhattan."

"What about the local police and Secret Service?" the anchorman asked. "Why haven't they been able to stop one cyclist?"

Liz pressed the headset against her ear, struggling to hear the studio feed.

"We have reports that the sniper set booby traps along his escape route to slow down his pursuers," she reported.

"What kind of traps?" asked the anchorman.

"One observer from the park said he used triplines to slow down police officers pursuing on foot. Our camera subsequently captured Detective Bannon pulled off his bike as he followed the sniper into a lane between two buildings."

The camera cut back to Morrison in the studio.

"The sniper's proven to be very resourceful in evading the police in previous attacks. Do you think these traps indicate he's following a planned escape route?"

Liz paused for a moment.

"It's hard to imagine he's been able to stick to any plan with so many pursuers converging from every angle. Thousands of police and citizens are chasing by foot, car, and helicopter. Tracking dogs are only a few blocks further behind."

"How can he possibly hope to escape to under these circumstances?" Morrison asked.

"I can't speculate, but he must know that his life lies in the balance. With everything he's done, the police and the mob won't hesitate to kill him if given the slightest chance."

The camera cut to the street scene where the riders approached a wall of flashing cruisers at the end of 94th Street. Scores of uniformed police officers crouched over the hood of their cars with their pistols pointed at the lead cyclist. The sniper veered into a cluster of high-rise buildings on the south side of the street and disappeared.

"He's turned off 94th Street," Morrison said. "Where is he now?"

"We've lost sight of him," Liz said, "but there's a police helicopter hovering over the block, continuing to move south. Citizens have reported a blood trail following the path of the riders. We believe Detective Bannon may have nicked the sniper and that he's using the trail to track the killer's movement in the maze of buildings between the main streets."

A cyclist suddenly shot out between two buildings and turned westward onto 93rd Street.

"There he is!" Liz shouted. "The sniper's camouflage clothing and face paint are unmistakable. Detective Bannon is close behind. It's only a matter of time before he catches the sniper."

Morrison leaned toward the monitor.

"He's turning off 93rd now."

Liz nodded excitedly.

"He's on Riverside Drive, headed south. Police cruisers are converging on his position from the north and south. He's got nowhere to go."

Weir's bike suddenly skipped over the roadside curb and disappeared under some trees at the side of the park. Joe raised his pistol and fired three shots into the trees then followed him into the park.

"Detective Bannon just fired at the sniper," Liz announced. "We've temporarily lost them in the trees."

The camera darted back and forth over the forested greenspace trying to pick up the riders. A few seconds later, the lead cyclist broke into a clearing headed toward a monument in the center of the park.

"The sniper has reached the Sailors and Soldiers Monument. His bike is chattering down the steep steps leading from the plaza to the Hudson River Greenway. The Detective is following close on his heels."

Morrison shook his head.

"It looks like he's running out of real estate. There's only a narrow patch of land between him and the Hudson River. Where else can he go?"

Liz nodded as she scanned the area to the south.

"He's shaken off the police cruisers and the mob following from the streets on the east side. But the park is narrowing as he moves toward its southern terminus. He's blocked by a trail of police cruisers on his left and the river to his right. He's headed toward a dead end."

Chapter Sixty-Four

Riverside Park

1:00 p.m.

W eir banked his bike onto the park's central esplanade and glanced over his shoulder. Joe had followed his path down the monument steps and was only a hundred feet behind. Overhead, the police helicopter swooped down over the top of the trees, blowing debris in all directions.

Shit, Weir cursed. *He's one persistent son-of-a-bitch.*

The Hudson River Greenway ran the length of the park. With two wide pedestrian lanes separated by a grassy median, it provided little protection from above. The sniper's only defense from police sharpshooters taking aim from the helicopter was to zigzag his bike along the path.

Weir could hear the sound of bullets striking the concrete pavement as he veered back and forth over the median. He glanced to his right. There were six lanes of heavy traffic on the Henry Hudson Parkway separating him from the Hudson River. Even if he could scale the concrete roadside barrier and avoid getting run over trying to cross, he'd be too exposed to the sharpshooters flying above.

To his left, he saw a row of flashing police cruisers lining Riverside Drive. Uniformed cops were streaming down the side of the hill through the trees trying to cut off his flank.

He was pinched on both sides, and the vice was closing.

His only chance was to get to the end of the park where there was an underpass to the river. He knew it would likely be blocked, but he'd deal with that when he got there. Right now, he had to keep the swarm of approaching police on his left side at bay.

He pulled out his pistol and began firing in the direction of the cops. Some of them paused to take cover behind the trees. Weir still had the speed advantage on his bike. So far, his unpredictable course changes had bypassed the blockades. The cops were still playing catch-up, trailing slightly behind.

Detective Bannon and the copter were his biggest immediate threat. He could feel the pain from the bullet wedged in his shoulder and knew that he was losing blood. All he had to do was preserve enough energy to get to the Hudson River. The cold water would constrict his blood vessels and slow the bleeding. Then he could hide under the surface, and the current would carry him out of harm's way.

Weir squinted toward the end of the path. He only had a few hundred yards to go. The park narrowed as it approached 79th Street and the police were moving in on both sides. He had a narrow window before the wedge closed. He stood up on his pedals and pumped his legs. Bullets were flying from every direction. A few pinged off his bike and another one ricocheted off his kevlar vest.

Fifty yards, twenty, ten...

Weir suddenly veered off the esplanade and hopped over the Parkway exit ramp onto 79th Street. Just ahead was the underpass leading to the Boat Basin Quay. Two police cars formed a wedge across the road, and four cops pointed their pistols in the sniper's direction. Weir reached to his side and unclipped a grenade attached to his belt. He lifted it to his mouth and pulled the safety pin out with his teeth then flung it forward as hard as he could.

Three seconds later, a loud explosion rocked the two cars in a cloud of smoke. Weir raced straight into the smoke and slammed past the shell-shocked cops to the other side of the underpass.

Just past the Boat Basin Cafe, he saw the wide expanse of the Hudson River. He only had another hundred yards to go. Then he'd be in God's hands.

Chapter Sixty-Five

The Boat Basin, Hudson River

July 24, 1:05 p.m.

W eir stormed through the police blockade and sped onto the circular drive surrounding the Boat Basin Cafe. The helicopter pilot saw him shoot out of the tunnel and swooped down, clipping his shoulder with one of the chopper's landing skids. Weir winced in pain and wobbled his bike for a few seconds then regained his balance and raced down the ramp leading to the quay.

Across the promenade, he saw the pretty array of yachts moored in their slips. It was the end of the line. A few yards away, the opaque surface of the Hudson River slid southward like a giant slab of rolled steel. He smiled at the irony. The sniper who dispatched those stepping into the light would save himself by slipping under the cloak of darkness.

Weir glanced over his shoulder. Angry diners streamed out of the cafe in his direction. The chase scene had played on the restaurant's big screen TV, and its patrons had talked about what they would do if they got their hands on him. Recognizing he had his back to the river, this was their chance to exact revenge on the killer who'd tormented them for weeks.

There was only one way to go. Weir hopped off his bike and flinched. From the adrenaline of the chase, he hadn't realized he'd also been shot in the leg. As he hobbled down the narrow dock, he heard the pounding steps of the mob closing in. He wheeled around and fired two shots into the crowd. One man near the head of the line dropped onto the wharf, and the group paused.

Weir pulled the trigger, but his magazine was spent. As he pumped his hand, the pistol clicked harmlessly. Seeing that he was out of ammunition, the crowd surged toward the sniper. A burly man caught a piece of Weir's vest as he tried to hop over the railing into the water and pulled him back onto the dock. He slammed the sniper's body onto the platform and began pummeling his face with his fists.

Weir's body shook as the man worked him over. Realizing he had one last chance, Weir pulled his hunting knife out of his side pocket and stabbed the man in the neck. Seconds later, the sun disappeared as scores of citizens piled on top of him, knifing him repeatedly with steak knives.

The last thing Weir remembered before passing out was hearing the familiar crack-crack-crack of a Glock pistol being fired into the air.

Chapter Sixty-Six

The Boat Basin, Hudson River

July 24, 1:10 p.m.

J oe stormed through the Parkway underpass onto the Boat
Basin circular drive. He'd paused just long enough in the
tunnel to check on the condition of his colleagues and call for
medical assistance. From his elevated position above the
docks, he could see a swarm of people in a pile at the end of
the jetty.

The police helicopter hovered overhead, barking orders
over its loudspeaker for the crowd to disperse. At the bottom
of the pile through glinting flashes of steel, he saw the
unmistakable pattern of camouflaged clothes. It was obvious
the crowd had closed in on the sniper and was taking matters
into their own hands.

Joe sped down the ramp and skipped his bike over the
riverside path onto the pier. He raced down the dock and
skidded to a stop at the edge of the crowd. He tried to pull
people off the heap, but the angry mob clung to the sniper's
clothing, refusing to be checked.

Joe stood up and hesitated. For many days, he'd dreamt
of the moment when he would be able to watch Weir suffer as
he'd made so many others suffer. It would be a fitting end to
the vicious killer, at the hands of his victims. But this wasn't
the way he envisioned it. Whether it was his desire to see the
life drain out of the sniper's eyes or to kill him himself, he
couldn't stand by.

He pulled his service pistol out of its holster and pointed
it over the top of the pile. Then he fired two shots in rapid
succession. He'd kept track of the number of times he'd fired

his gun since the chase began.   He'd purposely saved one round.

The mob stopped moving momentarily and looked back at the Detective.   He was pointing his gun directly at the crowd.

"Police!" Joe shouted. "Back away immediately!"

People slowly pulled off the pile and backed away in a circle around the stricken sniper.   Joe looked at Weir's battered face and bloody clothes, unsure if he was dead or simply unconscious.   On the dock beside him was a long breathing tube with a transparent float attached to one end. As the Detective took a step forward, Weir groaned and lifted his eyelids.

The sniper and the Detective regarded one another for many long seconds.   Then Weir's lip curled into a strange smile.   As he reached for his empty pistol, Joe raised his gun and pointing it squarely at the sniper's head.

Joe pressed his finger against the trigger. No one would fault him for ending the sniper's life here and now. Not the angry crowd and certainly not the cops looking on from the copter above. Everybody was lusting for revenge. Joe could justifiably say he acted in self-defense when the sniper reached for his gun, but it would hardly be necessary. Nobody would step forward to impugn the Detective if he killed the sniper in cold blood.

Joe gripped his gun with shaking hands, deciding whether to empty the chamber.   Weir lifted his hand and curled his finger beckoning for Joe to approach.   The Detective crept up to Weir with his pistol locked on the sniper's head and kicked the gun and knives away from his body.   Weir tried to say something, but he was too weak. Blood oozed from the corner of his mouth as he tried to talk.

Joe kneeled down beside Weir. He looked him squarely in the eyes, placing the barrel of his pistol on the sniper's forehead. If he flinched one millimeter, Joe wouldn't hesitate to blow a hole in his head just as the sniper had done to so many others.

"Do it!" he heard someone in the crowd whisper in the background.

"Kill the fucker," another one said. "He doesn't deserve to live."

"Joe," Weir wheezed. "There's something you need to know..."

Joe looked into Weir's eyes, and the sniper nodded faintly. The Detective bent down and moved his ear close to Weir's mouth. The sniper whispered something to the Detective then his body went limp. Joe pressed his index finger against Weir's carotid artery and felt for a pulse. There was no sign of life. The killer of his wife and a dozen other innocent New Yorkers was finally dead.

Joe reached into Weir's pant leg and pulled out a cell phone. He pressed a button on the side then slid his finger over the surface a few times looking at the screen. Then he stood up and peered down at the lifeless body of the sniper. His face was expressionless. After a few seconds, he shook his head and walked through the parted crowd toward the cafe with his gun hanging by his side.

Hannah's car skidded to a stop on the drive above the cafe. She rushed out to see Joe trudging up the dock. He glanced up at her briefly then walked up the ramp to her position. When he got to the car, he looked into his partner's eyes as he reached into his back pocket. He pulled out a set of handcuffs and slapped one end on her right hand.

"What...?" Hannah said.

"Don't even try," Joe said. "I have incontestable proof you gave up the Mayor."

He swung Hannah around and connected the other end of the handcuffs to her left hand.

"Before I read you your rights," he said, "just tell me one thing. Did you tell him where I live?"

Hannah's eyes filled with tears.

"Joe, he threatened to kill my *children.* After your wife was shot, I was terrified. But I swear—I had nothing to do with Jane's murder."

Joe looked at Hannah coldly.

"You have the right to remain silent..."

Chapter Sixty-Seven

18th Precinct, Lieutenant O'Neill's office

July 25, 9 a.m.

B rady O'Neill carried a tray of Starbucks coffee into his office the morning after the sniper chase. Joe and Kate were seated opposite his desk talking quietly.

"I see you're bringing us the good stuff finally," Kate joked.

"Yeah, well, I thought we should celebrate and all," O'Neill said.

"I'm afraid I'm not in much of a celebratory mood," Joe said.

O'Neill looked at Joe steadily. He knew the Detective was still grieving the loss of his wife and feeling conflicted about his partner.

"You might not want to mention that to the Commissioner. He's nominating you for the Department's highest award, the Medal of Honor."

"Great," Joe sighed. "That and two bits will get me..."

Joe held up his cup of coffee, signifying what he thought of the honor.

O'Neill ignored the comment and turned toward Kate.

"Kate, we couldn't have done this without your help also. I've called the Director personally and recommended you for the FBI's Meritorious Achievement Medal."

Kate sighed.

"I just wish we were able to include one other person in all this," she said. "This just doesn't feel right without Hannah. We were a team all along."

"Not as much as it seemed," Joe said.

O'Neill paused to consider his words.

"It's unfortunate about Hannah. But the sniper presented her with an impossible choice."

Joe cocked his head skeptically at the Lieutenant.

"Really, Chief? She could have told us about the threat. We might have been able to use that to prevent the Mayor's killing. Not to mention some of the other shootings."

O'Neill paused, not wanting to address the elephant in the room.

"Possibly. But I'd be willing to bet that he told her if she mentioned it to anyone else, he wouldn't hesitate to kill her kids. After your wife was targeted, the whole department was on edge..."

Kate cleared her throat to deflect the subject.

"If the sniper hadn't recorded Hannah giving him the details of the Mayor's scheduled address, we might never have known."

Joe nodded.

"She started acting increasingly skittish after the explosion at Weir's apartment," he said. "But I didn't suspect anything until she missed him at point blank range during yesterday's chase."

"You don't think she hesitated because you were in the line of fire?" Kate said.

Joe shook his head dismissively.

"Weir was too clever to leave that to chance. He probably told her he'd go public about her treachery if anything happened to him. I think he was using her as his safety net all along."

O'Neill leaned back in his chair and looked out the window.

"How long do you think he had her in the fold?" he asked.

"I didn't put it together at the time, but I think he approached her the morning of the Mayor's assassination. I think he placed a threat in the card attached to a flower delivery at the hospital. The handwriting on the map we found in the Long Island camp was similar to the script on the card envelope."

"That wouldn't have given him much time to prepare for the Mayor's shooting," Kate suggested.

"Four hours, to be precise," Joe said. "Assuming she called him immediately after her visitors left that morning."

"Clever indeed," O'Neill said. "It's impressive that he was able to set up the diversions in Union Square with so little time. We still don't know for sure where he fired from. The tracking dogs traced his scent to the top of three buildings in the area."

Joe nodded.

"That's where he placed the remote-controlled gunfire simulators. I'm pretty sure he fired from the water tower atop the co-op building on the west side. It had the clearest and most direct view of the platform."

"How did he escape from there?" Kate asked. "Your team got up there within minutes. There was no closed-circuit video of him leaving the building."

"I don't think he left the building. At least not that same day. I think he hid in the water tank until everything died down."

"But you said you checked the tank when you were up there?" O'Neill said.

"I did. The flashlight didn't penetrate the full depth of water to the bottom of the tank. I waited long enough for any reasonable person to hold his breath. But the hose I found beside him at the Boat Basin suggests he rigged a breathing apparatus that allowed him to stay underwater longer than anyone would expect."

Kate shook her head.

"I guess we got lucky he didn't jump into the Hudson River with that thing. It's wide and fast enough that our divers might never have found him in that murky water."

"It wasn't very sophisticated," O'Neill nodded, "but just effective enough to work. This guy had the full bag of tricks."

"Speaking of tricks," Kate said. "How the hell did The President manage to dodge the sniper's bullet? I'm surprised the Secret Service even let him go into that situation. Their whole M.O. is using secrecy, so no one knows where he's going to be speaking until the last moment."

O'Neill took a sip of his coffee.

"I spoke with some of the agents at the scene. Apparently he never even got on the platform. The whole thing was an elaborate ruse. The President was speaking from a separate sound stage hidden from view."

Kate's eyes widened in amazement.

"You mean they projected his image onto the platform? It was so realistic!"

"The glass surrounding the main stage had sophisticated electrochromic sensors. While simulating the image of the park setting in the background, they projected a 3-D holographic image of The President onto the stage."

"A *holograph*?" Joe said. "Maybe our Commander-in-Chief isn't quite as courageous as his handlers would have us believe. Too bad the Secret Service didn't share this technology with the Department a little earlier. We might have been able to save a few other lives besides the President."

"Let's keep that secret between us," O'Neill said. "The White House wants the country to think The President put his life on the line to catch the killer. We should be thankful it worked."

"Just barely," Joe said. "The sniper damn near got away again."

Kate looked at Joe and nodded.

"You're the real hero here, Joe. If you hadn't single-handedly chased him down on that bicycle, we might still be looking for him. How did you know where he was hiding anyway?"

"That was just pure luck. The dogs tracked his scent to the Eldorado building on the west side of the park. When we found the dead woman in her apartment, I figured he'd scoped the park from that location to choose his sniper position. I guess he didn't count on anyone looking at the trees from above to find him."

"That was pretty ballsy," O'Neill said. "He fooled me, that's for sure. Everybody was scanning the high-rises around the perimeter of the park. We figured the dogs had the park covered if anybody was stupid enough to try anything from the grounds."

Joe nodded.

"If he hadn't tried to hide his bicycle in the leaves, I probably wouldn't have found him either. He was very ingenious using the bike to throw off the dog's trail."

"We finally found the murder weapon there," O'Neil said. "I guess he was in too much of a rush to get the hell out of the tree to take it with him. Speaking of dogs, were you able to track the sniper's last location? I'm concerned he locked his pet up somewhere with no one to come back for it."

"That dog was the only thing in the world Weir cared about. He left a detailed map on his phone with directions to his new camp in the Adirondacks. I called the SPCA and they retrieved the animal. He's safe in their Albany shelter for now."

Kate shook her head.

"Let's hope he doesn't have to be put down like his owner was. Hopefully, he'll find a more stable caregiver." She looked at the Lieutenant. "Has ballistics traced the murders to the weapon? Is the case now closed?"

"All but the three most recent ones for which we have the copycat killers in custody. Nobody else has proven to be as resourceful and slippery as the original killer. Now that he's dead, hopefully anyone else who was looking at him as some kind of anti-establishment hero will think twice about trying to copy him."

Kate looked over and noticed Joe sitting pensively in his chair.

"If anyone gets any bright ideas," she said, trying to cheer him up, "the A-Team is still at your disposal, Lieutenant."

Joe looked at the empty chair opposite the Lieutenant's desk.

"It's the A-minus team now."

Epilogue

Battery Park, Lower Manhattan

July 31, 7:00 a.m.

Joe rested his elbows on the promenade railing overlooking the Hudson River. He'd come to Battery Park to watch the sun rise over New York Harbor and clear his head. It had been almost a week since the rooftop sniper was captured, but he was far from settled.

The murder of his wife and Hannah's betrayal had opened a gash that refused to heal. He felt more alone than ever. In spite of the recognition he'd received from the police department, he still carried a heavy burden of guilt. As a peace officer, he'd been unable to protect the two most important people in the world to him. Thirteen people had died in New York because of his failure to stop the killer. Countless others across the country lost their lives at the hands of copycat killers who were encouraged by the success of the New York sniper.

Weir had not only managed to drive an entire city underground, he'd drawn out a new legion of killers to terrorize the country. Compared to his accomplishments, Joe's efforts seemed puny. His wife was right—the sniper had controlled the behavior of virtually everyone he targeted. His undoing had more to do with bad luck than Joe's detective work. If the wind had shifted the leaves in a slightly different direction the day of the President's address, he might never have been found.

Joe looked toward the Statue of Liberty across the harbor. In the morning sun, she shined stronger than ever. Her raised beacon had provided hope for countless generations of New Yorkers. And yet, the promise of freedom and liberty on the shores just beyond her isle rang hollow. How could anyone ever feel truly free with the threat of violent death lurking past every corner?

Joe lowered his gaze to the water's surface. It was a quiet morning. The harbor's gentle waves reflected the rising sun like the facets of a giant gemstone. To any other observer, it was a beautiful scene. The copycat snipers had retreated back into the woodwork after their hero was vanquished. New Yorkers had emerged from their hiding places and resumed normal lives.

Joe peered a few hundred yards to his left. The first ferry of morning commuters was docking at Whitehall Terminal. He watched as the ship opened its prow and passengers streamed down the gangway. He glanced reflexively toward the top of the Ritz Carlton Hotel and shook his head. It had been too easy for someone to take the life of another. There would be more killings, because that is the nature of man. For now, at least, Joe could enjoy a moment of peace.

As he closed his eyes to feel the warmth of the sun on his face, he heard the unmistakable sound of a rifle shot. His eyes flew open and instinctively flashed toward the ferry terminal. The passengers had begun to stampede into the terminal. Two seconds later, their panicked screams wafted over the channel to Joe's position.

With sweaty hands, he reached for his police radio.

So it begins.

Other books by J. R. McLeay:

Dr. Richard Ross has discovered a miracle cure for aging. But it comes at a price. Everyone who wants eternal youth must undergo an operation before passing into adulthood that locks their body in the form of a preadolescent youth. When seniors die off, immortal juveniles rise to power and take over the world.

But not everyone is happy with the new arrangement. A group of rebels from the Garden of Eden church plots to overthrow the new regime and return the world to its natural order. When juveniles suddenly begin rapidly aging, the entire population is set on a course of imminent extinction.

Building to a chilling climax, Dr. Ross and his endocrinologist girlfriend must find and rescue the one remaining person who carries the genetic link for saving the human race.

A mind-bending technothriller based on Nobel prizewinning research.

http:getbook.at/cp

Independent authors such as myself depend upon your feedback to continue our passion for writing. If you enjoyed this book, please post a brief review on my Amazon book page at:

http://getbook.at/ud

Follow, share, comment or like at:

https://www.facebook.com/thecicadaprophecy

https://twitter.com/jrmcleay

www.jrmcleay.com

Acknowledgements

Writing a bestseller is no easy task.

The first step is coming up with an interesting and original theme. Sometimes it's hard to find inspiration for a new book, but the best ideas always come from real life experiences. For this, I'd like to thank my friends and one or two adversaries for providing the underpinnings for this book.

The next step is developing a workable outline that will provide immediate engagement and maintain reader interest all the way to the end. A number of resources provided invaluable assistance in this endeavor. K. M. Weiland's book Outlining Your Novel was my go-to reference to ensure I had all the bases covered. Syd Field's book The Screenwriter's Workbook provided the central foundation for establishing the necessary three-act structure for any good story.

Then the really hard part begins. Which is actually writing the story. It takes a superhuman effort to create an engaging piece of literature that works from beginning to end. There are so many elements to balance: the opening hook, building conflict, pacing, chapter endings, overall length, diction, character development, dialogue, point-of-view switches, secondary plot lines, finishing with a smart ending, etc.

Whew! How can any normal mortal weave all these elements into a cohesive and compelling story? For me, the best guidance comes from readers. I'd like to thank the many people who reached out and contacted me or who posted reviews for my first book The Cicada Prophecy. I learned from honest and candid readers what works and what doesn't work. I have tried mightily to correct the stipulated shortcomings from my initial foray into publishing and hope this book raises the bar.

Of course, the best way to be a successful writer is to listen, watch, and read what other successful writers do. Stephen King's instructional book On Writing provided many excellent tips. Katherine King's book Plot with Character provided many good ideas for developing rich and compelling characters. Nabokov's Lolita showed me how to write beautiful and elegant prose. Robert Patterson's and Dan Brown's hugely successful books showed me how to structure and pace my books to create page-turners. All of these writer qualities are a work-in-progress for me.

Once the first draft of the manuscript is finished, the difficult job of editing begins. Some of this can be done by the author himself, but not exclusively. I found the software application Hemingway particularly helpful in controlling my sentence length, overuse of adverbs and adjectives, and minimizing use of passive voice. Another application, Grammarly, corrected my improper comma usage, repetitive words, and spelling and grammar errors. How did writers function in the days before word processing programs and specialized software applications?

Of course, self-editing—even with sophisticated software tools—only goes so far. Every writer gets too close to his/her work and loses sight of both the forest and the trees from overthinking every single word. For this reason, arms-length editors are essential. They bring fresh eyes and see things only new readers can see. I'd like to thank John Dreese for bringing his excellent writer's eye to my first edit. If you're looking for a fun sci-fi/space exploration book, check out his highly-rated two-part novel Red Hope and Blue Hope. My good friend and ever-faithful reader Alicia Dougherty provided helpful feedback from a reader's perspective on how my novel could be tightened and improved. And Patricia Hadding, who is a prolific and detailed book reviewer, provided invaluable guidance on the technical ballistics and public security elements of my book. Check out her excellent book review blog at piratepatty.wordpress.com.

Once the manuscript is finished and vetted, it's ready to be published and uploaded to the major book marketing sites. The book formatting software Vellum took my rough Microsoft Word document and transformed it into a beautiful piece of literature. Thanks also to my friends at Amazon Kindle Direct Publishing and CreateSpace for all their assistance in uploading and configuring my ebook and paperback.

Did I mention earlier the hard part? Yeah, well forget that. The REALLY hard part of being a successful author is marketing your product. There are thousands, probably millions, of really good self-published authors who never got picked up by a major publisher and never figured out how to move their books on the primary e-commerce forums.

I've learned a tremendous amount about successfully marketing my book in the roughly two years since my first title was published. It's impossible to share all my learnings here, but suffice to say that no book will sell unless it attracts eyeballs. Getting eyeballs to your Amazon product page is an art and a science and is an extraordinarily complex moving organism. I'd like to thank my good friend John Dreese for partnering with me after my first book floundered for almost a full year to help me understand how to get optimal results.

Being a writer can be a lonely and frustrating job. If you don't have a strong support network, it's too easy to give up and sell out for a corporate job. None of this would be possible without the unconditional love and support of my amazing wife Tricia. Thank you, babe, for believing in me and never letting me let go of my dream.

Made in the USA
Lexington, KY
01 September 2017